THE BRATVA'S HEIR

(UNDERWORLD KINGS)

JANE HENRY

SOPHIE LARK

SYNOPSIS

Prison's a dark, bleak place.

But Clare brings me light.

My sweet little bird will be my ticket to freedom.

The first time I saw her, I had to have her.

From her big, dark eyes, to the curves she can't conceal…

The way she can only hold my gaze so long.

The way she shivers every time I move inside these chains.

And most of all, the way she'll bend the rules when I order her to…

I know a natural submissive when I see one.

Her degrees and titles don't change who she is: a woman who will bend to my will.

She doesn't know it yet, but Clare is mine.

Mine to train. Mine to protect. And mine to control…

CHAPTER 1

CONSTANTINE

I've been locked in solitary confinement for three weeks now.

The guards don't call it "solitary confinement" anymore—now it's "restricted housing," which is supposed to sound more humane. I'm still trapped in my cell twenty-three hours of the day, barred from phone calls or visits, so maybe they should call it "slow death by boredom" instead.

I got chucked in here after the Irish tried to cut out my liver in the courtyard. That's where most fights happen. This wasn't intended to be a fight, but an assassination. Three of those whiskey-drinking bastards cornered me with makeshift shanks—razor blades melted into toothbrush handles—and I didn't need the commentary to know what was happening.

"This is for Roxy," one of them said.

"No shit," I replied.

Then I caught his wrist and head-butted him right in the nose.

They got in some good cuts. Slashed me down the shoulder and the back. Stabbed me in the thigh, even.

As far as I can tell, they got a broken nose, a dislocated shoulder, and a knee that ain't never gonna be the same in return.

I've been my father's main enforcer since I was fifteen years old. I know how to take a man down so he doesn't get up again.

It's the one thing I'm good at: violence.

If Connor Maguire wants revenge for his daughter, he's gonna have to send a lot more men. With something better than razor blade toothbrushes.

They did manage to snap off a piece of that shank in my thigh. The prison doctor had to dig it out, and stitch up my back as well. As soon as he finished, the guards chucked me in "restricted housing." That's where I've been ever since, bored out of my skull.

Which is why I don't argue when the guard tells me I'm up for a mandatory meeting with a shrink.

I have zero interest in therapy. But I wouldn't mind seeing a new set of walls.

I let them cuff my hands and ankles, and I shuffle out of my elevator-sized cell, through the numerous checkpoints and locked doors that lead from Block 8 back toward the infirmary.

We take a hard right turn into a series of offices I've never visited before.

They set me down at a plain table on a wooden chair. Clip an anchored chain between my cuffs so I can only move my hands maybe a foot or so in any direction. Then I sit there and wait for exactly eight minutes.

Prison time is by the clock. 6:00 a.m. the lights snap on, jolting you out of sleep if you were asleep at all. 6:05 the guards come around to count the inmates. 7:00 a.m., breakfast time—hope you like oatmeal. Time allotted for meals, for showers, for exercise, for AA meetings… so on and so forth throughout the day, every minute accounted for, until it's time to sleep and start all over again.

I've gotten pretty good at counting the minutes passing, whether I want to count them or not.

So I know exactly how long it's been when the door cracks open and a woman walks in behind me.

I can smell her perfume before I can actually see her. Subtle and warm, hints of rose and anise.

It catches in my nose, dilates my pupils, gets my heart beating. After all, it's been three months since I've even seen a woman, let alone smelled one.

The prison fucking stinks. It smells like industrial detergent, institutional food, mildewed cells, and dank bodies.

By contrast, the scent of this woman's skin has my mouth watering before she's a foot inside the door. It's like an olfactory glimpse of paradise from the bowels of hell.

The sight of her is just as good.

She takes a wide berth, skirting the table, coming around to the other side to sit directly across from me.

She's trim and petite—dark haired, dark eyed. She might be in her thirties, but she looks younger because of the smattering of brown freckles across her cheeks that remind me of a dappled fawn.

She's trying for professionalism with her suit and dark-framed glasses, but she's left her hair down. And she can't hide the tension

3

in her shoulders, or the slight tremor of her hands as she arranges her folder and pen in front of her.

"Good afternoon," she says, politely. "My name is Clare Nightingale. I'm a correctional psychologist here. You've been assigned as my—as one of my patients."

Her voice is lower than I expected—soft, but clear. As she rests one pale hand atop the folder, I see that she's gone to the trouble of getting a manicure, only to paint the nails with clear polish. No ring on her left hand, and no mark of one recently removed.

She waits for me to respond.

I say nothing.

So she ventures a question she thinks I'll surely answer. "Your name is Constantine Rogov, correct?"

I watch her in silence.

As I suspected, the longer the quiet drags on, the pinker her cheeks become. She shifts in her chair.

After almost a full minute, she says, "Do you not intend to speak to me? The guards said you consented to this meeting."

I answer at last.

"What do you hope to accomplish, Ms. Nightingale?"

Even though she was trying to provoke me into answering, the roughness of my voice in this small space makes her jump. She's angry with herself for startling, her cheeks flushing brighter than ever.

"I'm here to help in the process of rehabilitation," she says. "By meeting with me regularly, I hope to help you pass your time here

4

more effectively, and to prepare you for a successful return to normal life."

"Return to normal life." As if I or any of my brothers ever had that luxury.

She's a crusader.

One of those women who thinks they can make a change in the world. The more dramatic the change, the more satisfying it will be for her. She could be vaccinating orphans in Guatemala, or sifting plastic out of the ocean. Instead she's here trying to reform the scum of the earth.

I look at her gleaming shoes, her leather briefcase, her tailored suit. All deliberately simple and unadorned, but discernibly expensive, nonetheless.

"What's a little rich girl like you doing in a place like this?" I say. "Surely there were better options once you graduated from… Columbia, I'd guess?"

Her lips bleach white as she presses them tightly together.

This is too easy.

"We're not here to talk about me," she says.

"But you think I should bare my soul to you. A stranger. Who doesn't want to answer a simple question about herself."

I can see her chest rising and falling under the modest blazer. I see the flutter of her pulse in the delicate hollow of her throat.

"Anything you say to me is confidential," she says. "It can't be used against you in legal proceedings."

"That's closing the barn door after the horse fled," I say. "I'm on a twenty-five-year sentence."

"Yes," Clare says, her fingertips flexing ever so slightly on the manila folder that surely contains a record of all my misdeeds. All the ones they know about, that is. "For the murder of your fiancée, Roxanne Maguire."

"I don't want to talk about that," I snap, rougher than I intended.

"We don't have to talk about it today," Clare says, with a slight emphasis on the word *today*, implying that it's a topic she will certainly return to in the future.

She won't like the response she gets if she tries.

Irresistibly, her eyes are drawn to my two massive hands folded on the tabletop. The thick, calloused fingers. The blunt nails. The tattoos on my knuckles and the backs of my hands. Her eyes roam up my heavily veined forearms and then to my biceps which are straining the limits of the XXXL prison uniform that still barely fits.

The words in that folder must be echoing inside her head.

Sexually assaulted…

Skull fractured by a wine bottle…

Cause of death: strangulation…

"Isn't it an impediment to your work to be beautiful?" I ask her.

She lets out a huff of air, half disbelieving, half flustered.

"I'm not—please don't try to manipulate me with flattery."

"I'm not flattering you. You're a stunning woman, trying to work with murderers and rapists. You're telling me that's not a distraction?"

She frowns.

"It's not an issue."

"That's impossible."

Now she looks almost angry.

"I'm nothing special," she says, bluntly.

I don't know why she's so intent on considering herself plain—she may not have the obvious flashiness of a certain sort of woman, but Clare's beauty is all the more powerful for its subtlety. The delicacy and luminescence of her skin, like the slightest touch would bruise it... those large, dark eyes, so liquid that they almost seem tearful...

Her fragility makes me want to do terrible things to her.

And yet, I almost want to protect her, too... like a little bird that could fit in the hollow of my hand... a nightingale, singing only for me...

"Don't be modest. You've seen the way men look at you. Tell the truth, Clare."

She bites the edge of her lip, irritated at my use of her first name, and at my commanding tone.

Still, I see the way that tone takes hold of her, compelling her to answer me.

"Men always stare at women," she says.

"They stare at you more... how could they not?"

"Mr. Rogov," she says, sharply. "I told you, we're not here to discuss me."

"I remember," I say.

But I think she will discuss herself if I push her. Because no matter how hard Ms. Nightingale tries to be stern, to maintain professionalism, I see the truth behind her thin façade. I see how she flinches when I bark, how she squirms under my stare. How her eyes flit up

o meet mine when I use a gentler tone, and how her cheeks flush
ink when I compliment her. Clare has been raised to respect author-
y. To crave it, even…

How exactly do you plan to rehabilitate me?" I ask.

he tip of her tongue darts out, moistening those pale lips.

Often it's useful to examine whether there's an underlying psychi-
ric issue that may contribute to negative behaviors. We can do
sts to determine if schizophrenia or depression might—"

'm not crazy," I say, flatly.

Mental health is a spectrum," she says. "There's no bright line
tween mental illnesses and sound, rational minds. And in any
se, even without a diagnosable condition, I can still help you to
derstand your triggers and correct your behavior."

eally," I say. "And how many prisoners have you helped in this
y?"

e shifts in her seat. "That's not really—"

ow long have you worked here?" I demand.

eard her stumble while introducing herself. I'm pretty fucking
e she was about to admit that I was her first patient.

n new to this prison," she says, with a valiant attempt at dignity.
t I assure you, I'm a fully licensed psychologist with—"

th?" I laugh. "When'd you get that license? Is the ink dry?"

e takes a slow breath, trying to shake off my taunts.

esn't work. As she moves to open my folder, her hand jerks,
king her pen onto the floor.

ls between us.

8

She leans far out of her chair to retrieve it, that long sheet of shining dark hair slipping over her shoulder and hanging down toward the dingy carpet.

She grabs the pen and pulls herself up again.

As she's rising, I lunge forward, all the way to the end of my chain. I seize that sheaf of hair and wrap it tight around my hand, jerking her out of her chair toward me. I don't have much room to maneuver, but even chained I overpower her with ease.

I pull her all the way inside the circle of my right arm, my hand wrapped up in her hair, my fingers clamped around the base of her neck. I yank her against me until her petite little body is pressed up against my chest. We're eye to eye, nose to nose, my other hand clamped over her mouth.

In this position I could kiss her or strangle her with the same bare minimum effort.

"That's how I know you're a fucking amateur," I snarl, looking into those terrified doe eyes. "Because a professional would know better than to wear their hair down, or even to pick up their pen. Hell, I doubt they'd bring a pen within a hundred feet of a man like me. They'd know I could stab it through their eye quicker than they could blink."

Her whole body is shaking. Tears glint in the corners of those big dark eyes.

To her credit, she doesn't scream or try to fight. She knows it would be pointless.

She can feel my arm around her. She knows I could snap her spine before the guards could make it through that door.

She looks in my eyes, searching for something. Maybe some spark of humanity. Maybe some hint of the horrible fate in store for her.

She won't find what she's looking for.

I snarl, "Consider yourself warned. I'm no fucking social experiment. I won't be reformed. I'm a criminal. A monster. A killer. I always have been, and I always will be."

She breathes heavily, unable to mask the way she trembles and pants in my grasp. She's terrified, humiliated, struggling not to burst into tears.

She thinks she can run tests on me. Well, I'm running a test on her right now. And there will be many more to come if she dares to visit me again. I have my suspicions about Clare, a condition I could diagnose in her just as easily as she could label me a sociopath and criminal.

I take one last inhale of that heavenly perfume.

"Go home, Clare. Find a nice stockbroker, join a country club. This is your one and only warning."

I release her, allowing her to stumble away from me.

She's shaking so hard that she can hardly pick up her folder and briefcase.

She casts one last horrified look at me. Then she runs out of the room.

Twenty minutes pass until the guards return.

I expect them to rough me up for putting my hands on the pretty little psychologist—or at the very least toss me in my cell as punishment.

Instead they take me back to solitary like nothing happened.

Which tells me all I need to know about my future interactions with Clare Nightingale.

CHAPTER 2
CLARE

The lights in the staff restroom flicker on then off, and for one wild, terrifying moment, I'm afraid they'll turn off altogether.

I've never been afraid of the dark, but after today…

The lights flicker and go back on, flooding the room with light so bright it's blinding. I blink and look around the small room.

Even though there are several stalls in here and the entrance should stay open, I kick it closed and bolt it. I lean my forearm against the cold steel, brace my forehead on my arm, close my eyes, and breathe deeply.

Inhale.

Exhale.

Inhale.

Exhale.

Inhale—I can still smell him. Raw and earthy, like freshly cleaved stone swept bare by a landslide. Clean, with the barest hint of pine. Unapologetically male.

Exhale.

I'm okay.

I'm okay.

I stand up straight and imagine what my mother would say if she knew I'd just leaned against the bathroom door in a *prison bathroom*. She'd probably have me bathe in hand sanitizer and take an STD test.

It's surprisingly clean in here, unlike the rest of the prison. Like a teacher's lounge in a rundown school, it's a little slice of normalcy in an otherwise dismal setting.

Thank God for that. I need something clean right now. Something normal and predictable.

I should have filed a report. He could be in major trouble for what he did, and it's my duty to report any incidents of abuse or misbehavior to the authorities. And if my father finds out... this would prove him right in spectacular fashion.

I'm usually the rule follower... but for just this once, I can't do it. I won't make the same mistake twice.

I glance in the mirror above the sink, half expecting to see bruises where he gripped my neck, but he left no mark. I tilt my head to the left, then right. A faint tinge of pink, no more. I swallow, watching my throat work.

I'm weirdly disappointed there is no mark, as if I need a badge for what I've been through. But there's nothing. I'm fine.

My hair, on the other hand, is another story. I straightened it today and worked hard to make sure I hit the professional vibes I was aiming for, but thanks to that *meaty fist of his,* my perfect hair's all messed up.

I've never been touched by hands like those. Ever.

No woman could ever be touched by hands like those and forget them.

Large, competent hands with thick, rough fingers, toughened by years of hard work and marked with faded ink. I can still see them, twisted around my hair and over my mouth with shocking strength. An expert hold that kept me immobile but promised violence if I disobeyed, quiescent power roiling beneath the surface. Ready to ruin.

I'm so shocked by what he did, I can't remember the color of his eyes. I'm half tempted to find him again, so I can piece his image together in my mind. His eyes, hard and flinty, narrowed in fury at the audacity of my claims, my purpose. Like many inmates, he doesn't believe in reform. Or so he says. I suppose if he did think reformation was possible, he'd have to admit being locked away like this serves a purpose.

I square my shoulders and attempt to right my hair. I have places to go and won't let some unlawful, immoral *criminal* shake me.

His voice, though. God, his voice, tinged with the rough edge of a Russian accent, a deep baritone that rings with authority. I can still hear it.

A professional would know better than to wear their hair down.

He spat the words out as if to strike me with them.

I shiver.

He was right. It's the first rule of self-defense for women. Never, *ever* wear your hair down. The second stupidest thing to do is to put it up in a ponytail, which is a ready-made handle practically inviting someone to grab it and assault you.

I knew this. *I know this.* And yet, today, for my first-ever visit to the infamous DesMax—the Desolation Maximum Security Corrections Facility—I *just had* to be all professional and put-together.

Frowning, I scour my bag until I find a hair tie and a few bobby pins. I quickly braid my hair, then twist it into a plaited bun at the nape of my neck. I looked average before. I look damn near homely, now.

Everything about me's absolutely, perfectly *average*.

Brown hair. Brown eyes. Average lips. Standard nose. Freckles.

I know his comments on my "beauty" were just a taunt, trying to get under my skin. I went to school with the most stunning socialites in the city. I've never stood out, and I'm fine with that.

With a rebellious flourish, I grab my lip gloss from the bottom of the bag, yank the cover off, and swipe it across my lips.

Oh, right. This was the nude color. My lips are the same shade, only now they're sticky.

Sigh.

My phone rings in the Cruella de Vil theme song, and I make a mental note to tell my bestie Felicity to stop changing my mother's ringtones. One of these days, she'll find out, and I'd rather not deal with the guilt trip. I silence it, thankful for the momentary distraction.

"Yes, Mother," I mutter to myself. "I'm well aware my birthday party's in thirty minutes. Excuse me while I tidy myself up after being assaulted by my latest client, who happens to be serving life for murder."

Imagining the look of horror on her face actually perks me up a bit.

I look my clothes over. Nothing's torn. Nothing's so much as even ruffled or wrinkled. The prison has very clear rules for what visitors are allowed to wear, but professionals who work here are given a bit more leniency. I chose this suit on purpose—a classic, double-breasted charcoal gray blazer with matching pencil skirt. Professional, and anything but sexy. Maybe it's the years of fear of men my father instilled in me, but for some reason, I felt I couldn't show so much as a flash of skin or femininity when coming into a men's maximum-security prison.

Didn't stop him from finding the most feminine thing about me and violating it.

Jerk.

Why did I do this again?

Because I believe in reform.

Because I believe that all humans are capable of greatness.

Because I believe in the power of redemption.

Someone in my family has to.

My phone rings again, and this time I look down to see not my mother but my father on the line. I shake my head, release a sigh, and go to pick it up. I'm twenty-nine years old, and my mother still goes to my father to make me behave when she doesn't get her way immediately. Charming, really.

"Hello?"

"Clare, your mother's frantic." By the muffled sound of his voice, I'd guess he's sitting by the bar on our back deck, surrounded by his cronies. Politics laid down for a few hours, let the imbibing begin. "Are you on your way?" He's attempting to sound casual, but I can almost see the tight-lipped question, practically feel him seething because she hounded him in front of his friends. Somehow this is my fault.

"I'm leaving now. I'll be there in about thirty minutes."

I'm only about ten minutes away, but Desolation city traffic is notorious for grinding to a standstill during rush hour.

It will give me enough time to compose myself, but first I need to get ready for the party. I can't exactly wear a suit to a birthday party. I might as well wear a sign across my forehead that says *Licensed Therapist. Ask me about my job.*

They'll ask me anyway.

I prop my bag up on the counter and take out the dress I brought to change into, specifically to coordinate with my suit coat and designed not to wrinkle. Felicity said it was "the cutest little off-the-shoulder midi dress, crush pleated," but I'd just call it a fancy summer dress. With the door locked, I have enough privacy to quickly change, then toss the suit coat on.

Lovely. The little ribbons tied at the top of the dress make the shoulders of my suit coat stand up like they're stacked with shoulder pads. Either I walk out of here with this ridiculous look, or I walk out of here showing skin.

I choose to look ridiculous. It's the safer option.

I grimace at my image. My mother would have a coronary.

Before I leave, I pump soap into my hands and wash them with the hottest water I can, as if to wash the memory of today's assault from my mind.

It doesn't work.

I unlock the door, sling my bag over my shoulder, and walk with purpose to the faculty parking lot.

I half expect shouts or a prison riot behind me when I leave. There's the clanging of metal and the murmur of voices in one room, but the rest is silent.

I look over my shoulder, only yards away from the cells where they keep the inmates.

Where is he now?

Why do I care?

My pulse accelerates.

After I left, how long did he sit in the room?

What did he imagine doing to me?

I read the file. I know how badly he hurt the woman he murdered.

Sometimes, you look at a criminal and can't imagine him or her ever committing the crime they were convicted of. Pretty, boyish-looking boys guilty of school shootings? Never.

But one look in his eyes, and I'm confident Constantine Rogov is absolutely capable of committing murder.

THE NEXT DAY, I wake at the crack of dawn. Party animal that I am, I came home from my birthday party by ten, removed my makeup and finished my skin care routine by ten-fifteen, and slid my eye mask on to get some shut-eye by ten-thirty.

By the time I left, my mom was plastered and teetering on her four-inch stilettos, and my father had broken out his cigars. The irony of the district attorney of Desolation recreationally smoking is not lost on me, but it isn't a party at the Nightingales until we hit what I affectionately call the plattered and flattered stage—when my mom rolls out the platters of petit fours and shots, and my father's friends start shining their halos in mutual admiration.

It's not my scene.

I stretch and slip off my eye mask, blinking at the time on my phone.

5:45.

I don't have to work until noon, so I've got some time to myself this morning. And I know exactly how I'll spend it.

I make myself a cup of coffee, sit in front of the computer, and type in his name.

Constantine Rogov

THERE ARE FEWER HITS than I'd anticipated, precisely two, as the following dozen or so are all LinkedIn profiles of anyone but the man I met in prison yesterday.

I click the first article. My coffee goes cold as I read.

THIRTY-FOUR-YEAR-OLD CONSTANTINE ROGOV, *originally from Moscow, convicted of first-degree murder. Rogov has a history of serving time for crimes of violence. His victim's skull was fractured with a blunt object, though the cause of death was strangulation. Although Rogov pled not guilty, the jury unanimously found him guilty. Rogov will serve a life sentence.*

. . .

I DRINK MY COLD COFFEE, my mind trying to piece this together. Yesterday, I'd thought to myself he was a man capable of violence.

But violence against someone he loved?

I keep reading.

"THEIR RELATIONSHIP WAS VOLATILE, to say the least," one source reportedly said. "They fought constantly, and last year on Valentine's Day, she slashed his tires when she suspected he'd cheated on her. Sources say theirs was to be an arranged marriage, aimed at forming an alliance between the Irish Mafia and the Russians."

SO HE BEAT HER. Bludgeoned her with a wine bottle. Then strangled her to death. In my mind's eye, I imagine him wrapping my hair around my neck and pulling.

Could you kill someone by strangling them with their own hair?

I swallow the bile that rises in the back of my throat, when my phone rings.

I don't recognize the caller I.D. Blocked number.

"Hello?"

Click Click Click. A brisk male voice comes on the line. "Desolation City Corrections Facility. Looking for a Miss Nightingale."

"Speaking."

A chill erupts down my spine, sending the little hairs on my arms standing on end. This isn't the number my supervisor uses.

"You have a requested call from an inmate by the name of Constantine Rogov. Will you accept this call?"

My knees grow weak, and I sink into a chair. I put all my energy into pretending that I'm not somehow both paralyzed with fear and dry-mouthed in anticipation.

"I do."

I do, like wedding vows.

I close my eyes at the sound of more clicks.

Then it's him. His voice is deeper than I even remember, huskier, his accent more pronounced.

"Hello, Miss Nightingale." He pauses and I can actually hear the sneer in his tone. *"Doctor."*

"It's uncustomary for inmates to call their doctors, Mr. Rogov."

"You accepted my call."

I swallow, my hand on the phone trembling.

"I did."

I do. I did. I got a doctorate for this?

"I won't keep you, Miss Nightingale. I'd just like to issue you a warning."

My pulse races.

"You're due to arrive this afternoon. But that won't happen. At ten a.m., they'll find out the doctor who's scheduled for the morning shift is unfortunately incapacitated and won't be able to attend as planned. They'll call you, Miss Nightingale. They'll ask you to come in early."

I force all the air out of my lungs just to answer. "Ah, will they, then?"

He doesn't even bother to respond to me. "You'll come in for the earlier shift. You'll take it. Then you'll make sure you see *me*."

Click.

"Hello?"

The line's dead.

I put my phone down gingerly on the nightstand and stare, unblinking, into the mirror. I don't know if I was just threatened or baited. But I know I have no choice.

CHAPTER 3

CONSTANTINE

After I return to my cell, I spend a long time thinking about Ms. Nightingale.

Prison is torturously tedious, so the simple act of dwelling on another person is not, in and of itself, significant.

Still, I pass an unusually long time recalling the specific details of her person. The feathery fringe of her lashes and the way they fluttered up and down like a distress signal. The constellation of her freckles that she had unsuccessfully tried to dampen with powder. The exact tone of the gasping noise she made when I seized her.

So many sounds women make are inherently sexual, no matter the circumstances.

Sometimes violent circumstances only make them more sexual…

I lay on my back, my cock stiffening inside the loose prison scrubs until it stands straight up. I lift my hand to my face, inhaling the lingering scent of Clare's perfume off my fingers.

Now my cock is throbbing hard, each heartbeat pulsing all the way up to the head.

This is a welcome distraction from the deep depression gripping me these last six months.

I reach inside my pants with my other hand, gently stroking my shaft. I imagine Clare's slim, pale hand wrapped around my cock, how her fingers would hardly meet. I picture her plain, clear-painted nails, their delicate pink color, and the softness of her skin that I experienced when I put my hand around her throat.

I imagine putting my heavy hand on her shoulder and pushing her down to her knees. I can almost see her looking up at me with those big, dark eyes. Terrified mostly, but with a hint of something else in her gaze... Curiosity. Fascination...

I saw it when we met.

She's frightened of me.

But I intrigue her, too.

She's read about men like me, or at least she thinks she has.

She chose to work with criminals for a reason.

She gets a thrill thinking she can help us. Reform us.

Clare is about to learn a harsh lesson.

I can't be helped, and I can't be changed.

Clare, on the other hand, is soft clay, unformed... she doesn't know what she really is. But I do...

I was wrong to think she was a fawn.

Feeling her frantic heart beating against my chest, I realized she is perfectly suited to her name—a little bird, easily ensnared so she can't fly away...

A bird that can be captured and trained.

Of all the things I observed about Clare, the one that interested me the most was what happened after she disappeared from sight.

She failed to report our encounter.

Which tells me a very useful piece of information about the crusading doctor.

Though she may look polished and earnest, the consummate good girl, it seems that Ms. Nightingale is not opposed to bending the rules. Especially under pressure.

And it just so happens, I'm the fucking Mariana Trench of pressure.

I imagine telling her to open her mouth. How those soft lips would part, and that little pink tongue would extend...

Then I'd lay my cock on top of it. I'd slide the head all the way inside her mouth, my hand wrapped up in her hair, just like when I grabbed her in that tiny room. I'd hold her tight so she couldn't escape and pump into her mouth over and over again until I exploded...

With a groan, I erupt all over the back of my hand, imagining coming directly into the little doctor's mouth.

The come flows out in spurt after spurt, a surprising volume built up in my balls from the hour I spent in her presence.

I lay on my back, drained but not satisfied, because I want what I was picturing. I want Clare on her knees in front of me.

And I begin to plan how I'll make that happen.

THE NEXT MORNING, I conduct a second experiment.

I use my one hour outside of solitary to reconnoiter our new shrink. I discover her phone number, her home address, the university from which she graduated (Columbia, of course, just like I guessed), and the make and model of her car.

And then I call her.

The first part of the test is to see if she'll answer.

The second is to lay out the bait: I give her an order. A simple, seemingly innocuous order.

I tell her to accept a shift at work this morning.

She likely would have accepted with or without my phone call.

But I want to see if she'll do it after I tell her to.

Will she arrive at 11:00, as I commanded?

Or will this tip her over into reporting me to the prison authorities?

I need to know exactly how far my little bird can be pushed.

Because if she's curious…

If she's stubborn…

If she comes pecking after my breadcrumbs…

She could be very useful to me.

ε

I'VE OFTEN THOUGHT that I don't possess the usual range of human emotions. So many seemingly common experiences are utterly foreign to me. I've never felt the need to wear a Halloween costume, or visit Disneyland, or coo over a baby, or watch a reality TV show.

Even situations that are supposed to elicit extreme emotion—like the first time I pulled the trigger of a gun while the barrel was pointed at a man's chest—I simply felt… nothing.

When I do experience emotion, it's as bright and keen as the blade of a knife. It slices through me, leaving no doubt as to what I feel.

I hear the clank of my cell door opening, and the guards calling out, "Rogov… psych appointment."

And I'm hit with a bolt of pure, electric excitement.

She's waiting for me.

Sure enough, as I enter the cramped, gray office space once more, Clare Nightingale is already seated, her expensive briefcase sitting next to her chair, her manila folder arranged at a perfect 90-degree angle to the edge of the table.

She faces me boldly, defiantly.

She thinks she's here to reclaim her power.

Today she's wearing a dark button-up shirt and trousers, all impeccably tailored. She's covered wrist to throat to ankle, and yet this is not as plain an outfit as yesterday—she's trying to project an image of dominance. Her hair is a shining knot at the base of her neck.

As soon as I'm chained in place at the table she says, "What is your intention in manipulating the time of our meeting? In calling me at home? Are you trying to threaten me?"

"Clare," I say. "I would never try to threaten you. I would simply do it. And you'd have no doubt of the message."

I see her flinch at the use of her first name, though she attempts to repress it.

I'm the one chained to the table, yet she seems hardly able to move while my eyes pin her in place.

"Why did you want to meet with me today?" she persists.

"I want us to get to know each other," I tell her. "That's what you want too, isn't it?"

Those thick, dark lashes tangle together as she narrows her eyes at me. "You're not going to control these sessions."

"Do you think you're the one in control? Here and now?" I ask her.

I tap one heavy finger on the desk, making a hollow sound that seems extraordinarily loud in the close space.

A shiver runs down her slim frame.

"You can cooperate with me, or you can go back to your cell," she says, coldly.

She's stubborn today. On the offensive.

I wish I weren't chained to this table so I could make her pay for her insolent tone.

Instead, I'm forced to negotiate.

"Cooperation implies a mutualistic arrangement," I reply.

"What do you mean by that?"

"In our last meeting, you refused to answer any questions about yourself. How do you expect us to converse together, to build a relationship, if I'm expected to tell you everything while you're a closed book?"

"It's not necessary to be personally acquainted with your psychologist," Clare says. "In fact, it's better if you aren't."

"Says who?"

"Decades of clinical research," she responds, tartly.

"I'm not writing a textbook. I'm telling you my conditions."

Clare considers this, her brain working rapidly behind the still mask of her face.

"You want an exchange of information?" she says. "A question for a question?"

I nod, repressing my smile. "That's right."

She taps her own fingertip lightly on the table, in unconscious imitation of me. Then she says. "Why don't you go first?"

Ah. Ms. Nightingale prefers to play black, does she?

"Certainly," I reply. "What did you do for your birthday?"

Her dark eyes swoop across my face, and she begins to say, "How did you—" before cutting herself off.

It took one call on an illicit cellphone to get a basic background check on Clare Nightingale. My *obshchak* Yury will dig up more information over the weekend, but for now, I'm already aware that Clare won a Distinguished Student Research award in school, that she lives in a posh apartment far outside the budget of a recent graduate, and that she turned twenty-nine just four days ago.

"My parents threw a party for me," she says, stiffly.

There's no affection in her tone. No gratitude. I don't think that's out of irritation with *me*.

"What did you do at the party?"

"That's more than one question," she says.

"Come now, you don't want to enforce that rule—I'm sure you'll have follow-up queries of your own."

She purses her lips slightly, considering, and then acquiesces. "We played cribbage and poker."

"You like cribbage and poker?"

"Not particularly."

"Why did you play, then?"

She frowns. "I suppose you never do anything you don't want to do?"

"Not very often… until I came here."

We both become aware, once more, of where we're sitting, of the chains on my wrists, of our relative positions in this room. For a moment those elements had seemed to dissolve around us, to become pale and foggy, while Clare's face and mine stood out in sharp detail. Now it all comes rushing back into focus.

"My turn," Clare says, firmly.

I expect her to ask about Roxy. My stomach clenches in anticipation.

Instead, Clare says, "You came to Desolation when you were sixteen?"

"That's right."

"Where did you live before?"

"Moscow."

"But you're an American citizen?"

"My mother was American."

Clare sits back slightly in her chair, her dark eyes flitting over my hulking person.

"What was she like?" she asks.

I'm sure she's wondering what sort of woman makes a son like me. She might be picturing an addict, a prostitute, a stripper…

The impulse to correct that assumption is overpowering.

"She was a pastry chef," I say. "She worked in a Michelin star restaurant. Her pastries were literal art—people hated to eat them. She was educated and cultured. She would have fit in just fine at your birthday party." I give a small smile. "Unlike me."

I can see the curiosity in Clare's face. She's wondering how a woman like that becomes the bride of one of the most notorious Bratva bosses in Desolation.

But that is a topic I don't wish to discuss.

So I say, roughly, "What about your mother?"

I already inferred that Clare Nightingale has a fraught relationship with her parents. Sure enough, she stiffens like frost, while attempting to answer in as bland a manner as possible.

"I suppose you'd call her a socialite. She's on the boards of several charities. An excellent tennis player, too."

Poor Clare is no poker player. She's got mommy issues written all over her—possibly daddy issues, too.

Time to press on the bruise.

"Expectations must be high in the Nightingale house," I say. "Little rich girls don't become doctors unless they're trying to impress someone. And yet, this is the last place a parent would want to see their daughter working. Is it possible to submit and rebel at the same time?"

I lean forward on the table, the chains shifting with a hissing sound. I steeple my fingers under my chin, watching Clare closely.

"What does Daddy do?" I muse.

"He's a banker," Clare says, through pale lips.

She's lying.

I file that little inconsistency away for future reference.

"When did you start working for your father?" Clare demands.

"Young," I say, which is true. I was twelve years old the first time he put a gun in my hand.

I could lie right back to Clare in return for her fib, but for all my flaws, all the sins I've committed, I do have one line I never cross; I always keep my word. For better or worse, if I say I'll do something, you might as well engrave it on fucking stone tablets.

"You said you don't believe in rehabilitation," Clare says. "You don't think people can change."

"I know they can't," I growl. "Liars lie. Thieves steal. Gamblers flush their money away. A man's nature is his destiny."

"How do you know your nature is to be a criminal, just because you were born into a Bratva family?" Clare asks, her keen dark eyes fixed on my face. "What if you had been born in my family instead? Aren't you just describing the effects of environment? And after all, environment can change… circumstances change…"

"If my father was a banker," I say, "then I wouldn't be me. What's born of a cat eats mice."

"You're wrong," Clare says.

Her contradiction gives me a pleasant thrill of annoyance.

I rather enjoy how this little bird will argue right to my face, as if I couldn't snap her in two if she irritated me.

But I don't want to snap Clare in two. I want to teach her better manners.

I want to squeeze her… twist her… bend her over this table…

I want to put my fingerprints all over that pale skin, and see if she bruises the same color as those freckles…

Until she gives in to me. As she's dying to do, deep down inside…

"I'm surprised a man like you gives so much of your power away to 'destiny'," Clare says. "Aren't you in control of yourself? I choose what I want to be. Not my family, not my circumstances."

"You like to think so, Clare," I say, softly. "But give it a year. Give it five years. This crusading fire will die inside you, smothered by the ugly realities of this place. By your complete inability to make a difference in anyone's life. Eventually, you'll return to the comfort of parties and charity boards, to people like yourself. You'll look in the mirror and the person staring back at you will be all too familiar to you."

My words bring a kind of nauseated fear into her face.

Stubbornly she replies, "You'll see for yourself that you're wrong. I'll still be here in a year, in five years, and so will you. I hope it won't take that long for you to see the possibility of a different road ahead of you."

I appreciate Clare's spirit.

I even appreciate her misguided concern for me.

But there's no fucking way I'm going to be in DesMax a year from now.

CHAPTER 4

CLARE

I gather up my papers and tap them on the table. I try to use them to quell the shaking in my hands, but it doesn't work. I hope I can at least hide the trembling, but the knowing look in Constantine's eyes tells me he doesn't miss a thing.

He notes everything about me... that he can see, anyway. And for some reason, I wonder if he notes things that he can't, like he somehow has a sixth sense or a fine-tuned power of perception.

My notes tell me he's an enforcer for the Bratva—and heir to the throne of his father Artyom Rogov.

Enforcers are the ones who make others pay, that much I know.

Men of his caliber in the Bratva don't get there by being nice guys and maintaining the status quo.

I don't like how easily he affects me. I've poured blood, sweat, and tears into my degrees, into working my way toward a prestigious career, and one hot, testosterone-laden alpha undoes me with a crooked smile.

No… no, it's far more than his smile.

I need to get laid. Or… something. Maybe drunk. Possibly even high. I'm confident Felicity has a good ol' store of edibles she'd share with me if I asked her. Whatever it is that's in my system needs to be eradicated, and now, so I can resume a professional demeanor when working with Constantine.

I glance at the clock. "Our time is up for now, Mr. Rogov, but before you go, I'd like you to take this form, fill it out and sign it for me before our next session."

"Call me Constantine, Clare."

Heat flames my cheeks, and my heartbeat quickens. "I'd prefer if you call me Dr. Nightingale."

His eyes narrow ever so slightly. "I don't know any Nightingales in Desolation," he says.

I swallow hard. "As you've enjoyed pointing out, we don't exactly run in the same circles."

"Yes," he says, in that low, rumbling voice. "And yet, not much escapes my attention…"

I try to squash the panic that wants to distort my features.

"You said your father's a banker?"

Why did I have to pick banker? "Yes."

Another long silence stretches between us.

I'm beginning to wonder if "enforcing" involves interrogation. Constantine could have had a career at Quantico, in an alternate universe.

I force myself to remain perfectly still. Not to speak, not to move, not even to breathe.

Finally, he shakes his head as if to dismiss me, scowling down at the paper in front of him. "What is this?"

"A simple intake form to screen you for mental illnesses."

He chuckles mirthlessly, a sound that chills me to my core. "You think I'm crazy."

"No, I don't." I swear it's the first protest every damn one of my patients makes when I do the intake.

"This paper asks me if I hear fucking voices."

"Yes."

"Only a crazy person would hear voices, Clare."

"Constantine, most of us would benefit from professional help at one point or another. This form only tells me where we should begin."

I flinch when he reaches for the paper. He pauses, lifting those dark, heated eyes to mine. "You're like a frightened little mouse, you know. So easily spooked." He releases a breath as he slides the paper over. "I like that about you."

He's called me a mouse and a little bird, imagery that smacks of submission and fear.

I swallow hard. He likes how easily I spook?

I definitely *don't*.

I watch as he glances over the intake form. His scowl deepens, and his eyes narrow.

I flinch when he barks a laugh. "This is bullshit." God, there I go again spooking like a frightened filly. "You think these little check-marks on a paper will indicate if I'm mentally ill?"

When he tips his head to the side, he almost looks boyish, for the barest fraction of a second.

"Not really, no. It only gives us a starting point."

"Real, bona fide crazy people know how to lie, Clare, so well you'd never detect the slightest hint of untruth. Real crazy people justify evil so thoroughly, they've muted the semblance of conscience before they graduated grade school. Real crazy people revel in pain and equate power with pleasure." He scoffs at the paper. "No tally of checkmarks on a page would tell you that."

I've had it with his know-it-all attitude and scorn for my field of study. I've had it with the way he makes me fear the next breath I take.

I push myself to my feet, bend over the table, and reach for the paper. Quick as a flash, he snags my wrist, his thumb pushing on my pulse. At the feel of his warm, rough fingers on my skin, my heart skips a beat. My skin flames at his touch, and I'm consumed with an irrational, all-consuming need to *run*.

"Ah, ah," he says with a cluck of his tongue. "You did it again, *Ptichka*."

My voice is a mere whisper. "Ptichka?"

Holding my gaze with his, he drags his rough, masculine thumb over my pulse, almost gently. "It's a Russian term for little bird."

"Ah," I say, feigning bravery. "The big bad Russian uses terms of endearment?"

A slow, wicked grin spreads across his face. Oh, God, I can't look away. A flash of perfectly straight, white teeth and full lips makes me tremble, the unmistakable promise of destruction written in his features. He's the type that would win your heart then tear it to pieces and scatter it like so much confetti.

I won't let him.

I blink and pull my arm away from him. I feel cold without his touch, like someone snuffed the fire out and I'm left in a chilly, dark room.

It makes me want him to touch me again, and I hate that.

"You were saying I did it again. What exactly did I do?"

He leans across the table, straining on his chains. "Came close enough for me to touch you."

"You overstep, Constantine. I'm your doctor."

"No, Clare. I didn't hire you. I didn't ask for you. I never signed on the fucking dotted line. You're not my doctor."

I don't respond. I'm not sure how to.

"I'll tell you what you are," he says, with a note of disdain I'm all too familiar with.

My temper ignites, and my hands clench into fists. Heat flares across my chest, and I heave a furious breath. I sit just close enough to him so he can see me, so he has to stare into my eyes, but not so close he can actually touch me. I've spent my entire life either being judged by the wealthy elite for not meeting their perfect criteria, or dismissed by everyone else for being wealthy elite. It's a lonely, lonely place to be. I won't let this asshole judge me.

"Go ahead, Constantine. Sitting across from me for an hour of your life, knowing literally nothing more about me than my hair and eye color, you've got me all figured out. Let's hear it. What am I?"

I watch a vein pulse in his temple, and his nostrils flare. I'd be scared of assault if he wasn't chained. Hell, I'm still afraid of it even now.

"You're either a virgin, or you're a girl who's never been with a man who knows what to do with a body like yours."

I blink, too surprised to respond. Fear and desire are so intimately acquainted, I don't know which is taking root in my belly, but I know I'm powerless to stop it.

I listen to him, my mouth gaping and my fingers clenched into claws on the table's surface as he continues.

"You're a good little girl. You follow the rules. You're charming and creative, and you work hard. You're witty and enthusiastic, drawing many to you as friends, but only a select few are in your inner circle. You cross every 't' and dot every 'i.' You don't park in handicap parking spaces and haven't made a late payment in your life. Your daddy paid for college, so you have no student loans."

Am I that predictable?

He leans closer. Thank God he's chained. The distance between us is the only thing right now keeping me from incinerating.

When he lowers his voice to a rumble, I need to lean in closer to hear him. A wicked gleam glints in his eyes. He licks his lips.

"You've made yourself climax, but you've never had an orgasm that took your breath away, that left you boneless and wrecked. You've never had your legs spread and your pussy licked until you screamed yourself hoarse." He swallows. "Have you, doctor?"

I'm on my feet. I don't remember standing. I reach a trembling hand to my briefcase and right myself.

"You've overstepped, Constantine." I draw in a breath and release it again. "And if you think I'm that easy to read, you're sadly mistaken."

I reach for the paper and tuck it back into my portfolio. I place it in my bag, then look for the pen.

The pen is gone.

Shit.

Fuck.

I mask my fear so he doesn't know how scared I am, and mentally berate myself. He warned me. He *warned* me. And like an idiot, I left the pen right there on the table for him to take.

I should report directly to my supervisor. At the very least, I should mention to the guard that Constantine may have taken my pen. But then they'd know that I was the negligent one that left it where he could take it.

The *jerk* talked about sex and made me all flustered and used that time to take advantage of me. He took the pen when I wasn't even looking.

Argh!

I walk away from him with my head held high, thankful he can't know my belly still quivers with want. I shake my head at the door.

"This isn't about me. This is about you. This is about finding your way back to who you're meant to be." I turn to look at him and note the surprise in his eyes. Holding his gaze, I reach for the clips that hold my hair in place and tug them loose. My heavy hair swings from the clip onto my shoulders. Taunting him. "Things aren't always what they seem."

I turn on my heel and walk out the door.

I'm shaking so badly I feel faint.

It was a ruse, of course. I lied through my teeth. He was right about goddamn everything.

How fucked up am I that I'm letting him get to me?

Does he have my pen?

I rummage through my bag in the staff room, scattering papers and folders onto the table. My fingers find the barrel of a pen. I breathe a sigh of relief.

When my phone rings, I answer it with shaking hands. "Hey."

Felicity.

"Hey, honey. You okay? I've texted like ten times and haven't gotten to you yet." Even Felicity doesn't know about my job at the prison. No one does.

"Oh, yeah, I'm fine. Sorry. Just finishing up work."

"Okay, chickie, just checking."

She goes on about how much she enjoyed the birthday party, how Spurgeon McDowell asked her on a date, and how Gideon Benedict wants my number.

My thoughts are with the man sitting in the other room.

You've never had your legs spread and your pussy licked until you screamed yourself hoarse.

Would Spurgeon McDowell and Gideon Benedict know how to do that? I idly wonder.

Nope.

Would Constantine?

No! God, no. No no no no no!

I must be out of my mind to even begin to think about this. But there's something about a large, muscular guy with tattoos that tells you this is a man that isn't gentle in bed. This is a man who knows what to do with a woman.

The man gives me *one little taste* of attention, and the next thing I know, I'm imagining exactly what it would be like to do the things he… told me he'd do to me.

I focus on the sound of my heels clicking on the concrete as I walk toward the exit.

I should give my resignation. I have to complete my residency, but there has to be another opening somewhere. Anywhere.

Being around Constantine will be my undoing.

CHAPTER 5

CONSTANTINE

Clare hustles out of the room, ringing the buzzer on her way out to let the guards know it's time to take me back to my cell.

I'm back in gen pop now, my tedious stint in solitary at an end. I prefer the convenience of meeting with my fellow Bratva in person, accessing contraband cell phones and passing instructions with ease. The only problem is that the Irish are not going to be satisfied by our encounter in the yard. Roxy is dead. They're going to demand my death in return, or at a bare minimum, severe physical damage. A little dustup won't cut it—they'll attack again.

That's not the reason I need to get the *fuck* out of here, however.

I need to get out because the Irish aren't the only ones who want revenge.

Roxy drove me fucking nuts at times. It was going to be an arranged marriage—we hadn't dated so much as planned the alliance. How the Bratva and the Irish would share territory around Brighton Beach. How we'd supply them with access to our casinos and they'd sell their product with impunity to our gamblers, splitting the profits 50/50.

I liked Roxy. Respected her, even. But we were never in love, and she made me want to strangle her half the time. She was wild, irresponsible, forgetful, insane with money to the point where you would think she was deliberately setting it on fire. We fought constantly.

Still, I never laid a hand on her.

Punched holes in the wall, yes.

Threw a vase an inch from her ear once, after she slashed the tires on my Maserati.

But I never hurt her. Never harmed a single hair on her head. That wasn't part of our agreement.

The night Roxy was killed is as much a mystery to me as it is to everyone else. I woke up on our bathroom floor covered in her blood, the wine bottle smashed on the tiles, my hands inches from her swollen throat.

It was the worst moment of my life. Not because of Roxy—I was sorry for her, but like I said, we were never in love.

The thing that ripped my guts out was the loss of the baby. She was only eight weeks pregnant. He was the size of my thumbnail. But I had heard his heart beating, strong and persistent inside of her.

He mattered to me in a way that nothing had before. He gave me something that almost felt like hope.

And then he died inside of her, snuffed out before I ever saw his face.

I may have blacked out, but I know I didn't kill Roxy.

I know what I'd do and what I wouldn't.

I've killed plenty of people in my life... never a single one by accident.

I never would have lost my temper to the point of losing my mind.

If I had any doubts on the topic, the speed with which my arrest and conviction was rammed through the legal system was all the additional proof I needed. DA Valencia attacked the case with an intent and ferocity that showed months of forethought. "Evidence" materialized amongst the police with detail and consistency that could not simply have been the result of a little money and a few twisted arms over a matter of days. There was planning in this. Skill. Finesse.

I was thrown in jail with an actual, solid, conviction. This was no slap-up job from the DA, designed to keep me in jail a couple of months before easily being overthrown on appeal. This guy really intends to put me away for life.

Obviously, I'm not going down without a fight.

If he thinks I'm going to rot in here, waiting for my lawyer to beat against the closed doors of the legal institution, he's sorely fucking mistaken.

I'm getting out of DesMax.

I'm going to find out exactly who shoved me in here, and I'm going to make them fucking pay for it. Every minute I spend in this hole is going to be repaid with a gallon of blood dumped down their throats with a nozzle. They'll fucking choke on the very idea that they thought they could put a knife in my back without even getting their hands dirty.

And most of all, they'll pay for my son.

They think the Irish will finish me off before I can seek my revenge? I'll fucking burn the lot of them. I liked Roxy but without our marriage happening, the alliance is shattered. I'll blaze a path through every person who stands in my way, including the Irish.

This is all to explain that I do have to watch my fucking back while I'm making my preparations to get out of here.

Preparations that intimately concern my little *ptitsa* Clare.

Clare fucking Nightingale, huh?

That's very interesting, considering that when I leaned in close to her, when my mouth was inches from that delicate, warm, achingly vulnerable throat, I saw something I had never noticed before.

Clare's fancy, expensive clothes are monogrammed.

Tiny silk monograms, tucked in the labels and sewn in thread the precise color of the clothing. Clare herself might not even know they're there.

In fact, she almost certainly doesn't know, because I assume she would be clever enough to use the same alias as in all her professional documents.

Her seamstress knows differently.

Clare Nightingale is actually Clare Somebody-else.

Clare "V".

I have an inkling who that fucking "V" might be.

I CALL Yury from a contraband cell phone so the call can't be tracked or recorded.

"What did you find?" I ask him.

"You're not gonna like this, boss," he says. "Or maybe you will…"

"Go on."

"Nightingale is her mother's maiden name. Your little rich girl is a whole lot more connected than she's letting on."

"Who is she?" I growl.

I've got no time for Yury's teasing. Get to the fucking point.

"Clare Valencia. She's the DA's daughter."

"I fucking knew it," I breathe.

Valencia was part of the conspiracy to frame me, I fucking know he was. He sent his daughter here to try to pick my brain.

He thought she could earn my trust. Leech information out of me under the guise of "doctor-patient confidentiality."

Well, he's gonna pay the price for putting his little bird within my grasp.

"Get everything ready," I tell Yury. "Friday is the day."

CLARE COMES to visit me at 2:00 in the afternoon on Friday.

I'm curious to see how she'll be attired after our last conversation.

When last we met, I told her she needed to be bent over, spread open, and fucked.

If that thought terrified her, disgusted her, then I'm guessing she's going to come in here armored in the frumpiest getup from her closet.

Instead she strides into the room in a dress with a knee-high skirt slit up the back, sky-high heels, and her hair long, loose, and shining around her shoulders.

A deliberate taunt.

An invitation even…

My hands tighten involuntarily at the sight of her. The chains make a noise like a sigh.

Clare doesn't notice that I'm overheated, my skin flushed from a double layer of clothing.

She likewise fails to see that while my hands still appear cuffed, I'm no longer tethered to the table.

In the seven minutes I was waiting for her, I made use of the clip stolen from her pen the other day. Mechanical locks are simple to pick—it's only the electronic locks in the prison that pose an issue.

Or at least they did before today.

Clare sets down her briefcase opposite me.

I toss back her ridiculous form, completed. It slides across the table, flaring open like a fan.

The idea that I could ever be quantified by such basic questions is offensive to me.

Questions written by academics who don't know the first fucking thing about what it means to be an actual killer—a man untethered from the bullshit bounds of conventional morality.

"What do you think you'll learn from that?" I ask Clare, not bothering to hide my sneer.

"I don't know if I'll learn anything," she replies, coolly. "I don't even know if you answered honestly."

"I don't lie," I snarl. "If I said I did something… I did it. If I say I will do something… you know I fucking mean it."

"Really," she says. "What did you tell Roxy Maguire you were going to do? Because according to witnesses, you said you were going to kill her."

I narrow my eyes at Clare, the air between us dropping twenty degrees in temperature. It's now 2:12, by my estimation.

"I'm sure you're familiar with colloquial speech," I growl.

"You two had a tumultuous relationship?" Clare says, picking up my form and pretending to peruse the responses.

She doesn't want to look me in the eye. There's an edge to her question.

Is she scared to walk over the thin ice of this topic? Or is it possible that my little bird is a tiny bit jealous?

Does she wonder how it felt when I put my hands all over Roxy's body? If I ever seized her hair and yanked her close like I did to Clare?

"You want to know if I loved her?" I ask Clare.

"Did you?" Clare murmurs.

She knows she's crossing a line—asking a question not as a doctor, but as herself.

"I've never loved a woman," I say.

Now Clare's eyes flit up, fixing on mine.

"Do you think you even could?" she asks.

2:14 now.

"I don't know," I growl. "What do you think a woman would have to do to captivate me? To please me? To satisfy me?"

"I thought *you* were the one who knew how to satisfy a woman," she says. "Isn't that what you told me the other day? You think that's what women like? Brutes who threaten them?"

I look up at Clare from beneath lowered brows.

"Oh, I know what you like," I assure her. "I know you better than you know yourself. You think you want a gentleman? A Prince Charming? Someone to buy you flowers and rub your feet?"

Clare's little pink tongue darts out to moisten the center of her lower lip. She's waiting, mesmerized. She really wants me to tell her.

"You want permission," I say. "To be as bad as you want to be. You want to be told to get down on your knees, to open your mouth, to do as you're told… so you don't have to feel guilty. Because you're just doing what Daddy said…"

She's barely noticed that I've leaned much further across the table than I would have been able to do if I were securely tethered. We're only a foot apart.

2:16.

"I don't get on my knees," she says.

"But you will open your mouth…"

Her lips part, probably to argue with me.

It doesn't matter. I lunge forward, seizing her face between my hands, pulling her up out of her chair and shoving my tongue into her mouth. I kiss her like a conqueror, like an invading army with no boundaries and no mercy. I taste her sweet mouth and I steal her breath and I buy myself the seconds I need to wrap my hands around her throat before Clare can scream, before she can even blink.

2:18.

I look her right in the eye and I say, "Why did Valencia send you here?"

Clare's eyes widen and now she does try to scream, but I cut her air off with a squeeze of my hands.

"Don't even think about it," I hiss. "You're going to answer my questions, no more and no less. You try to call for help, or you even fucking think about lying to me, and that's the last sound you'll ever make."

Her pulse races beneath my fingers like that poor little heart might explode.

"W-what are you talking about?" she gasps, against the pressure of my hands.

"Don't fuck with me," I snarl, forehead to forehead, nose to nose with Clare. She's up on her toes, those expensive heels barely touching the floor, her slim fingers clutching at my much larger hands, desperately trying to disengage my grip. She might as well try to bend the bars of one of these prison cells. "I know your father's the DA. Why did he send you here? Who is he working with? What does he want to know?"

"He... doesn't... know... I'm here..." Clare wheezes, face suffused with blood, lips darkening.

I'm inclined to think that's bullshit.

But if Clare is going to keep lying to me under the circumstances, it means she's going to require a level of persuasion impossible to apply inside the prison.

2:20.

The lights go out with a popping of halogen bulbs.

The tiny, windowless room plunges into darkness.

I wrap my arm around Clare's throat, pull her from her side of the table and start dragging her toward the door.

It's ridiculously easy to haul her along. She can't weigh more than a buck ten. I'm more than double that size in pure muscle and bone. She's kicking, clawing, doing anything she can to break my grip. She might as well wrestle an oak tree—it's not even a contest.

I'm not worried about the guards. When the power is cut, the generators kick in, automatically sealing all perimeter doors. I'm trapped in D block, but the guards are likewise trapped outside these offices.

Luckily, I'm not trying to get out that way.

I only want to pass from the psych offices to the infirmary.

To do that, I need Clare's ID card.

2:21.

I haul her over to the infirmary door, swiping her card without bothering to remove it from the lanyard dangling around her neck.

She's kicking so hard that she's lost one of her shoes. She manages to connect the other heel with my shin, pretty fucking hard. I tighten my forearm around her neck, snarling in her ear, "Knock it the fuck off. Every bruise you leave, I'm going to pay back on your ass."

As the infirmary door clicks open, I drag her through.

A chubby nurse catches sight of us. She shrieks, diving behind her desk.

She's got nothing to worry about—I've got everything I need already in place.

2:22.

I heave Clare over to the closest laundry chute and toss her down headfirst. I slide along after her, barreling down the dark metal slide

52

until we land in a massive pile of dirty sheets. Nikita and Erik are waiting, dressed in the dark coveralls, rubber boots, and thick gloves all the laundry workers wear to protect their hands from the harsh industrial chemicals.

"Hurry!" Erik hisses at me.

The sight of my two Bratva brothers galvanizes Clare. She realizes that the power outage was no coincidence, that I'm not simply acting on impulse. She leaps up from the sheets, trying to simultaneously scream and sprint away from us.

I slap my hand over her mouth, picking her up bodily and tucking her under my arm like an unruly toddler.

We hustle over to the empty prisoner transport truck pulled up to the dock.

The driver looks at us with a horrified expression. "We agreed on one person," he sputters. "Not two. And not a fuckin' hostage!"

I thrust Clare into Erik's arms, stripping off my prison scrubs, revealing the stolen guard's uniform beneath.

"Double the fee, then," I say. "You're taking us out either way—take the carrot before I have to use the stick."

Nikita passes me a guard's cap.

Erik is gagging Clare, tying her hands in front of her.

When she's trussed up like a turkey, the driver reluctantly pulls up the false panel to the cabinet in the floor of the truck the guards use to smuggle drugs and other contraband inside the prison. The space was too small for my bulk, but Clare fits inside just fine.

Meanwhile, I take my seat on the passenger side.

2:24

"Hurry," the driver says, nervously. "If we're not at the gates by 2:25…"

"See you in a couple months, boss," Erik grins.

He's inside on a petty larceny charge. He'll be out again soon enough.

Nikita has another year. He looks at the truck, his sullen face transformed by child-like longing.

"Couldn't have put me on the manifest too?" he grumbles.

"Don't worry, brother," I tell him. "You might both be out sooner than you think."

The overhead lights snap on behind us, full power restoring in just under five minutes.

Anything under five minutes isn't reported.

It doesn't trigger a full lockdown.

I pull the heavy truck door shut. The driver starts the engine, heading toward the gates where the sentries are resuming normal protocol after the brief glitch.

In one to two minutes, the guards in D block will check on Dr. Nightingale. They'll see that the psych office is empty. They'll discover that we're both missing.

With the doors unlocked, the nurse in the infirmary will raise an alarm.

D Block will be thrown into full shutdown, fully armed guards searching room by room.

But right here and now, I'm already passing through the three sets of gates, the driver waving to his friends, my head down beneath the stolen cap, the tattoos on my neck covered by the high collar of the uniform.

Below my feet, I can just make out the muffled thumping of Clare knocking her bound knees against the walls of the false compartment.

I give a sharp rap with my heel to tell her to shut the hell up.

She's got a lot worse coming if she doesn't start telling me the truth.

CHAPTER 6

CLARE

I scream as loudly as I can, on the off chance we're in a place where someone might hear me. That proves fruitless. First, I'm gagged so my screams are muffled. Second, there's definitely no one here to help me.

Instead, I'm shoved into this tiny, dirty, dank little compartment where I imagine they bring in contraband or something. It's definitely not big enough for a person, but lucky me, I'm a small person, so it worked for his purposes just fine.

I hate small places. *I hate them.* When I was five years old, I got stuck in an elevator with my mother. We were there three hours before firefighters were able to rescue us. I can still smell the cloying scent of her perfume, still feel the humid air that made it feel like I was in a coffin. I've been claustrophobic ever since.

Tears wet my cheeks, tickling my nose. I'm sweating bullets and trembling. My body temperature vacillates between hot flashes and chills. I try to draw in a breath and can't. My lungs feel constricted, like someone's squeezing them, as hard as he squeezed my neck. If my hands weren't bound, I'd check to see what was choking me, but in my mind, I know.

It's only fear.

Fear. Something I can control.

I close my eyes and whisper to myself. The sound of my raspy voice makes my racing heart slow a little.

"You're safe," I whisper around the gag. "You're not suffocating."

I can still feel his hands on my throat, still feel the burning sensation. My cheeks are too hot and my skin is all prickly.

My chest feels too tight, not helped by the fact that I can't draw in a deep breath.

I have to will myself to be calm.

"You're safe. You're not suffocating," I whisper again. Slowly, my pulse begins to slow.

I give up kicking after a few minutes. When my voice begins to grow hoarse, I remember what he said to me.

You've never had your legs spread and your pussy licked until you screamed yourself hoarse.

I will not scream myself hoarse and give him any ideas.

Not that he needs any assistance there.

I didn't give him enough credit. I'd thought that I knew what he was capable of... I'd read the files. I know how he killed his fiancée. But I put way too much faith in DesMax and way too little in Constantine.

He'd orchestrated his escape with military-like precision. He's had this planned for weeks. Months, even. He knew exactly where to go, when, and how. All he needed was one little piece of the puzzle for it all to fall into place—me.

How did he find out who my father is? My heartbeat accelerates when I think about the venomous sound of his voice, dripping with hatred and fury. He hates my father—most inmates do. It's why I assumed a pseudonym when I came here to work.

My eyes water as shame fills me. I thought so highly of the value of my work, so highly of my plan... but I underestimated the danger I was in.

I feared him when he was chained. What might he do to me now?

God.

I'll have to be careful. I'll have to play my cards just right.

We're cruising along at a rapid speed, I can tell that even from where I am. He's talking on the phone in rapid, furious Russian. I don't know any Russian, but a few words are clear.

Petrov.

Yama.

Valencia.

Petrov I've heard of. The name's familiar from the research I've done on Constantine. Head of the New York Bratva, he's known for running illegal gambling and fighting. I'm not sure where or how, but I know it's how he and his Bratva group earn the majority of their money. Constantine is Bratva, so he'll have something to do with Petrov sooner or later.

My mind starts to grow fuzzy, and my mouth dry. I startle when a harsh kick bangs right beside my head.

"You alive in there?"

I recognize Constantine's familiar growl and mentally flip him off. I'm conserving energy, and I kind of like the idea of him thinking I'm dead. I reason that if I don't answer right away, he might assume I'm dead and let me the hell out of here sooner rather than later.

So I don't respond.

He curses under his breath in Russian, and I feel us cruising to a slower speed.

"If I open this and find you're fucking with me..." his voice diminishes off into a string of Russian curses.

What? What will you do, kidnap me?

Asshole.

In my head, I know that it's probably wisest to play along with him. Not to goad him on. I'll play nice, but only so I can get my way. I want out of this fucking tight space *now*.

I hear voices. I close my eyes, concentrating. If these voices are police... if we've gotten pulled over... I'll have to use what little energy I have left and scream my ass off.

My heart sinks when I hear guttural Russian. Constantine sounds almost... friendly.

Great.

We start moving again. There's a crick in my neck and my wrists hurt from the restraints.

"Take the tunnel." He's talking to his driver.

For a minute, I'm almost glad I'm locked where I am, because tunnels almost freak me out worse than tight spaces. I imagine myself in another place. Anywhere but here.

We come to a quick stop, and my head smacks against the wall.

Voices again. Harsh, angry, then a bark of laughter that makes my pulse spike. We're clunking along, probably still in the tunnel. There aren't that many tunnels in Desolation. I go through what I know.

There are a few tunnels in New York and a few bridges as well. If he's only using the tunnel as a decoy to avoid being followed, using the tunnel's darkness to hide him, he may have gone right back out on the other side.

We could be anywhere in the State right about now, and time goes by so slowly when I can barely breathe.

Finally, *finally*, we cruise to a stop. Voices again, some more banging. I can hear Constantine's voice above them all.

I'm listening as hard as I can but can't make out anything between the muffled sounds and the thick Russian accents. I startle when the panel above me grates open. I blink in the blinding overhead light.

"Get out." Constantine reaches for me even as he commands me. I stifle a whimper. His meaty fists clasp around my forearm, hauling me out as I'm already getting out. He yanks me out of the truck and onto the ground. My feet hit the ground, wobbly, and I feel as if I'm going to fall. He yanks a knife out of his boot, slashes at the bonds at my knees and ankles, then catches me when I stumble.

I want to curse him out, but I'm still gagged. Looks like he doesn't plan on changing that anytime soon. Still, I draw in a deep breath to quell my nerves. It feels good to breathe fresh air again, but I haven't calmed down. I feel like I've gone straight from the frying pan into the fire.

My eyes haven't yet adjusted to the lighting, so at first, I don't notice the other men there until one of them speaks. I look up and stifle a gasp of shock.

We're in an old, abandoned warehouse, likely still in Desolation.

No... not a warehouse. A slaughterhouse. Huge meat hooks hang from the ceiling, and the concrete floor's stained with blood. Through broken windows, I see a rusty chain-link fence surrounding paddocks outside. My eyes come to rest on the blood-stained floors.

I don't like to think of whose blood that could be.

With my eyes adjusted to the light, I stifle another gasp. There are dozens and dozens of men standing around. Large, bulky, tattooed men, some brandishing knives and others, guns. Some wear harnesses with multiple guns secured in place. They stand in small groups, dressed in faded clothes and hoods, as if to make a quick getaway or hide their identity if necessary.

One thing is very clear to me. They're here for a reason, and they're not happy that I'm with Constantine. They shoot furious looks my way, and if Constantine wasn't standing right next to me, I'd be dead, or worse. Some of them I'm sure would be happy to use me well before they did me in.

Constantine speaks in Russian, words I don't understand, but I hear my name. He says my father's name.

No. Oh, God. If they know who I am... And they do. I can tell by the look in their eyes, probably half of them have had a run-in with my father, and they didn't part friends.

I'm dizzy with fear. My eyes come to rest on a massive metal table. I look away. I imagine back when this was a slaughterhouse, what they'd use that table for. I can imagine what they use it for now.

I look back at Constantine when I realize he's speaking English again. For my benefit? But no, not all the men here are Russian. For some reason, he wants me to hear this.

"No one touches Clare. She's mine to deal with, mine to bargain with. I want her father to know I took her and why, because he'll answer for what he's done."

What has my father done?

"Are we clear?"

A large man with longish, graying hair comes up to Constantine and gives him a huge bear hug, then smacks his back so hard I wince.

"Welcome back, brother."

Constantine hugs him back in a fierce, manly hug that makes a surprising lump rise in my throat. He's been separated from these men... his brothers... for how long? It's like he's a prisoner of war returned home. Greetings all around, and someone produces a case of beer. They pop the tops, slamming the cans into each other in a cheer, and beer and froth slosh onto the floor. Constantine closes his eyes, throws his head back, and guzzles like he's dying of thirst. I imagine that's his first drink in a long, long time.

"Petrov's at Yama," a slight blonde Russian man says to Constantine. "He's kept the Irish out of there since you were locked up."

"Yeah, brother," a man with a shaved head says from the back. "We all fucking knew you were framed. All of us but the Irish knew it."

Now there's a wrinkle I hadn't uncovered yet.

He's telling them he was framed?

It's the first time I've considered the fact that he may not have done what he served time for. And he thinks that somehow... my father... *is* involved.

A heavy, dark haired man with tattoos everywhere there's skin steps to the front of the crowd.

"Your name's Clare," he says, scowling. "Related to DA Valencia?"

I nod shakily.

He shakes his head from side to side, his eyes narrowed to slits. "You fucking know who your father is, bitch?"

Constantine tightens beside me, his grip on my arm painfully tight.

I don't respond. I don't breathe.

The man takes a step toward me. I've never seen such fury before in someone's eyes. "Your father killed my brother."

What?

My father didn't kill anyone. Of course he didn't. I can't respond or defend his honor because of the gag, but I look away as if to dismiss him. With a grunt, he raises his hand, steps toward me, and I flinch, prepared for the blow. Constantine spins and tucks me against him, putting himself between me and the other man's fist.

"Touch her and you'll lose that fucking hand."

The other man backs down.

"She's mine to bargain with. You want to get to Valencia, find your own fucking daughter." There's a tense silence, then the gray-haired man barks out a laugh. The man that threatened me shakes his head and walks away. In the distance, I spy a younger man with wide, vacant eyes, watching me. I stare at him until he turns away.

Constantine finishes his beer like he's on a lunch break, crushes the can, then tosses it into a pile of smashed cans behind one of the brick walls. The men scatter with promises of meeting at a place called "Yama" tonight after the sun sets.

"Gives me plenty of time," Constantine says to me as he drags me to a small black car parked in the shadows outside.

Plenty of time for what? I want to ask him. But the truth is, it's plenty of time to do fucking anything. I'm completely at his mercy, and the man is bent on vengeance.

I try to note where we are but can't. I've never seen this place in my life, and it has the distinct feeling of being both desolate and inhabited. As we make our way to the car, I see a rickety old steel sign.

Butcher and Son

I'll remember that.

So far, I've pieced together that he's likely called in favors to escape. He thinks I had something to do with my father and worked with him so that I could find out information. Something tells me he doesn't believe the truth, that my father didn't even know I was there. He's met up with his Bratva brothers and likely some neutral alliances or friends who also owe him favors. And he's going to do something with Petrov?

What is he going to do with me?

He opens the door to the sleek black car. I don't know the type of car, but it smacks of luxury and grace, with a matte ivory leather interior, gleaming chrome accents, and a roomy interior. I'm not here to admire the car, though. He drops me unceremoniously on the passenger seat.

I watch as he walks around the car and opens the driver's side door. He folds his large bulk in the driver's seat with a sigh of contentment. Bet it feels good to sit in the driver's seat again. The engine comes to life and purrs when he turns the key.

Still, he doesn't speak. I have so many questions and so few answers.

I watch as he takes something out of his bag, reaches over, and ties it like a blindfold around my eyes. I'm plunged into darkness. This I can handle better than small places, but I still hate the feeling. I'm guessing I'm not allowed to see where we're going next. Like the warehouse, it's probably a safe place for men like him to go.

I startle at the sound of his voice because I don't expect him to speak.

"You may say that you're innocent, Clare. You might tell me your father's not the DA, or that he is but you have no idea what he's planning." I startle at the feel of his hand on my leg. "But know this. I'm very, *very* well-versed in the art of hostage interrogation. In fact, my brotherhood often calls me in just to perform that job. One might even call it my specialty."

I knew it. I could tell just from his stare, even when he was the one in chains on the other side of the table.

My stomach clenches. He can interrogate me all he wants, but I won't give him the answer he wants because I can't.

I freeze when his hand travels further up my leg. He shoves my dress aside.

"You wore this to taunt me, didn't you?" I don't respond. I jump when he gives my leg a sharp smack. "Answer me when I ask you a question. Now let me ask you again. You did this on purpose. The dress. Your hair. The entire outfit, just to show me you could, didn't you?"

I absolutely did it as a power play.

I think before I respond, but finally nod my head. Yeah. Yeah. I did.

"That was a very bad girl thing to do. Do you have a bad girl fantasy, Clare?"

Bad girl fantasy? I don't even know what that is.

I shake my head from side to side.

When he clucks his tongue, I startle. "Now, Clare, no lying, or I'll have to punish you for that, too. Are you lying to me?"

I shake my head vehemently from side to side. I do not have a bad girl fantasy or whatever the fuck.

"You sure about that?" he says in a low taunt that almost purrs. "You don't get wet when you think about being punished?"

I gasp around the gag when his thumb travels to the inside of my leg, my senses magnified with my eyes still blindfolded. He brushes one large, calloused finger along the tender skin. "I won't interrogate you the way I'd interrogate a man, Clare." I can almost hear the smile in his voice. "No, little *ptichka*. I have much different methods in mind for you."

He threatened to hurt the man that wanted to hurt *me*. What does he mean, then?

Am I safe from everyone but him?

CHAPTER 7

CONSTANTINE

It feels intensely good to be back amongst my brothers again.

I had friends on the inside of DesMax, but nothing compares to my inner circle of soldiers. The men who would lay down their lives for me. The ones who obey without question. Who can be trusted with even my darkest orders.

They wanted to fall on Clare like wolves on fresh meat.

They fucking despise her father, especially Yury. Valencia ordered the cops to rough up his brother during an interrogation. Either the cops went too far, or they did exactly what Valencia asked—either way, they cracked his brother's skull, and he died of a seizure in his cell later that night. The city said Yury's brother had a "pre-existing condition," and the cops were never charged for the killing, let alone Valencia himself.

Yury would love to do the same to Clare: handcuff her hands behind her back, beat her black and blue, and dump her off on her father's doorstep.

But no one is going to lay one fucking finger on her.

Nobody but me.

I decided that Clare belonged to me the moment she walked into that room. When she sat down across the table from me. When I heard her say my name in that low, clear voice of hers.

I wanted her as soon as I laid eyes on her.

The fact that her father is my enemy only makes this all the more delicious. It adds a wickedness to my lust, like pepper on steak.

At this very moment, I'm sure Valencia has been informed that his daughter is missing, and that I'm the one who took her.

He'll send a fleet of cops into Desolation to try to hunt us down.

He'll rampage through my casinos, my strip clubs, my warehouses.

But he's not going to find Clare.

Because I'm taking her somewhere much safer than that.

Somewhere the two of us can really get to know each other. Just like my little bird wanted.

I start the engine of Yury's Bentley. I'd love to sit behind the wheel of my Maserati again, but unfortunately, it's too recognizable—it'll have to stay in storage a little longer.

Clare is huddled against the door, her mouth split by the gag, those big brown eyes blindfolded. She looks so helpless and vulnerable. My cock is an iron bar running down the leg of this detestable uniform.

I drive into the heart of Desolation—the Warren. The most dense, violent, broken-down part of the city, where even the cops are scared to go. Where ancient neon signs buzz and blink, where boarded-up windows outnumber glass panes, where half the businesses are fronts for something you can only find by entering through an unmarked door in the alley...

Like the Emporium.

From the outside, it looks like nothing more than an ancient hotel, the facade weathered, the steps cracked.

Inside, it has everything I need...

I park behind the hotel, coming around to Clare's door like the gentleman I am. I yank it open, catching her arm before she can tumble out onto the concrete.

Her legs are shaking so badly she can hardly stand. I pull down the blindfold so she can walk without stumbling.

"If you promise to keep your mouth shut, I'll take the gag down too," I tell her.

She stares at me for a moment, those dark eyes gleaming with rebellion. Then, slowly, she nods.

I pull the fabric out from between her teeth. She grimaces like she wants to bite me.

"Where are we?" she demands.

"You've never been here before?" I say, knowing full well that she's never been within twenty miles of this place. There's no chance Clare has stepped foot on the streets of the Warren. "I think you'll find it incredibly... educational."

Taking a firm grip on her arm, I lead her in through the back entrance.

The bouncer gives me a nod of recognition.

"Good to have you back, Mr. Rogov," he says.

He doesn't bat an eye at the sight of me leading a woman into the club with her hands bound in front of her. That's positively tame compared to what he sees going in and out of these doors.

Walking into the Emporium is like walking into another world.

The light is low and violet-hued, emanating upward from the baseboards. The thick carpeting, velvet furniture, and darkly papered walls give a hushed feeling like the padded rooms of an asylum. The dull beat of the music throbs like a heartbeat.

Even this early in the afternoon, the Emporium is full. This is Desolation's most popular sex club. Every hour of the day the lonely, the horny, and the depraved seek relief in their most forbidden fantasies.

Up on the main stage, three stunning blondes are taking a bath together in a claw-foot tub. One of the girls is stretched out in the water, her legs spread so that her knees bend over the rim of the tub, her feet hanging down on either side, the faucet pouring directly over her exposed pussy.

The second blonde kneels next to the tub, sucking the first girl's toes.

The third blonde perches up on the rim, soaping her extravagantly proportioned breasts for the enjoyment of the men seated directly around the stage.

Clare stares at the show wide-eyed, then back to me. It doesn't take a genius to see she's wondering what I'll do to her, what I have planned.

"You want a drink?" a waitress asks us.

The waitress is dressed in fetish gear—a complicated harness of leather straps that leaves her breasts completely bare. Her nipples are pierced, as well as her eyebrow, nose, lower lip, and tongue.

"I'll have a shot of Stoli," I say. "She'll have the same, with lime and soda. Bring it to our room."

The waitress nods, sauntering off on her eight-inch heels to retrieve our order.

Clare looks at me like I'm insane.

"I don't want a drink," she says.

"You're gonna need one," I inform her.

"Why the fuck have you brought me here?" she hisses at me, her eyes darting around at the patrons seated in their booths, some already well on their way to satisfaction as heads bob in laps and half-naked whores writhe on the laps of powerful men—powerful women too.

Go-go girls dance in cages. The bartenders wear body paint and thongs. Clare isn't the only person with her hands tied.

I'm enjoying her discomfort. And enjoying even more the gleam of curiosity that she can't quite conceal.

"We're here so we can have a little chat," I tell Clare, my fingers digging into her arm. "I can't check into any old hotel at the moment."

"My father will find me," Clare snarls, trying to pull her arm out of my grip.

"Oh, I intend him to," I bark back at her. "But not yet."

I drag her upstairs to the private suite on the topmost floor.

I've used this room before, though only with professionals. Never with someone I knew on a more… personal basis.

I've always had certain proclivities.

It's why I never had a serious relationship before Roxy.

I don't like kissing, I don't like cuddling, I don't like murmuring sweet endearments in the dark.

What I like is total obedience. Total control. The easiest way to get exactly what I want is to pay for it.

I prefer professionals. The women who simper and pose for my attention in daily life have no fucking clue how to please me.

But Clare… Clare is something different.

She's been sheltered, that much is evident. Tempting, to introduce her to what the world has to offer outside those white picket fences.

I've seen the way she responds when I give her an order. She wants to resist, but she can't. When I touch her, no matter how roughly, her pupils dilate, her skin flushes, her thighs tremble.

She can tell herself that she hates me, that she's terrified.

But the truth is… *she fucking likes it.*

The suite has all the tools I need to make this little bird sing.

The room is large and grand, in the same ancient, ornate style as the rest of the hotel. The four-poster bed is hung with dusty crimson drapes. Blackout curtains block the slightest sliver of daylight from entering, and thick rugs muffle the worn wooden floorboards. Up here the light has a reddish cast, tempered by the old-fashioned lampshades.

"Sit," I say to Clare, nodding toward the bed.

She eyes the mattress warily.

"*Sit,*" I bark.

Her knees bend without conscious thought. She sinks down on the edge of the bed, her bound hands resting on her lap.

I turn away to hide my smile.

A light tap on the door signals the arrival of the waitress. I take the drinks from her tray, closing and locking the door.

Clare flinches at the sound of the bolt turning.

"Listen," she starts blubbering, "I already told you, I have no idea about any grudge between you and my father. He doesn't tell me anything, we're not even close. Actually, I think he kind of despises me… like if you think he's going to pay a ransom—"

"Quiet," I say.

She falls silent, her throat convulsing as she swallows.

I carry the drinks toward her.

"Are you thirsty?" I say, quietly.

I know that she is.

Adrenaline will dehydrate you like nothing else. I can see how pale and papery her lips have become, how difficult it is for her to swallow.

She holds up her bound hands for the drink.

"No," I say. "Open your mouth."

She looks up at me, her dark brows drawing together in an irritated line.

"Open it," I growl.

Slowly, her lips part.

I dip my fingers into the vodka soda. Then I trace my wet fingertips around Clare's lips, moistening them.

She shivers at my touch.

Unconsciously, her lips part further, and her tongue slips out, seeking hydration, but sliding against the balls of my fingers instead, sending a jolt all the way up my arm.

That was just a little taste.

She licks her lips, wanting more.

"Open your mouth," I say again.

This time, Clare opens wider.

I take a sip of her drink, then I spit it directly into her mouth.

She rears back, horrified, sputtering.

"What the fuck are you doing!" she shrieks.

I seize her chin between my thumb and index finger, holding her tight, drilling her with my stare.

"Are you thirsty or not?"

"I'm not—don't you even think about—" she stammers.

"You don't seem to understand your position, Clare," I growl. "I stole you. And when the Bratva steal something… we don't give it back. You belong to me now. If you want to eat, you'll eat from my hand. If you want to drink, you'll drink from my mouth. You're going to answer my questions, and you're going to do what I say. Or you'll suffer the consequences."

"What consequences?" Clare squeaks.

Ignoring that, I take another sip of the drink, tasting the sweet freshness of lime and vodka against my tongue. Then I kiss her, letting the liquor mix between our mouths.

This time, Clare doesn't pull back. In fact, she gives in to the kiss, like this drink is drugged with much more than a shot of vodka. My mouth is the drug, my breath in her lungs the irresistible anesthetic.

Clare is a true submissive.

She just never knew it until this moment.

She kisses me. And she swallows.

"Good girl," I say.

Clare flushes pink.

"Stand up," I order.

Clare stands, stumbling slightly.

"Hold still…"

Pulling a knife from my pocket, I flick open the blade. Before Clare can shy away, I cut the dress off her body with five swift slashes. I make the cuts quick and brutal, but I'm more careful than she could know to protect that baby-soft skin.

Now Clare stands in her bra and panties, black and composed of thin, gauzy material. I can see her nipples through the bra, standing out in hard, dark points.

She stares down at her feet, unable to meet my eyes.

"Turn around," I say. "Show me what I stole."

Slowly she rotates, giving me a three-hundred-and-sixty-degree view of her body. Clare's figure is soft and surprisingly full. Her breasts are larger than I expected, well balanced by a plump white ass. Her waist nips in to form a pleasing hourglass shape, and her thighs are smooth and creamy. Every part of her looks gentle, vulnerable, exquisitely soft. She looks as if she's never been touched by a human hand.

I want to touch her.

I want to mark her.

I want to make her mine and mine alone.

"Did you wear that black underwear for me?" I growl. "Don't you fucking lie…"

Her cheeks flame and her legs tremble beneath her.

"Yes," she hisses. "Before I knew what an asshole you were going to be."

I grab her by the face, tilting up her chin, forcing her to look at me.

"You knew exactly what I was," I say. "I warned you right from the start."

"Yes," she whispers. "You said you were a killer. But now you're saying you were framed…"

"I *was* framed," I growl, my fingers sinking into the soft flesh of her jaw. "By *your* fucking father."

"Why would he do that?" Clare asks, her dark eyes wide and innocent looking.

She seems genuinely confused. But I've been around the block too many times to fall for a sweet baby face.

"That's what *you're* going to tell *me*," I inform her.

"But I don't know anything!"'

Her voice is practically a wail.

I let go of her face.

"That may be," I say. "But there's only one way to find out…"

Clare expects me to push her back down on the bed. Instead I shove her against the wall, where a bevy of shackles and bonds dangle from the ceiling, with manacles bolted directly into the plaster on either side.

If she were a man, we'd be handling this very, very differently.

Perhaps even if she were a different sort of woman.

But there's something about Clare that brings out a new creativity in me—a torturer's genius. She's my muse, and this body is a flawless canvas begging to be painted every shade of pink, red, and purple.

I winch her bound hands overhead, tying them in place. Then I kick her feet apart, stooping to shackle each ankle in a spread position. Finally, I grab the blindfold from around her neck, covering her eyes once more.

"What are you doing?" Clare cries, turning her head helplessly to track my movement, even though she can no longer see a thing. "What are you going to do to me?"

"Don't worry," I tell her. "I have a feeling you're going to enjoy this…"

I open the chest at the foot of the bed, perusing the tools at hand.

Clare flinches as the hinges creak open, her breasts rising and falling rapidly in the flimsy cups of the bra. Her nipples are harder than ever, from fear or anticipation.

I pull out a vibrating wand.

I flip the switch, the buzzing noise as angry as an agitated beehive.

Clare lets out a shriek, her arms stiffening overhead. She tries to close her legs but it's impossible with her ankles shackled to the wall.

"Now tell me, Clare," I say, making her jump as she realizes how soundlessly I've crossed the room, how close I'm standing to her. "Tell me who your father's been meeting with. Tell me who comes to the house."

"I don't even live with him!" she cries.

"Don't play stupid. You've seen something. Who came to your birthday party?"

"Uh… um…" she's panting, hyperventilating, unsure what tool I'm holding in my hand, and what I'll do to her if I don't get the answers I need.

I zap her nipple with the wand, making her jolt as if she was electrocuted.

"Chief Parsons!" she shrieks. "He came to the party! I saw him go into my father's office…"

"Good girl," I say again.

Then I press the wand against her cunt.

"Ohhhh Godddd…" Clare moans.

The vibration is intense; at first, it's too much, and she tries to twist away from it. But I press the wand relentlessly against her clit, rubbing it back and forth in slow strokes. Soon Clare hangs slackly from her bonds, rolling her hips against the vibrator, making a deep, groaning sound unlike anything that's passed those pretty pink lips before.

I see her pace speeding up. She's humping the wand, her breath quickening too. Her chest flushes pink, her nipples practically cutting through the thin material of the bra.

I yank the wand away from her.

"No!" she gasps, looking around blindly with her eyes still covered.

"Now tell me the security code to your parents' house."

She clamps her mouth shut, shaking her head stubbornly. "No fucking way."

I grab her right breast, squeezing hard, twisting the nipple.

"Answer me."

"Ow! Fuck you! No!" she cries.

I slide my hand down the front of her panties, feeling the intense heat of her pussy, how wet and slippery it has become. Her clit is swollen and throbbing, my fingers sliding easily through her folds.

Her knees buckle beneath her, and she leans against my shoulder, gasping and trying not to beg for more.

"Tell me," I whisper in her ear. "I won't hurt them. I just want to take a look around his office. He won't even be home…"

"I can't," Clare murmurs.

I rub my fingers back and forth across her clit, feeling her heart hammering against my torso, hearing her desperate panting in my ear.

"Tell me," I order.

"Promise not to hurt them…"

"I told you. They won't even be home."

"4719," Clare gasps.

"Very good," I grin.

"Now please… please…" she pants.

"Beg me to let you come."

"Please, make me come, Constantine!"

I press the vibrator against her again. I massage it in slow circles around her clit, allowing the climax to build and build. Then I press it on just the right spot, until her whole body starts to shake, until she's screaming herself hoarse, just like I promised her.

I watch the waves of pleasure wrench through her.

Once she collapses, hanging limply from her bonds, I give her a short break. I spend that minute or two admiring the luminescence of her skin, the way it glows faintly pink, like cherry blossoms, in the aftermath of her orgasm.

I yank off her blindfold. "One more question, Clare. You answered it before, but I want you to look me in the eye and answer me now. The full fucking truth."

Slowly, she raises her head and meets my gaze, her expression dazed and unfocused, drugged with pleasure.

"Who sent you to meet with me?"

"No one," Clare mumbles. "It was just… they assigned me a stack of inmates. I picked up your file first."

"Hm," I say, not letting her see that I actually do believe her.

I press the wand against her clit again, turned all the way up to maximum.

"No!" she gasps. "It's too much!"

It's not too much.

She's already starting to come again, relentlessly and helplessly, her whole body jolting like she's strapped into an electric chair.

I don't stop until she's come three more times, until she's begging me to stop with tears running down her cheeks.

Only when she's completely exhausted, limp and helpless as a newborn babe, do I cut her down, and lay her across the bed.

CHAPTER 8

CLARE

I wake from a sex-induced coma. I didn't even know that was a thing.

The room is darkened, luxurious, imbued with the sweet, seductive smell of sex. It takes me a moment to remember where I am, and when it comes back to me, I jerk upward. I can't move. My wrists are tied in restraints, my feet cuffed and set apart with a... bar of sorts.

I've never been into anything like this. I've never seen anything like this in my life.

And yet...

I lick my lips and remember the taste of his mouth, the taste of lime-soaked vodka on his lips and mine. I draw in a hoarse breath and try to keep still.

I need to know where my captor is. I need to prepare for what he'll do to me next.

I take a mental tally of my body.

I'm weak from what he did to me, but I'm not injured. I look down at my body, half-expecting bruises or evidence that he forced himself on me, but no.

I close my eyes and listen. There's the sound of running water, then Constantine's thick Russian accent. I look around the room as my eyes adjust to the darkness. A sliver of yellow light peeks from around a doorframe. There's a small bathroom, the door's ajar, and he's filling what looks like a kettle with water.

When he enters the room again, his eyes meet mine. He's showered, wearing only a towel around his waist. I stare. I've never seen a man like him naked up close and personal. Ever.

How many have?

He's huge and bulky, but there doesn't seem to be an ounce of fat on him. His neck's solid muscle, his shoulders so strong I imagine he can bench press my entire body weight. No, more. I remember the way he tucked me under his arm and carried me like a child. Ink scrolls down his neck, his shoulders, his arms, and when he turns toward a table with the kettle he holds, I see his back is a pattern of tattoos as well.

The towel is snug around his trim waist.

He utters something in Russian, then hangs up the phone.

"So you've wakened, little bird. Are you ready for our next discussion?"

Something tells me our next "discussion" involves some of the accoutrements that lie like snakes in grass on nearby tables and shelves—whips, a supple chain, a thin rod, something that looks like gathered strings of leather, a mask of some sort.

"No."

His low, dark chuckle makes me shiver in anticipation of what he'll do next. He's neither amused nor happy. I wonder if it's the sound of a man crazed.

He sets the kettle on a table a few yards from me and, dropping the towel, reaches for a clean set of clothes. I watch, looking in unabashed awe at every muscled, chiseled inch of him before he dresses himself.

"No?" He shakes his head, plugging the kettle in. There's a silver tray on the table I didn't see before. My mouth waters. God, I'm starving. "Haven't you learned yet what will happen to you when you disobey me?"

Disobey? Is he delusional? Where does he get off thinking it's okay to talk to me like this?

Then I remember he kidnapped me, tied me up, dragged me to this club, and made me climax to the point I was boneless and begging him to *stop*.

At this point, the way he talks to me is almost moot. He treats me like he owns me. Maybe he thinks he does.

He lives a way of life so foreign to me, and I don't just mean head of the Bratva. I don't know what to expect.

I don't like that.

"Hungry, little bird?"

My stomach growls as if to betray me.

When I remember how I'll be fed... how he gave me my drink... I decide I'm maybe not so hungry after all. I turn my head away from him and don't respond, but he doesn't like that. In the next moment, the bed creaks, bowing under his weight, and his fingers wrap around my jaw.

"You'd do well to remember your place, Clare," he says in that deep voice of his tinged with the Russian accent, something I will forever associate with *danger.* "If you disobey me, I'll punish you. And I won't always be so kind as to make you orgasm for punishment."

He's threatened punishment before, and a crazy little part of my brain's both curious and horrified. I never quite realized that climaxing can be painful and punitive. I suppose like any appetite, there's discomfort when overindulged.

"Now," he says, as if we've got that all sorted out. "I asked you a question. Answer me, or I'll take you straight across my knee to teach you manners."

Right, then. *That's* what he'll do.

"I'm not hungry." My stomach growls again.

"Liar." His eyes narrow. Reaching for the platter beside him, he lifts a steaming mug and gives it a stir. I watch, mesmerized, as his big, inked fingers lift a tea bag out, then nestle it on a little plate. He's surprisingly gentle for such a large, rough man. I watch as a trickle of tea makes a pattern on the tiny saucer. He lifts a small steel carafe and pours milk in, then takes a long gulp before he releases a pleased sigh.

"Ahh. *Christos,* that's good. You should talk to your father about the swill they call tea in the Desolation jails." His tone's gotten an edge to it. I really wish he'd stop bringing up my father.

My mouth waters when he places a thick slab of cheese on a wedge of crusty bread. It looks delicious.

His eyes close when he takes a bite. He chews, swallows, then wipes his mouth with a napkin. I'm a little surprised by his good table manners.

"Also delicious."

He makes good work of the little finger sandwiches, the antipasto platter, a mound of olives, and some grapes and berries. It seems this location, in the grimy underbelly of Desolation, serves only to throw people off. Or maybe it's Constantine who's all smoke and mirrors. It seems he has connections in every corner of the city.

"That's fancy fare for a guy like you, no?"

I'm faint with hunger, my belly gnawing at me.

A corner of his lips quirks upward. "What do you really know about me, Clare? For all you know, I'm a connoisseur of fine wine and cheeses."

"Perhaps. And you're right, though you did say your mother was a pastry chef. It seems her fine pastries weren't the only delicacies you have a taste for."

He leans over and brushes a lock of hair off my forehead. The tender touch unnerves me, it seems so unlike him, but I remember the way he protected me in front of the others. It seems Constantine is a complicated man.

"I have a taste for many fine things," he says in a low, raspy voice. He drags the pad of his thumb across my cheekbone. It's warm and calloused, but the touch is so intimate, a thrill of fear skates down my spine. Holding my gaze, he traces the edge of my lips with his thumb.

I want to kiss it. I'm not sure why.

He cups my face, but his eyes are masked.

"Why would my father frame you?"

I'm not lying here in bed, naked, at his mercy, and chatting about cheese and olives.

He sits up straighter, an instant reminder of the imbalance in power here.

"You believe me, then?"

"I don't think you're lying."

"You don't think I'm lying, but you can't say you believe me?"

"Why would I believe a man who broke out of prison and kidnapped me over the man who raised me?"

I need more evidence. More proof.

There was way too much truth in the tone of his voice when he threatened me, his hand on my neck. I haven't caught him in a single lie.

I won't say he's lying to me, but I need way more evidence for proof.

His eyes hold mine for long moments before he responds. "Because of the two of us, only one of us will protect you."

"Why would you protect me?" I whisper. I shake my head. It's clear enough to me that if he was framed, he'd want to get out. It's clear he has the power and connections to do so. It's also clear that I was an easy target for him to use to get out, and he at least initially believed that I had something to do with a conspiracy against him.

But it isn't clear why he cares for me at all.

He doesn't answer my question.

"I am not a good man, Clare. To tell you so would be a lie. And I do not lie. And I'm telling you the truth when I repeat: your father *is* a liar, and he *would* hurt you. The woman I was engaged to died because of him. Why, I don't know." He leans in. "I will find out. And it will go far, far easier for you if you help me instead of hinder me in this."

It's a proposal of sorts, I know it is. He wants to know if he can depend on me, if I'm someone he can rely on. I don't know how to respond at first, because I need to find out more information. But I'm also naked and tied to his bed in a sex club, so I'm hardly in a position to negotiate anything.

"You're asking me to betray my father."

"I didn't ask you to betray anyone. I'm asking you to help me find answers."

"But you'll demand things from me, and you'll use what you can find to get to him. You'll kill him."

At first, he doesn't respond, but he doesn't look away. He leans closer to me, bracing himself on his hand by my side. I can smell the masculine scent of the soap he used. Like him, it's potent and powerful, and it does unexpected things to my body.

I swallow hard. My breathing's labored. My pulse races.

"Killing your father would be a mercy, Clare."

He wouldn't kill him, then. He'd torture him first.

I stare at him, mouth agape, unsure of what to think. My mind is cluttered with thoughts that unnerve me, and the least of my worries is my current state of affairs.

If what he tells me is true… though he has no proof of my father's guilt and I have no proof of his innocence… my father killed an innocent woman. Brutally. It's an unforgivable sin, one he deserves to be punished for.

I can't reconcile the father I know—the professional elite who plays golf on weekends—as the man behind the murder. He wears *argyle socks.*

It can't be possible.

It can't.

But why else would Constantine insist on his own innocence? Why else would he break me out of jail and assume I was in cahoots with my father?

I can't cave so easily. I shouldn't believe what he says so readily.

"How does your father treat you, Clare?"

I look at him, surprised by the question. "What?"

"Does he hurt you? Or are you special to him?"

I look away. I don't like this topic of conversation, but there's no point in going mum now.

If I wasn't cuffed, I'd shrug. I try to appear nonchalant. "He isn't a *bad* father. He doesn't… hurt me. Well, physically anyway."

A deadly calm comes over Constantine. "How did he hurt you?"

"Well, he just… expects many things from me. I have to look perfect, behave perfectly. I had to get perfect grades, drive a perfect car. Anything less than perfection taints his reputation, and on more than one occasion, he's upbraided me for not being the daughter he expects me to be."

To my surprise, a lump rises in my throat. I hate thinking about this. I've gone to therapy for years to deal with this, but apparently, I've just buried it all.

"I see. So this is why you hid your job from him. He'd never approve of his perfect daughter soiling herself by working in a prison."

So he believes me, then? I nod. "Yes. Why do you want to know?"

"It's simple. If he hurt you, too, I'll remember that when I get my hands on him."

I stare at him. He'd... get revenge for *me*? I don't know how to respond.

I try to stifle a yawn, exhausted with everything that's happened. Constantine's eyes go to the shackles above my head.

"It's difficult to sleep cuffed. I can remove the restraints, but if you try anything remotely stupid, I'll tie you up and whip you. Do you understand me?"

A jolt of fear spikes through me. Not a doubt in my mind he would.

I nod.

"Outside this door are three armed men. They all obey my command. I've paid good money for a good night's sleep, and I've waited way too fucking long to jeopardize that."

I nod again.

"First, eat."

I open my mouth and allow him to feed me. Rich cheeses, small bites of dainty finger sandwiches you'd find at a party, and olives, followed by water he mercifully lifts to my mouth. I turn my mouth away from his hand when I've had enough, and he doesn't press the issue.

When I'm done eating, he unfastens my cuffs, and my wrists swing free.

"I have to use the bathroom."

"I'll go with you."

I make a face, but he only chuckles. "You can have a measure of privacy, little bird, but make no mistake, I don't trust you."

I push myself to standing and stretch my aching limbs. I'd give half my inheritance for a massage right now.

I'm in a temper after all that's happened, so I toss over my shoulder, "You're the one who broke out of jail, shoved me under the floor-boards of the escape vehicle, took me to a disgusting slaughterhouse, then interrogated me, and *I'm* the one you don't trust?"

I gasp when his palm cracks against my ass so hard I nearly stumble. I gape at him, but he stands behind me, clearly prepared to deliver another smack if I talk back.

"Watch that tone of voice, *ptitsa*. You'll do as you're told."

My cheeks flame. I walk to the bathroom on tenterhooks, scared of what he'll do to me next, but he only follows and waits outside the door. I stare at myself in the mirror. My hair's wild and untamed, my makeup long since faded. There are rings under my eyes and little red marks along my shoulders and chest, probably from being chained and dragged around like a rag doll.

I look savage and fearful. I don't like that. I stand up taller, splash water on my face, and drag my fingers through my hair.

My parents must be frantic. I can't imagine what they're going through. But if my father did what Constantine says he did... he might be afraid for an entirely different reason.

I need sleep. I need to put this away for now. I need to think about what to do next and prepare for what *Constantine* will do.

I close the door, stand up straight, and walk straight back into his lair.

CHAPTER 9

CONSTANTINE

I have to leave my little bird caged at the Emporium while I attend to a few personal matters. She's carefully guarded by three of my soldiers, but still, I feel a strange sense of unease at leaving her, even after barking at Yury on my way out of the club, "Nobody goes in my suite, and no one comes out. Don't speak to her. Don't look at her. Keep that door locked."

"Yes, boss," Yury said, humbly.

The thought of Clare—messy-haired, sleepy-eyed, and naked in that rumpled bed—is constantly on my mind as I meet with Emmanuel, catching up on the state of each of my many businesses.

Emmanuel is my cousin and one of my closest friends.

Our fathers are brothers.

Uncle Ivo is nothing like my father. He loves food, wine, and women —usually in that order. He likes to joke how pleasant it is to be the younger brother, with none of the responsibilities of leadership, and all of the accompanying rewards.

"Probably more rewards," he teases my father, "since I'm the only one who has time to enjoy them."

Emmanuel is just as irreverent as his father, and one of the only people who can truly make me laugh. He's a good *Avtoritet*, someone I can always rely on—as long as he hasn't been over-indulging. Much like his father, Emmanuel likes to sample the wares of the underworld a little too frequently.

Emmanuel takes after his mother in appearance—slim build, dark hair, dark eyes, sallow complexion. Though he's tall and reasonably good-looking, he's no favorite with women. Roxy never liked him—he probably made a few too many jokes at her expense.

"He just talks too much," I told her.

He's talking a mile a minute right now, telling me, "The cops are everywhere looking for you. They rampaged through the Bleak Street casino and smashed a bunch of the slot machines."

I grit my teeth, furious at the expense to have those machines fixed.

Chief Parsons has gotten pretty fucking bold if he's ordering his officers to attack my casino.

Then again, he was already pretty fucking bold when he assisted Valencia in framing me.

Clare's admission that her father is personal friends with Parsons is no surprise to me—the trumped-up evidence was too good. It's a conspiracy that goes all the way to the top, as they say.

But for what purpose?

Prior to my alliance with the Irish, I would have said that Connor Maguire was my number one enemy. He's the one who stood to benefit most if I was tossed in prison for the rest of my life.

But I think he was happy with our arrangement. And there's no way on God's green earth he would allow his beloved daughter to be slaughtered as collateral damage.

I don't need the Irish's furious assassination attempts to assure me that they are genuinely fucking pissed that Roxy is dead.

Speaking of which—

"The Irish are looking for you, too," Emmanuel says. "They're telling everybody how they're going to cut out your heart and feed it to Chopper."

Chopper is Roxy's pit bull.

"No way is that mangy mutt getting so much as a lick of me," I growl. "I hated that fuckin' dog."

"Didn't like sharing the bed with him?" Emmanuel snickers.

"His breath is worse than yours," I tell Emmanuel. "Plus, I find it pretty fucking strange that he didn't even bark the night Roxy was killed. Didn't do shit to save her. A bad guard dog is no good at all."

"Yeah, that is weird," Emmanuel says, without much enthusiasm to discuss the topic further.

My men all stand by me. But sometimes I think one or two of them might not actually believe that I didn't go off in a rage and pop Roxy with the wine bottle. Like right now, something in Emmanuel's tone makes me think that he believes the reason Chopper didn't attack is because he knew Roxy's attacker on a personal level... like 'cause we lived in the same damn house together.

"Set up a meeting with Maguire," I say. "We need to put this bullshit to rest. I didn't kill Roxy and I want to find out who did just as much as he does."

Emmanuel raises one dark eyebrow. "I don't know if they'll agree to that," he says. "And even if they do… it might only be so they can get you within heart-hacking range."

"Do it anyway," I order.

I had planned to check in with my father next, but I keep having the nagging sensation that I shouldn't leave Clare alone any longer. I drive back to the Emporium and practically run up the stairs to the suite.

"She still in there?" I say to Yury.

"Of course," Yury says, clasping his heavily tattooed hands in front of him and looking nervously toward the doorknob like I'm making him doubt himself.

I barge into the room, startling Clare, who is standing at the window looking down at the uninspiring view of the parking lot.

"Thinking of jumping out?" I say.

"Or throwing someone out," Clare replies, frowning and crossing her arms over her chest.

Ha. She's recovered a little spirit in the hour I've been gone.

"You couldn't lift one of my fingers if I didn't want you to," I say.

"You think you can do whatever you want to me just because you're built like a gorilla," Clare snarls.

"Oh, I don't *think*," I say. "I *know* I can."

Clare is so angry that her whole body is stiff as a cardboard cut-out.

"What's your plan for me right now?" she demands.

"You're coming with me."

"Where?"

"To my father's house."

That seems to surprise her. Her shoulders drop involuntarily, and her mouth opens in a comical little "o" shape.

"I don't have any clean clothes," she stammers.

"Here."

I toss a bundle of clothes directly at her chest. She catches them lightly, one-handed.

As she unwraps the faded T-shirt and jeans she frowns slightly.

"Did these belong to…"

"No," I say, sharply. "They're Yury's sister's clothes."

Is she… jealous? Does she dislike the idea of wearing the clothes of a woman that mattered to me?

"Oh," Clare says, relieved and mildly embarrassed.

I would never dress Clare in Roxy's clothes. I already feel like Roxy is an angry ghost, following me everywhere I go, constantly watching over my shoulder.

I know she isn't angry with me. If spirits exist at all, Roxy's would be the one and only creature on this planet who knows for certain that I didn't kill her. Well, her and Chopper. And whoever the fuck actually did it.

Still, that ragey little Irishwoman will never rest easy until the person responsible for her death, and the death of our child, has paid dearly for his crime. The bloodier and more protracted his suffering, the happier Roxy would be.

Clare pulls on the jeans, socks, T-shirt, and sneakers that Yury so helpfully provided. I can't help smiling at the sight of her—Yury's sister is only fifteen years old, and the T-shirt is emblazoned with a bright pink K-Pop album cover.

"Are you serious?" Clare says.

"It's that or you can come along naked," I say. "I'm sure you can guess which one I'd prefer."

Flushing, Clare stuffs her feet into the sneakers and follows after me.

Honestly, she looks pretty cute in the T-shirt, and those jeans are clinging to her ass in a way they never could on some teenage girl. I have no interest in adolescents—I like a woman with shape. Clare's got more curves than a motor speedway. I'd like to drive my tongue down every inch of them.

No time for that right now, however.

I take her to my father's ornate, rococo-style house on the edge of Blackwood Park.

This neighborhood of stately mansions is less than a seven-minute drive from the Warren, yet I might as well have crossed into another country. In Desolation, wealth and power reside only a few streets over from abject poverty. My father straddles the borderline; invading the galas of the elite when it suits his purposes, but more comfortable amongst the desperate and depraved—the people who would cut your throat for fifty dollars in a dark alleyway.

My father is the definition of ruthless acquisitiveness. There is nothing he won't do to get what he wants.

He used to be able to accomplish his goals with his fists. He was just as massive and brutal a man as me, a ferocious fighter known as the Dentist for the amount of teeth he'd knocked out of people's mouths. I learned from the best. I could have the same nickname now, for slightly different reasons…

His men feared and adored him. Sometimes when they were all rip-roaring drunk, he'd box with them for fun. It was an effective way to remind even the boldest up-and-comers why he was at the top of the heap.

Until he was shot in a drive-by by a pack of Armenians back in Moscow. He took eight bullets, including the one that lodged at the base of his spine.

The other seven shots hardly inconvenienced him any longer than it took the doctor to dig the metal out of his body.

But that last bullet severed his spinal cord. There was no recovering from that.

He's been in a wheelchair ever since, unable to stand, walk, or even fuck.

As you can imagine, it hasn't improved his temperament.

I'm the heir to his empire, second-in-command, and whoever put me behind bars likely fucking knows it.

Whoever masterminded the frame-up job might just as well have been an enemy of my father. They know I'm his muscle as well as his successor. Hell, they might even have known about Roxy's pregnancy. We had only told our inner circle, but no ship is safe from leaks. If they wanted to end the Rogov line, they got damn close to accomplishing their goal.

My father knew about the baby. He hasn't offered me one word of consolation. It isn't his way—I've never heard endearments from him, or even compliments. Still, the loss of his grandson should have been marked in some way.

My resentment at that omission, even after all these months, surprises me.

I'm not glad to be back at this house. In fact, I despise it.

The only thing I don't hate at this moment is the woman climbing out of the car behind me.

Clare looks with awe at the sprawling facade of the house, though she must be used to mansions grander than this. She's probably wondering how the inside of a gangster's house differs from what she's seen before.

She follows me inside, staying extremely close and slightly behind my right arm like an off-set shadow.

I like how she clings to me.

Testing her, I pause for a moment in the entryway. Sure enough, she stops too, like a well-trained dog brought to heel.

My cock stiffens in my pants.

I'd like to train her to do so many things…

But for now, a less-pleasant encounter looms.

I take her directly to my father's study.

Since I was locked up for the better part of six months, you'd think my father might show a little excitement at my return. Instead, he hardly looks up from the open ledger on his desk, only giving me a passing glance and Clare a hard, dark stare, before he writes a few more lines and then lays down his pen.

He says, "This is Valencia's daughter?"

"That's right."

"What do you plan to do with her?"

"Use her as leverage," I reply.

This is partly true. But I have many other plans for Clare, before I'll even think about trading her back to her father...

My father seems to infer something along those lines, because he narrows his pale blue eyes at me, his upper lip curled in a sneer of disgust.

"Kidnapping her was... impulsive," he says. "It's bringing too much attention from the cops."

"They would have looked for me anyway," I say. "Valencia didn't go to all the trouble of chucking me in that fucking hole just to let me escape again."

"He smashed eight of our slot machines," my father says. "We should send him her pinky to remind him to watch his fucking manners."

Clare shrinks even closer to me, so close that I can feel her soft breasts pressing against the back of my arm, and even sense the fluttering of her heart as she watches my father, wide-eyed and terrified.

My own stomach does a long, unpleasant revolution at the idea of holding Clare's wrist against a table while one of my father's men swings a cleaver down on her hand.

Clare has beautiful hands—cream-colored with translucent nails and long, elegant fingers.

No fucking way is anyone touching them. Or any other part of her.

She's mine to do with as I wish.

Mine and no one else's.

"I have better uses for her," I say, shortly.

My father is silent, his expression judging.

"There's a fight at Yama tonight," he says. "Ilya will be there."

Ilya is a broker of sorts. In fact, he was instrumental in brokering the alliance between us and the Maguire clan.

Funnily enough, he's been damn hard to get hold of ever since I was chucked in jail.

He can dodge my phone calls, but not my hand around his throat.

"Perfect," I nod. "So will I."

With that, I close my hand over Clare's wrist and pull her out of the office.

I can feel her relief as we leave my father's dour presence, and the oppressive gloom of the house overstuffed with artwork, rugs, statuary, and furniture. Gangsters always over-decorate. The drive to transform illicit wealth into ostentatious belongings is too strong to resist. Vases and paintings are the trappings of a legitimate life—harder to claw back than a pile of cash.

"So you're not going to cut off my pinky," she says quietly, once we're out of the house.

"No."

She pauses, then asks, "Why not?"

I turn to look at her, at her large, dark eyes that gaze up at me with more than fear… with genuine curiosity. This fucking crazy little shrink—she can't stop analyzing me for a second.

"Because I don't want to," I say, roughly. Then I add, "I have much more interesting uses for those hands."

The statement comes out gruff, like a threat.

Clare doesn't flinch away. In fact, her soft little exhale carries more than relief—maybe, possibly, a hint of anticipation.

She's silent following me into the car. Then she says, "What happened to your father?"

"Shot by a rival," I say.

"When? Back in Moscow?"

I nod.

Almost as soon as my father was back on his feet—figuratively speaking of course—he began bringing me to work with him.

"He needed me to be his eyes, his ears, his legs," I say. "He was paranoid. He thought there was a mole amongst his men."

Someone who had tipped off the Armenians as to where he would be the day they drove by the Danilovsky market in their open-top Cadillac, spraying bullets out of two machine guns.

His physical reduction maddened him.

He needed someone to act as his avatar. And though I hadn't reached my full strength or height yet, he knew I soon would.

"How old were you?" Clare asks.

"Twelve."

She recoils, horrified.

"I was almost six feet tall already," I tell her, as though my mind had grown along with my body. As though I wasn't still a child inside. "He put a gun in my hand. He began to train me in his business— first the basics of extortion, theft, and vice. Then he took me to his whorehouses, his drug dens, the warehouses where he broke the kneecaps of men who owed him gambling debts."

Clare looks sickened. Her reaction is stirring something inside of me. I hear my voice coming out of my mouth without thought, without plan. Telling her things that I told myself were fine, were acceptable, were good business, good parenting—for a mafioso.

"I was still twelve when he popped my cherry," I say. "Not sex—that came a year or two later with one of his whores. No, he wanted to breach the one great barrier of the criminal world, telling me the sooner I got over it, the better. He wanted me to kill a man."

Clare's lovely, pale hands twist in her lap. She's watching me closely, but she doesn't say a word to interrupt or discourage me.

"He waited for a good candidate. Someone from the neighborhood who turned snitch for the cops. His men brought him into that same warehouse, the one where the floor was already stained, where the dumpsters out back often held parts of bodies wrapped up in black garbage bags.

"The man was skinny, shorter than me, but an adult with crow's feet around his eyes, and thinning hair. He was terrified. I had never seen a grown man beg and cry. He whined like a little girl, sobbed, offered us anything if we'd spare his life. Truth be told, he disgusted me."

Clare watches me, her chest barely rising and falling with her breathing.

"My father said, 'Shoot him.' I pointed the gun. Squeezed the trigger. I was surprised how small a hole it made in his chest. I thought it wouldn't kill him, that I'd have to do it again. But he slumped forward and after a few minutes he died."

Clare finally exhales, a long, sighing sound not unlike the last breath of the dying man. I remember that sound clearly. Also, the scuffed shoes he wore on his feet. And how he had a nick on his chin, like he'd cut himself shaving that morning.

"You were a child," Clare says. "You had no choice."

I look her in the eye, unflinching.

"I had a choice," I say. "There was only one finger on that trigger."

Clare's head gives an almost imperceptible shake.

"Do you hate him?" she says.

She means my father.

"Of course not."

She frowns slightly. "You said my father was a liar and a killer. That he caused Roxy's death."

"What of it?"

"Isn't your father the same?"

I snort, starting the car engine.

"This isn't a battle of good against evil, Clare. There is no good and evil. There's everyone with me and everyone against me. You can guess which side your father falls on. I'm giving you a chance to be with me instead. Because you don't want to be standing by your father when I pour napalm on his head."

CHAPTER 10

CLARE

Constantine is absolutely adamant that my father killed Roxy. There's not a doubt in his mind that my father is guilty. I, on the other hand, am not convinced.

I tell myself that he isn't going to hurt my father, not really. We'll find out who did kill her and why, and when we do, he'll have to give up his relentless pursuit and his desire for vengeance against my father.

Constantine makes a phone call, and though he's speaking in rapid Russian, I'm pretty sure he's conversing with one of his soldiers. I hear that tone he has when he's barking orders.

It brings a flush to my chest and neck that embarrasses and alarms me. Why on earth does he have this effect on me, when I don't want it, when intellectually I hate it? He's a criminal, a brute. He's done outrageous things to me and threatened worse. I should despise him.

Yet I find myself pressing my thighs tightly together to try to ease the throbbing between them, turning my face toward the window so he won't see the color in my cheeks.

"See you there," Constantine says in English, ending the call.

We're driving along the crowded streets of Desolation in another borrowed car, this one with tinted windows. I wonder what it's like to live like this day in and day out, the life of a nomad. Nowhere to put down roots, no real place to call home. Tonight, he might go back to the sex club, or camp out at a friend's house. He probably has a safe house or somewhere he can take us. It's clear he has no lack of resources at his disposal. But will he ever have a place where he can really settle down? Will he ever be able to walk the streets in broad daylight again?

Will I?

"You ever been to a fight, little bird?" Constantine asks.

"A… fight? What do you mean?"

His lips quirk up like they sometimes do when I say or do something that amuses him, which honestly happens fairly often.

"A fight, Clare. Like people hitting each other."

"For sport?"

He shrugs, clearly unconcerned with the concept of people hitting each other for other reasons. This doesn't surprise me, but it's still unsettling. His casual view of brutal violence unnerves me.

"No," I say honestly. "I've never seen any kind of fight before, in a ring, or otherwise." I stroke my chin thoughtfully, sifting through my memories. "Well… I mean, one time when I was in seventh grade, a few boys got in a tussle over something and got into a fight, but it was broken up before anyone really got hurt."

"They fought over you?"

I stare at him, agape. "Over me?"

He takes a turn, his eyes still on the road, but he tenses a little. "You act as if the very concept's preposterous."

"But it is."

He reaches for my knee and gives me a none-too-gentle squeeze. "That's enough of that."

Of what? I want to ask, but don't. My throat feels clogged and my nose tingles, and I'm not exactly sure why.

He doesn't have to say it aloud, but he'd fight for me. There's no question. He threatened one of the men already, and he defended me in front of his father.

Why?

"You've lived a sheltered life, little bird."

I look out the window and nod. "I have."

We drive in silence for long moments. The differences between us seem cavernous.

I twist a lock of my hair, still looking out the window, when he finally speaks again.

"Tonight, you'll see a fight unlike anything you've ever seen before."

I turn to him and blink. "Are you attacking someone?"

A sad smile flits across his features before he schools them again. "No, Clare. If I were planning an attack, you wouldn't be coming with me."

Why?

The question pops into my mind again, but I can't speak it aloud. I'm in a place with him where I need to watch and listen, to observe. Something tells me I'll have more than my fill of answers, and soon.

"Tonight, you'll come with me to *Yama*. In English, it means 'the pit'," he continues, taking a turn down a narrow, dimly-lit street lined with cars.

"Okay, so that doesn't sound like a nice, bougie place we might pick up a few cocktails," I mutter, to cover up the hammering of my heart. *The pit?* "The pit makes me think of Edgar Allen Poe."

"The Pit and the Pendulum," he says quietly. "My favorite."

He continues to surprise me. First, his surprisingly gentle edge. His appreciation for good food. Now, he's an Edgar Allen Poe buff?

"You like Poe?"

"Of course. What's there not to like?" He turns down another road, and the parked cars whiz past us so quickly, my stomach clenches and churns. We're driving deep into the heart of the inner city, and I've never been anywhere near this place before. I surprise even myself when I realize that I'm actually relieved he's with me. This isn't a place a girl like me should ever walk alone. But next to him, no one will touch me.

I shrug. "They say not to judge a book by its cover, but I've misjudged you."

"Shame, shame, doctor. You ought to know better than to jump to conclusions." For some reason I can't quite decipher, his scolding tone makes me feel a little shy. I squirm.

"Ah, the blush of a true submissive," he murmurs, almost to himself.

"I'm not blushing," I protest, turning fully away so he doesn't see the way my cheeks flame. I don't know if I like being called a submissive. I'm not entirely sure I know what that even means, but it doesn't sound like something I relate to.

"You are, little bird. I love the way your cheeks color like that. I look forward to knowing I'm the reason why you blush."

My body ignites, consumed by the thought of him doing... whatever it is he'll do to make me blush. *God.*

"You speak freely, Constantine."

"I speak truth, Clare."

I have to change the subject. "What have you read by Poe?"

"Everything, and repeatedly."

"Oh, wow."

He slows down, coming to a stop at a stoplight. "I had a nanny who gave me the collected works in a hard-bound version when I was ten. I was too young then to appreciate how brilliant they were."

"Same."

"In DesMax, I discovered them in English, and it was almost like reading them all for the first time."

"Oh, wow. Are the translations that different?"

"There are many translations, but most lack... nuances, I believe you'd say."

I look out the window and mutter softly to myself, "'Words have no power to impress the mind...'"

"'...without the exquisite horror of their reality'," he finishes. A Poe quote.

I'm in a car with an escaped convict, as his prisoner, having a more entertaining conversation than I've had on any date. The irony is striking.

We drive in silence for long minutes. When he speaks, I almost jump. I catch myself just in time. He already calls me his little bird. I won't scare like one.

"Yama is the underground fighting ring run by Petrov. It probably goes without saying that underground fights are held without legal approval. People have them on private property illegally."

"Who makes the rules?"

A muscle ticks in his jaw. "Usually, there are no rules. The fighters arrive and don't know which opponent they'll face."

"So without the legality of it, there are no taxes… no one to regulate the flow of money."

"Precisely. Large sums of money change hands."

"Do people die?"

He pauses before he answers. Frowning, I watch as he easily navigates the narrow rows of cars and takes a sharp left before he parks the car. "Yes."

"Wow. And we're here because…"

"Lots of reasons. You're a smart girl. Doctorate, isn't it? Let's hear your theories."

I don't know if I'm flattered or insulted. I draw in a breath, then let it out again. "Fair enough. You were told that Petrov kept the Irish away from here. They were the only ones who believed you guilty of Roxy's murder."

"Yes."

"So here, you're safe from blowback from the Irish. It's likely the place you're safest, because the only people who could do you real harm would be… well, legal authorities. Yes?"

"Right."

"And since you believe my father was the one who framed you, you're going to want to start asking some questions."

"I don't believe so, Clare. I know so."

I don't respond to that. He's far more certain than I am. I like to think my father's innocent still. I like to think we have a chance of him not dying by Constantine's hand. The very thought makes me sick.

"You've come to make inquiries or something, I'd guess?"

"Yes. I have to prove to the Irish more than I have to prove to the justice system that I was not the one responsible for Roxy's death. The Irish will kill me before I'll ever be taken into custody again."

"So what happens if... if you get the... justice you seek." My stomach roils. "And you are vindicated by whatever organized crime rings threaten you."

"Yes?"

"What then?"

He shakes his head. "You should know one thing that differentiates the two of us, Clare. People like you—well-to-do, wealthy, born with a silver spoon in your mouth."

I inwardly cringe.

"Their lives are planned out for them. Their parents know what schools they'll go to before they're born. They know they'll go to college, and in some cases, who they'll marry, and the list goes on. People like me?" He shakes his head. "We live day-to-day. I haven't given any thought to what happens next, because the light in front of me only goes as far as my next step. My next step is entering that club and vindicating myself."

Any day could be the last day he lives. I wonder if he finds the concept terrifying or freeing. Perhaps both.

"Stay in the car until I come to your side to get you."

Wow. He doesn't even want me to open the door and exit the vehicle alone? Lovely.

I don't even think about disobeying him. Right now, my very life depends on obeying him.

I flinch when the passenger door opens.

"So easily startled, little bird," he says with a sad shake of his head. "Don't you know you're safe with me?"

"Safe with the man who kidnapped me? No."

But I'm lying. I've never felt so safe in my life. Walking next to Constantine is like walking next to a demigod—I've never seen someone of his size and strength, his ferocity. Though he's a magnet for danger, I can't actually imagine him hurt or killed. By extension, I feel just as invincible.

He slows his pace so I can keep up, otherwise I'm nearly sprinting because he's so much taller than I am. "Stay by my side and don't speak unless you're spoken to."

"That sounds very medieval. Am I your serf?"

"You are adorably nerdy is what you are."

"Aww. No one's ever called me that before."

He gives me a crooked smile, a bright flash of teeth before he quickly sobers. "I mean it, Clare. Stay by my side. Don't talk to anyone. Don't answer questions. You'll shadow me here so I can keep you safe."

I nod. "Got it."

The Pit has the same vibe as the sex club, only when we go in, it's nowhere near as opulent. Instead, it's as grimy inside as it is outside. Dimly lit, it smells faintly of sweat and rubber, like a well-used gym. People walk past us oblivious to who we are, dressed in everything from torn jeans and faded tees to heels and miniskirts.

"*Jesus*, motherfucker." Someone comes up next to Constantine and smacks his back. "Heard you broke out, heard you took Valencia's daughter? Unfuckingbelievable."

Constantine bumps the guy's fist, then drags me along. I'm guessing that as Valencia's daughter I might not be the most popular person in here.

All around us, people congratulate him, greet him, welcome him back like he's a soldier back from war. It's a little awe-inspiring. He's clearly a man of stature here.

"Mr. Rogov, Petrov sends his warmest greetings," a large, beefy blond guy says when we reach one of the crowded rings. "He's otherwise occupied tonight, but says he'll catch up with you soon."

Constantine nods. "Tell Petrov I'd like that."

The look on his face tells me it's a lie, and it doesn't take a rocket scientist to figure out why. Any man who runs a place like this must be ruthless and cutthroat.

But there I go making judgments again, and so far, that's been a really shitty decision.

There's a snack bar along one wall with large tubs of popcorn and frothy beers, and along another wall, a long bar where bartenders serve drinks.

"Where are the fighters?" I have to practically scream above the noise of the crowd.

"We're in between fights. Wait and see."

I blink, surprised to find us in a room unlike the main arena. I hear some men and women speaking Russian in one corner, and in another, strings of Italian. I imagine this is a meeting place of sorts for the underground network of criminals.

People cheer when Constantine comes in, and someone smacks him on the back again. I'd be black and blue after all that back smacking, but he only smiles and greets everyone. They all seem genuinely happy to have him back.

"So glad to see you got out," a petite little blonde wearing death-defying heels says. "I knew you were innocent."

Constantine nods. "Thank you."

"We've told everyone we know," a tall, thin, but lethal-looking guy from another corner says. "We're spreading the word of your innocence."

"The only ones you need to watch are the goddamn Irish," a hefty guy with a white scar across his chin says. "They're out to kill, brother."

"I know."

"You'll have to get to them first," someone else supplies. I don't even know who it is. "You're safe here."

"I heard Petrov kept the Irish out."

"Some Irish. McCarthy's allowed in when he visits the States."

Constantine nods. "Of course."

So it seems there are good Irish and bad Irish, in his eyes. In all their eyes, really.

"I'm sorry about what happened to Roxy," a pretty redhead says. "That was awful."

"It was," Constantine replies. "The person responsible will pay."

Affirmations go up all around, cheers and agreement from all sides.

My stomach clenches.

If what he says is right... that my father, the man likely responsible for sending some of these people here to *jail*... is actually guilty of framing Constantine? He's dead. There's no way he'll escape from a literal ring of underground vigilantes.

"There you are, boss," one of Constantine's men says, catching up with us. It's Yury, the one practically soaked in ink, the one who hated me on sight because of his brother. I was terrified when Constantine left him to guard me, but I shouldn't have worried—his men seem too loyal and too well-trained to disobey his orders. And he's made it clear that no one is to lay a hand on me.

A second soldier joins us a moment later—this one tall and dark-haired. He gives me an appraising look that I don't particularly enjoy, his eyes crawling over my body in the ridiculous hot-pink T-shirt.

"Oh, cousin," he chuckles. "Now I understand why you had to take the girl along with you in your jailbreak..."

Constantine frowns, resting a heavy hand on the small of my back. The possessive gesture makes me feel oddly comforted in this tight press of criminals and gangsters.

"Be quiet," he says to his cousin. "I don't want to draw attention to her."

An irritated look flashes across the cousin's face, but Constantine either doesn't see it, or doesn't care. His attention has been drawn to a stocky man in a pinstriped suit with a bald head as polished as a bowling ball.

"Watch her a moment," Constantine says to Yury.

Without waiting for a response, he shoves his way through the crowd, planting himself in front of the bald man before he can make his escape. And escape is precisely what the man seemed to intend—I watch surprise, anxiety, and desperation flit across his face, before he smooths those emotions away and greets Constantine with a phony grin.

"There you are, my friend! I didn't expect to see you out and about, with every cop in the city looking for you."

"I'm sure you didn't," Constantine growls. "You've been avoiding me, Ilya."

"Not at all, my friend! But you know, things are so delicate at the moment with the Irish and—"

"I'm perfectly aware of how *delicate* it is. What I want to know is why. Who knew about our deal? Who was asking around? Everyone comes to you, Ilya, don't you fucking stonewall me—"

"You know I would never breathe a word of your business to anyone—"

"Unless the price was right," Constantine snarls.

I don't witness Ilya's continued protests, because Constantine's cousin steps in front of me, cutting off my view. It doesn't help that the first match has apparently started in the adjoining room—over the cheers and howls of the crowd, I can no longer eavesdrop either.

"So you're a shrink," the cousin says.

"I'm a psychologist, yes," I reply, shortly.

"Analyze me, then."

"Emmanuel…" Yury says in a warning tone.

Emmanuel ignores him, his dark eyes fixed on my face with equal parts mockery and challenge. His face is flushed, and I think I see the tiniest dusting of white powder around his nostrils. I know what that means—taking a bump in the bathroom was as common as swapping a tampon with the girls I grew up around.

"Psychological analysis is not a party trick," I say. "It can take years to drill down into someone's psyche, and that's *with* the full cooperation of the patient."

"That's funny," Emmanuel says. "'Cause I can size you up in five minutes flat. Guess I shoulda been a shrink."

"Oh really?" I say, coldly, trying to peer around his shoulder to see if Constantine is coming back. I don't like how close Emmanuel is standing, or the way he grins maliciously as he looks down at me.

"I know a spoiled little rich girl when I see one," Emmanuel says. "Trying to inch away from me. Wishing you didn't have to breathe the same air as us peasants. Well, you're in our world now, princess. And you're gonna learn the hard way that we're smarter than you, stronger than you, and we can do whatever the fuck we want with you…"

Yury clears his throat, another warning that Emmanuel ignores.

Constantine is still talking to Ilya.

It's funny—Constantine likes to remind me that I'm sheltered, but it doesn't bother me so much coming from him. Maybe because he doesn't vilify me as one of the elite. Whereas Emmanuel looks like he'd like to peel my skin off with his fingernails.

Taking a deep breath, I square my shoulders and look right up into his face.

"If that's the best you can do, you better stick to your day job," I tell him. "I'm perfectly happy to be here tonight—in fact, I'm rather enjoying it. From a clinical perspective, there's a fascinating array of socio-divergent behavior on display. You, for example—you seem to be overcompensating for feelings of physical inadequacy, which is understandable with all these powerful men around you. Yet you turn that aggression on me, one of the only women present. Which makes me think you may be compensating for sexual inadequacy as well."

Emmanuel's face goes rigid and pale with every word that flies out of my mouth. It doesn't help that Yury lets out a soft but discernible snort of amusement.

"You filthy little bi—" Emmanuel starts, before Constantine rejoins us and he falls instantly silent.

"What did Ilya say?" Yury asks, swiftly changing the subject before Constantine can notice the spring-loaded tension among our little group.

"A pack of bullshit lies," Constantine says. "Call Remo. Tell him to get over here and track Ilya everywhere he goes. Stick on him like a shadow. If he meets with anyone, if he makes a phone call, even a text, steal his fucking phone and see who he's warning. I shook the tree—he's gonna drop some fucking apples."

"You got it, boss," Yury says, ducking out to call this Remo person.

Constantine throws a sharp look at Emmanuel, like maybe he didn't miss the tension between us after all.

"Go get us some drinks," he commands.

I can tell Emmanuel doesn't like being ordered around like a waiter —not one bit. But he simply nods and heads off toward the bar.

"My apologies," Constantine says. "We've missed the first fight. Don't worry, I have excellent seats for—"

He's cut off when someone slams into him from behind. He rocks on his feet but doesn't lose his footing. He comes up swinging, fighting the men who swarm him from every direction.

Before I can scream, before I can even open my mouth, Constantine shoves me hard, pushing me back into the crowd, out of harm's way.

The move costs him a moment's attention that he pays for with a brutal slash of a knife across his bicep. Blood spatters the cement floor like a Pollock painting.

"Constantine!" I shout wildly, trying to see through the crush of bodies much taller than me.

I can't tell who's fighting him, who's helping, and who's trying to get away before they catch the edge of a knife. I see at least three blades, slashing at him from every direction. Constantine ducks and wheels with an agility that hardly seems possible for a man his size.

One of the men slashes at Constantine's face, howling curses, and Constantine chops his hand down hard on the man's arm, sending the knife clattering away across the floor.

"Feckin' Rogov," one of the attackers growls. Irish? Have the Irish infiltrated the fighting ring?

Constantine flings one of his attackers into another, but two more barrel forward, howling like demons. My God, they're relentless.

Any minute, I expect him to kill them. To shoot, or slice their throats, or at the very least land a blow.

But he doesn't.

He deflects every strike, dodging and weaving expertly, his eyes darting away from his attackers once more to find me in the crowd.

I'm fine, I want to tell him. *Focus on you.*

He dodges again, then rolls on the floor just as the youngest of the men stabs his knife down toward his chest.

"Constantine!" Yury bellows, shoving his way through the melee and barreling into the attacker. Yury hits him from the side, knocking him flat. Constantine dives on him, wrapping his thick arm around the man's neck, putting him in a headlock.

By this point, several more burly, bouncer-looking types come charging in, bellowing, "Fucking Irish. Alert Petrov!"

The attackers *scatter*. I'd imagine they're dead if Petrov catches them here. It's so crowded in here, so loud, that nearly all escape, except the one caught dangling like a mouse in a trap by Constantine's beefy arm.

It's only then that Emmanuel rejoins us, holding a bottle of beer in each hand.

"What the hell?" he says. "What happened?"

CHAPTER 11

CONSTANTINE

I drag Niall Maguire toward the doors, my arm wrapped around his neck in a headlock.

We're intercepted by Petrov and four of his men.

If anything, Petrov is more furious than I am, his face congested with blood and his teeth bared as he snarls at Niall, "You dare try to kill a Bratva in my club? I told your father every fucking one of you is banned."

Petrov is not defending me simply because we're both Bratva. He has his own beef with the Maguires, from all the matches they've fixed with Irish fighters. These days, the only Irish he'll allow through the door are the McCarthys.

Niall doesn't answer Petrov. His eyes are fixed on me alone, blood-shot and mad with rage, as he twists his face upward to spit at me, "We'll get you anywhere you go. You'll never be safe. Even after you're dead, Roxy will find you in the next world and tear your soul to pie—"

I cut him off with a tightening of my arm around his throat, turning his threats into strangled gurgling.

"I'll deal with him," I say to Petrov.

Petrov considers, jaw twitching with anger. On the one hand, this is his ring, and the Maguires transgressed, against his warning. On the other hand, possession is nine-tenths of the law, and he'll have to pry Niall out of my hands if he wants to punish him himself.

Besides, the main fight is about to start. Petrov has bets to take, drinks to sell, and plenty of other potential conflicts to break up on the floor.

"You can use the basement," he offers, reluctantly.

"Perfect."

I haul Niall down the dimly lit cement steps, followed closely by Yury and Emmanuel. Emmanuel escorts Clare along with us. For the first time since I broke us out of prison, her eyes are darting around looking for the exits, as if she wants to run away.

The basement is a bleak, damp place. So filthy and dark that it almost makes Yama look luxurious by contrast. The windowless space is lit by only a single bare bulb, the light veering left and right as the bulb swings from its wire, making it feel as if the whole concrete box is rocking.

"Stand there," I say to Clare, pointing to the far corner. "Don't move and don't speak."

Pale and frightened, she walks obediently to the corner, Emmanuel right by her side.

I fling Niall down on a metal folding chair, the rusty legs almost collapsing beneath his weight.

"We'll fucking get you," Niall snarls, spit spraying from his lips. "I don't care if you kill me. My father will come for you, and my uncles, and my cousins... there's a hundred of us and we're never gonna stop..."

"I'm well aware you Irish breed like rabbits," I sneer, annoyed by the deep cut down my bicep courtesy of Niall's knife.

On the other hand, I feel something almost approaching pity. It was fucking madness for him to attack me. Niall's a decent fighter but he's barely six feet tall, slightly built, and only twenty years old. He's Roxy's little brother, and we're acquainted enough that he knows his chances in a fight against me are fucking nil.

Despite his bluster, I can tell Niall is terrified, shaking like a leaf in the wind. He absolutely fucking should be. These goddamn Irish have been like a pack of rats swarming me everywhere I go. I should wring his neck right now. But Roxy always defended her little brother, even when he acted like a total shithead. She wouldn't want me to hurt him.

"Listen to me," I say to Niall, my tone as serious as it's ever been. "I didn't kill Roxy."

Niall makes a derisive scoffing noise.

Before I can say anything, Yury cracks him across the jaw with a punch that knocks the chair backward, the base of Niall's skull connecting with the cement.

Clare shrieks, "Stop! He's just a kid!"

She breaks away from Emmanuel, running at me, practically throwing herself on top of Niall to protect him from me.

"Get away from him," I snarl.

"No!" Clare cries. "I'm not going to stand here and watch you torture him!"

I grab her arm and yank her up, spinning her around to face me. I point my finger right in her face, hissing, "You don't fucking interfere with my business."

Clare shrinks back, terrified by the look on my face. Emmanuel seizes her again, rougher than necessary, and drags her back to the corner. I don't chastise him.

Clare needs to learn her place. Just because we talked about books, that gives her zero fucking leeway to defy me.

I likewise shoot Yury a look, silently telling him to dial it back. Not because of Clare, but because I have no intention of cracking Niall's skull open. At least, not right now.

Chagrined, Yury hauls the chair upright again. Niall flops forward with a dazed expression, blood running out of the side of his mouth. His sandy hair hangs down over his face and his blue eyes are unfocused.

"I'm not going to tell you again," I say to Niall, quietly. "I didn't hurt Roxy. And I'll prove it to your father. But I need time. And information."

Niall blinks up at me. I can't tell if he's half-conscious from the blow to the head, or if he's considering my words.

"Was Roxy still seeing Evan Porter?" I say. "I don't care if she was. But I need to know the truth."

Evan is Roxy's ex-boyfriend. He was not at all happy when she broke off their relationship to acquiesce to the terms of the marriage contract. He's just a two-bit hustler, nobody that Connor Maguire would have ever allowed to marry his daughter with or without me in the picture. But he's violent, and may have been angry enough to take out his rage on Roxy and me.

"No," Niall mumbles through swollen lips, after a moment. "She knew better than that. My father wouldn't have allowed it."

Possibly true. Connor Maguire is an intimidating man, harsh and authoritarian over his two wild children. Still, it wouldn't have been the first time Roxy defied him.

"Did you see Roxy the week before she died?" I demand of Niall.

He's starting to regain his wits, and with them, his opposition to helping me in any way.

"You're not going to fool me into thinking you give a shit," he sneers. "This Inspector Clouseau bullshit isn't tricking anybody—"

Yury takes a step forward again and I make a hissing sound to remind him to back off. Yury looks at me in confusion. Usually this would be the point in the proceedings where we'd be pulling out fingernails with pliers.

Well—he has a point.

Striding forward, I seize Niall by the throat and lift him out of the chair and off his feet.

"I may not have killed Roxy, but I'll snap your fucking neck if you don't answer me," I snarl, right in his face. "I'm trying to do your family a courtesy. If you force my hand, I will slaughter every last one of you. Every uncle, every cousin."

Niall sputters something I can't make out, because his face is purple, his lips turning blue. I loosen my grip a fraction.

"Yes," he wheezes. "I saw her three days before."

"Where did she get the wine?" I demand.

"What—what wine?" he gasps, his toes scrabbling for the floor as I keep him held aloft with one arm, my hand clamped around his throat.

"The wine we drank that night! Where did she get it? It was expensive, Chateau Margaux. Was it from your father's cellar?"

"He does—doesn't drink—"

I set him down so he can speak a little clearer, but I don't remove my hand from his throat.

"He doesn't drink wine!" Niall gasps. "Only whisky."

I let go of Niall, allowing him to collapse backward onto the chair.

I can hear Clare's whimper of relief on the other side of the room, though I don't look at her.

"Take him home," I say to Yury.

"Shouldn't we hold him?" Yury says. "In case Maguire comes after you again?"

"I think we should kill him," Emmanuel says, flatly. "They can't be reasoned with. And Petrov won't like it if you let him go so easy."

"I don't care what Petrov wants," I say. "This is between me and the Maguires." Then, facing Niall, I add, "You tell your father that if I killed Roxy, I would have killed you too. You tell him that whoever did this wants a war between us, and he's playing right into their hands. I'm not going to give them what they want."

I jerk my head toward Clare. "You. Here. *Now.*"

She's pale and sickened, staring between Niall's battered face and my right hand, shining red across the knuckles where Niall's blood ran down.

"*Now!*" I bark, making her jump to attention.

Reluctantly she joins me, though she's not standing as close as she did before.

I'm equally irritated with her.

Grabbing her arm, I drag her roughly toward the car.

"Let go of me!" she cries. "I can walk."

"You don't do a fucking thing without my permission," I hiss at her. "And you sure as fuck don't interfere when I'm working."

"That's working?" she cries. "Beating up some twenty-year-old kid who just lost his sister?"

I round on her. "Do you think there's an age limit to swing a knife or pull a trigger? I just fucking told you I killed a man as a child. Niall would have stabbed that knife right through my heart if I gave him the chance."

"He never got close," Clare says.

"This isn't a game. And if it were, I would be the one who understands the rules, not you. You have no idea who we're dealing with, and what they're capable of doing."

I yank open the rear door of the SUV and practically chuck her in the back seat. Then I climb in after her.

"You see any newspapers with your face on them?" I demand. "You hear your name on the news?"

"No," she stammers, "but I haven't exactly been watching—"

"You can watch all damn day and you won't hear a peep about Clare Nightingale, or Clare Valencia, or whatever the fuck you want to call yourself. Your father hushed it all up. He'd rather risk me shoving you in a suitcase and burying you in the woods over the negative publicity of his daughter being kidnapped. Not to mention the spot-light it would put on my conviction."

Clare swallows hard, staring at my furious face.

"You're lying," she says.

"When have I ever lied to you?" I snarl. "Name one fucking time."

Her mouth opens but no sound comes out.

"Do you want to find out what's really going on?" I demand. "Do you actually want to know the truth?"

"Yes," she whispers.

"Then you work with me. You help me. And you don't fucking inter-fere with my methods."

"Alright," she says, so quietly that I can barely hear her. "I understand."

"Not yet you don't," I say, unbuckling my belt.

"What are you doing?" she squeaks.

"I told you that if you disobey me, there will be consequences."

"I didn't—"

"Did I not tell you to stay in the corner and keep your mouth shut? I was never going to kill Niall. But if I decided to, it would be the right fucking decision. And either way, it's not for you to question me."

"I'm sorry," Clare says, her eyes darting from my face to the belt and back again.

"Not yet you're not," I reply. "But you soon will be."

Clare tries to bolt for the door, fingers scrabbling wildly with the handle.

Unfortunately for her, the doors of the SUV can only be unlocked by the driver. She might as well be in the back of a cop car. And just like a cop, I have a taste for punishment.

Seizing her by the throat, I throw her across my lap and rip her jeans down around her knees. Her underwear goes with them, baring that milky white ass that practically begs for a flogging.

"Let go of me, you animal!" she shouts, kicking and squirming and trying to get away. "Don't you fucking dare!"

That's the first time I've heard her curse.

"Watch your mouth, little bird," I say, "or I'll wash your mouth out with something you won't enjoy. Take your punishment, and I'll go easy on you. Say, 'I'm sorry Daddy, please forgive me'."

"Let me go this fucking instant!" Clare shrieks.

"Wrong answer."

I swing the belt, bringing it down hard on her ass.

Crack!

Her flesh ripples under the impact, and a bright pink stripe marks her snowy flesh.

Clare howls.

"*Oww!* What the—"

Crack!

I strike the other cheek, even harder.

"*Owww!*" Clare cries again, and now there's a distinct sobbing tone to her voice.

A tone isn't good enough.

Crack!

This time I hit the backs of her thighs, and her shriek is high enough to shatter glass.

"Stop, please, I'm sorry!" she blubbers.

Crack!

"That wasn't very convincing. Make me believe you're sorry."

"I'm sorry, Daddy!" she cries.

"A little better. But I told you not to curse."

"You curse all the time!"

Crack!

"*Ow!* You motherfu—"

Crack! Crack! Crack!

Now she really is crying, and not just a little bit.

I drop the belt. Then I unzip my trousers, letting my cock spring free, heavy and swollen.

"Beg for forgiveness," I tell her.

I don't force her head down on my cock.

I wait for her to wrap that slim little hand around the shaft and bring the head to her warm, wet mouth.

Still sobbing softly, she takes my cock in her mouth and begins to suck.

"Good girl," I growl.

I feel the shiver of pleasure run down her spine at my compliment.

I stroke my thick fingers through her hair, gently massaging her scalp.

Her throat relaxes and her mouth sinks further down my cock, her silky tongue dancing around the head.

Her technique is tentative, unpracticed, but she's as eager to please as I knew she would be. She goes to work on my cock, licking and sucking, attentively listening for my moans of encouragement that spur her on to even greater enthusiasm.

Just as she hates to be disciplined, she loves to be rewarded. Just like the good little submissive she is.

"Deeper," I order.

Obediently, she tries to force my cock further into her throat, though it makes her gag.

I reach down and begin to massage her ass, red and throbbing from the whipping.

She whimpers a little as I touch the raw flesh, the whimper turning into a groan of pleasure as I slide my hand further down, cupping her pussy.

She's wetter than an oil spill, my fingers plunging into her with ease.

She moans around my cock, arching her back, begging for more.

I fuck her with my fingers, pushing them in and out of her in time with the thrusts of my cock into her mouth. The deeper she takes my cock, the harder I finger her.

She's panting around my cock, riding my fingers, her whole back flushed almost as red as her ass.

Her eager amateur blowjob is more pleasurable than cock sucking from any professional whore. She wants to please me desperately.

She's trying anything she can think of, pushing herself harder and faster to earn my touch on her pussy, to convince me to make her come.

"Time to wash out that dirty mouth," I growl.

I ram my cock down her throat, pumping hard.

At the same time, I push two fingers into her and rub my index finger against her clit.

Clare lets out an anguished gurgling sound as she starts to come. I feel her pussy clenching and twitching around my fingers.

I unload my balls into her mouth, a hot rush of come directly down her throat. Clare doesn't even seem to notice—she's lost in the throes of her own orgasm, insensible to taste or sound or the need to breathe.

My whole body shakes as I keep coming, the longest orgasm I've ever experienced. It seems unending, wave after wave of pleasure pulsing through me as I accomplish exactly what I'd pictured in that prison cell.

Reality is so much better than fantasy.

I could never have pictured Clare so eager, so compliant, and so shamefully flushed as she finally sits up, wiping her mouth.

She's embarrassed by how hard she came, and how she bent to my demands. She can't even look me in the eye.

I pull her close against me, stroking her hair again.

"Don't be ashamed, little bird," I murmur in her ear. "You cannot fight me. See how good it feels to submit…"

And though she won't answer me, though she won't admit it out loud, I feel how her body relaxes against me, how she sinks into the warmth of my chest.

CHAPTER 12

CLARE

Somehow, I'm back in my seat. Buckled. I look down at the fastened seat belt in a daze. Everything feels surreal.

I can still feel the fiery lash of leather across my ass and thighs, but already, the painful ache of the punishment he gave me has begun to fade to a warm flush.

I'm sure the way he brought me to orgasm had something to do with that.

He's wrapped a bandage around the cut on his arm that's already begun to heal, like he has some kind of superhuman strength. I, on the other hand, am still nursing my wounds.

"Is this what you do?" I ask in a low murmur. I try to keep the pout out of my voice.

I don't know where we're going, but this road isn't familiar. Makes sense. Though I'm sure he'd love to drag me back to the sex club, he's being targeted and can't return to the same place twice.

"What do you mean?" he asks. It's faded to dusk outside the window, a lightish gray blue with a melancholy edge. His large, rough hand—the same hand that made me climax just moments ago—comes to rest on my left thigh. He releases a breath. I wonder if he realizes he did.

"When you're in a relationship. She defies you; you punish her. You dominate her. You make her climax. That's how you bring her to heel."

Such a funny expression, to bring someone to heel. I read it online once, and thought it bizarre, but for some reason it seems to fit quite well now.

Why are we talking about this? Why did I bring this up? I don't want to talk about what he did with other woman any more than I want to feel that unrelenting bite of his belt again.

At least for now.

He smirks. I love that smirk.

"No."

"Constantine, don't lie to me. You're better than that."

"I told you, little bird, I have not lied to you. What I'm telling you is the truth. Have I dominated women? Yes." The rough edge of his accent makes each word cut sharply, and for some reason they seem to have more emphasis that way.

He gives a shrug, before he takes a hard left and we ascend a small hill. "Have I spanked a woman before? Also, yes. I like things kinky, and I like to be the one in control. That much is likely clear to you."

Ah, yeah. You could say that.

"But I don't have relationships with women, Clare. So, no. You know Roxy and I were engaged for an arranged marriage with no wasted love. What we did here, me and you, was between us." He pulls into a parking garage and cruises to a stop on the first floor in a space marked *private parking only*. There's a contemplative look on his face, as if he wants to say something more, but can't quite bring himself to do it.

He turns himself fully toward me, the full force of his gaze penetrating. "We've had a long few days. For one more night, we're free from the hounds of hell at our heels, as it were." He suppresses a sigh, but I note the weariness that crosses his features.

Touching my cheek with surprising gentleness, he says, "Tonight, we rest."

I nod. The thought of escaping or getting to my family has become distant and muted. I feel it in my heart that he was framed. That he didn't kill Roxy. There was an authenticity to the way he questioned the man in the basement earlier that can't be denied. But there's more to it. The way he's conducted himself, the questions he's asked.

If he were guilty of her murder, why would he spend his time so close to the place of his escape? If he were guilty of her murder, he'd be so far from here by now they'd never find him. He has the money, the connections, and the resources. But here he is, scouring the underbelly of Desolation for the person responsible for Roxy's death, because he knows he's an innocent man.

I believe Constantine. In fact, I even believe that I'm special to him. And yet...

"What?" he says, instantly spotting the turmoil I'm trying to conceal. "Speak, Clare. Tell me what troubles you."

Taking a deep breath, I admit, "I know it was an arranged marriage you would have had with Roxy. But you seem... very intent on avenging her."

Constantine sighs. For the first time I see more than weariness etched on his face; I see deep sorrow. It cuts me to the core.

"I am not avenging Roxy," he admits. "I'm avenging our child."

My heart sinks like a rock.

"She was pregnant," I whisper.

"Yes. She was only two months along, but she carried my son and heir."

"I'm so sorry. It wasn't in the report…"

He laughs bitterly. "I wasn't charged with that murder. And no one will pay for it—unless I make them pay."

My sympathy is like a whirlpool in my guts, collapsing me from the inside. I don't know what to say. There's nothing I *can* say to comfort him.

Instead, I simply slip my hand into his and hold on tight.

Constantine squeezes back, hard enough to crush my fingers.

"Don't let this trouble you, little bird," he says. "This is my burden to bear."

Large, open windows give us a view out of the parking garage to the buildings around us. We've arrived at a building of such size and grandeur that I look up, startled.

"Where are we?" I ask, climbing slowly out of the vehicle. My voice hushes in awe as I look about the most decadent entryway I've ever seen. I've traveled at length with my family and have never seen opulence like this. The floors are inlaid with sparkling marble accented in gold, strings of soft music play from overhead speakers, and the elevator doors gleam. Large vases of fragrant, fresh pink and white flowers sit on the tables, and uniformed guards bow when we enter.

"This way, sir," one of the guards says to Constantine.

With a sweep of his hand, the elevator glides noiselessly open, revealing plush burgundy carpet and recessed lighting, again lined with mirrors. The picture of luxury.

"Would you like an escort or a private ride, sir?" The man's drawn face shows no emotion. He's either ignorant of who Constantine is and what he does, or he's got an excellent way of hiding it.

"Private, thank you." I notice him slip the guard folded bills before he leads me onto the elevator. The door glides to a close in front of us. I blink, staring at a brilliant reflection of myself. My cheeks are pink, my eyes bright. At the memory of what made me flush, my blush deepens.

"This is a private elevator in a hotel," Constantine says in my ear. Ah, a privacy entrance that politicians or famous musicians might use. He anchors his hands on my waist, drawing me close to him. I feel the length of him pressed against my butt.

"Did spanking me turn you on?" I ask, in a husky voice I don't recognize as my own.

"You have no fucking idea, little bird. Overpowering you, punishing you, the way you fought and squirmed, made me hard. But watching your mouth open when you came finished me off... I've been painfully hard ever since."

I flush. "That doesn't seem quite fair."

"Never said it was."

The elevator door slides open, revealing a luxurious hallway similar to the one downstairs, outfitted in opulence with gold finishes.

Gleaming marble, thick, plush carpet, flowers in large, generous vases, their fragrance enchanting.

He wants a night off.

A night off from fighting people and hiding from the chase and finding who's responsible for Roxy's death—and the awful loss of his son. A night off from carrying the weight of everything.

His large, rough hand finds mine as we walk down the hall. Every step makes my striped ass ache. I still can't believe he had the audacity to whip me like that. I still can't believe I… liked it? Did I? Well, no. It was too painful to really *like*, yet… the way I climaxed afterward is another story.

It's impossible to tell where I am. I've traveled, but never in Desolation, and outside of the city proper there are too many hotels to count. The question remains, though. If I knew where I was, would I try to escape? No. I'm in too far now. I have to help him find Roxy's murderer. And if it is my father… I can't think of that.

With a quick flash of a card, the door unlocks. He pushes it inward and tugs me in behind him.

"Oh my God," I breathe when he lets me in. I've traveled before. I've even lived in the lap of luxury before, but this is amazing. Comfortable furniture, simple with clean lines and soft contours, the room is decorated in earth tones with great accents. There has to be at least five more rooms adjacent to this, one a spa-like bathroom, and one a full jacuzzi and bar that leads to a balcony.

"Wow. This is incredible. Have you been here before?"

He looks around and shrugs. "I haven't. I came here because Emmanuel's father owns it."

"Ah. So you're safe here?"

His eyebrows go up a bit. *"We're* safe here, yes. The men at the door that let me in are armed men of the brotherhood. No one will get to either of us before they get through them."

I notice a weariness about him. His knuckles still show faint traces of blood from his interrogation of Niall Maguire, and there are a few lacerations I didn't see before.

"Come, Clare." He reaches a hand to me, his large palm face up. Waiting for me.

I take a step toward him and slide my palm against his. Gently, so gently I hardly notice what he's doing at first, he tugs me over to him and kisses my cheek. "Sweet girl," he murmurs in my ear. "Sweet, beautiful, lovely girl."

I don't know what fascinates him so much about me.

I still see nothing more than an average girl who's a bit haggard after everything that's happened. I'm not someone he should be interested in, or proud of. I'm as plain as plain can be. And yet, when he looks at me...

I step toward him. He frames me between his legs, his heavy arms coming to rest gently on my shoulders.

"You look perplexed, Clare. What is it?" His brows furrow as he waits for an answer. I shiver, remembering what he did the last time I got a stern look like that.

I shake my head, but he makes me look at him by grasping my chin. "Ah ah, little bird. I asked you a question."

There's gentle correction in his tone that makes my heart beat faster. I'm still raw from the punishment I got for disobedience.

"You're an enigma to me," I say baldly. It's the truth. He's so brutally violent and vicious, yet there's this tender side I'd bet very, very few have ever seen...

He doesn't ask me why, or question my statement. He only sighs and nods. "Now that, I understand."

"Do you?"

"Of course. Every relationship in my life from my parents to my friends has been complicated, for the exact same reason."

I don't question this. I believe him.

His phone vibrates in his pocket. "Stay right there." I don't move. I hardly breathe. I think I'm physically incapable of defying him after today.

And just like that, the gentle side of Constantine's gone, the ruthless killer taking its place. He curses in Russian, then asks some questions in a deep, harsh voice that rings with authority. I don't speak his language, and even I'm quaking.

I turn away from the harsh sound of his scathing words, but he grabs the back of my shirt and yanks me over to him. My body slams into his. He shuts off the phone and flings it. I gasp, but it lands on a pile of cushions on the large, fluffy sofa. He swallows my gasp with a kiss.

With a harsh groan, his tongue lashes mine, and my body gives a spasm of pleasure, as if remembering the echo of orgasm not long ago. His fingers tangle in my hair and give a painful, erotic tug that travels low to my core. I groan, and that only encourages him more.

Fingers clenched, he tugs my head back, and when my mouth opens on a gasp, he deepens the kiss. Constantine may have a gentle side to him, but another side's unleashed in this kiss. His lips bite, his fingers pull, his body presses mine to his, like he wants to swallow me whole, and the way my body responds it's like I know intuitively where this goes next.

His mouth travels from my lips to my jaw, unhurried but insistent, while at the same time he's rapidly undressing me. "I want you naked, little bird. I want to see you. I want to taste you. Then, I want to devour you."

I nearly moan just at his words, as I quickly help him undress me. My clothing pools at my feet, discarded, and when I stand in front of him naked, he takes a minute to admire me.

"Fucking beautiful," he says, his eyes alight with wonder and lust. I gasp when his huge hands cup my aching ass and squeeze. "Still sore, Clare? Say no, and I'll reignite that fire for you," he warns.

"Oh, absolutely dying over here," I mutter, which earns me a lopsided smile. I feel strange undressed while he's still fully clothed, as if it emphasizes our imbalance in power.

He cracks his palm against my ass which *hurts like hell*, then he cups my butt and yanks me up. My legs wrap around him by instinct, my body on fire. My head falls back, and he laves his tongue along my neck, my breasts, his massive hands firm yet gentle. We walk like that to the bedroom. I'm vaguely aware of a large glass window and twinkling lights and when we enter the room, the largest bed I've ever seen.

With reluctance, he slides me off his body and sets me onto the floor. His voice rumbles over me like broken glass. "Undress me, *ptitsa*."

I reach for his shirt and tug it up, the fabric bunching in my fingers as I desperately undress him. The shirt falls to the floor. I've never been up close and personal to him when he's undressed like this, and I can't help myself. Mouth agape, I run my fingers along his ink, his chiseled shoulders, those powerful, muscular arms as big as small trees. I anchor myself on his shoulders, wrap my hands around him, bend my mouth to his chest and drag my tongue along his nipple.

"Khristos," he curses. I smile to myself when his pants tent with the power of his erection. I clench my thighs together, my core aching to feel him in me.

I lick my lips and slowly lower myself to the floor. Soft, velvety carpet hits my knees. My fingers tremble when I reach for his belt buckle. I remember how he liked it when I sucked him off, and I'm eager to taste him again. I'd never done that for a man before, and I got wet just hearing him groan with pleasure. I unfasten his belt as quickly as I can, then tug it through the fabric loops. I go to toss it on the bed so I can work on his pants, but he takes the belt from my hand.

"Ah ah, Clare. Hand it to me."

I freeze. He's not going to spank me *now*? But no. With a wicked gleam in his eyes, he glides it over my head and fastens a loop around my neck. My pulse quickens. What's he doing?

"Take them off."

Hands shaking, I unfasten his pants and shove them down his legs. His erection springs up. I swallow hard, overtaken by unmitigated lust. I reach for his boxers and shove them down, cup his balls, encircle his thick, veined shaft, and bend closer. I drag my tongue across the very tip, then moan out loud at the salty taste of precum.

I close my eyes and take him fully in my mouth, just as he tightens the belt around my neck. I can breathe, but I have to concentrate. I'm heady with arousal and slightly affected with the choking sensation, but the only thing I can feel right now is vicious, unparalleled lust as it flows through my body like a current. I suckle and tease, before I thrust my mouth along his shaft, over and over.

I love the way he tightens the makeshift noose around my neck, a warning of how dangerous he is, how close to the edge of insanity we skate. I love the feel of his free hand in my hair, weaving and tugging and guiding my head to please him.

"That's enough," he grates. "I want to be in your pussy when I come."

The belt slumps around me, and he makes quick work of removing it and tossing it to the side.

"Up," he orders, yanking me to my feet. Impatient with my slowness in following on my wobbling legs, he lifts me up and brings me to a small room—no, closet? He flicks on a light and a faint ivory glow lights the room. I gasp. It's a walk-in-closet of sorts, fashioned with mirrors. There are no walls, no windows, just mirrors.

Wordlessly, he takes my hands and presses them on one of the mirrors as he stands behind me. The surface is cool under my touch. With his foot, he gently pushes my inner calf. "Spread for me." My pussy clenches. *Fuck.*

I stare in the mirror as he takes his position behind me, his huge, inked fingers such a contrast against the creamy white of my hips. My whole body fits inside his in our reflection. I'm fully outlined with raw, muscled, inked alpha male, and *I. am. here. for. it.*

My hands in front of me, my legs spread apart, he lines his cock up at my entrance. His deep, masculine groan makes me impossibly wetter than I've ever been. I can't breathe. I can't think. I can feel, and I can watch.

His eyes hold mine in the mirror when he glides himself inside me. The feeling's exquisite, like nothing I've ever felt before. I'm so full. So perfectly, blissfully *full.*

"Oh God," I mutter when he thrusts his hips. Perfect bliss shoots through my body, and I haven't even climaxed yet. There's something about the angle, his size, and my insanely aroused body that makes every thrust feel like a mini orgasm.

"You stay right there," he orders, with a warning slap to the thigh.

I groan in response, just as he thrusts again. Over and over, he shoots frissons of euphoria through my limbs, never once breaking my gaze.

"You're mine," he grates, with a ferocious thrust that takes me to the very edge. "Fucking *mine*."

He holds my gaze with the final thrust that nearly splinters me. I cry out, the intensity of my orgasm too much to take. My body fragments, utter ecstasy painted through every nerve. He growls his release; his fingers tightening on my hips is painful, but I don't want him to stop. It's everything I didn't know I needed.

"Yes," I moan, my body jerking with spasms of pure, unadulterated bliss echoing through me. *"Constantine. Yes."*

CHAPTER 13

CONSTANTINE

I wonder what Clare meant when she said 'yes'?

Was she agreeing that she belongs to me, or was she simply lost in her climax?

I had plans for Clare. I intended to use her as a weapon against her father.

But the more time I spend with her, the less I want to trade or barter for her life.

I don't want to give her away at all.

I've never felt an attraction like this.

Her skin doesn't feel like normal human skin—its silky texture is as unlike other women's as velvet is from wool. Her scent intoxicates me. And the grip of her pussy around my cock—it's fucking bespoke, like it was made for me.

Her natural stubbornness against her need to please me is a delicious dichotomy that I can't help but exploit. I love how she tries to resist, only to sink helplessly into a desire that equals my own.

I let her sleep as long as she needs, watching the innocent blankness of her slumbering face, the rise and fall of her delicate shoulders.

She's naked under the sheet.

Already I long to pull it back again, revealing that body that brings the blood rushing to my cock before I've even laid a hand on her.

It takes every ounce of willpower I possess to leave her alone.

Instead, I ponder my next move.

Yury tracked down the supplier of that expensive wine. Apparently, it was delivered to our house the day Roxy uncorked it. She was a fool to accept a gift without confirming the sender, and I was a fool to drink it with her, not considering that Roxy never would have spent so much of her own money on anything that wasn't diamond encrusted.

Obviously, I need to find the sender of the wine. The *real* sender, not whatever bullshit name was written on the invoice or receipt.

I explain this to Clare when she finally wakes.

"I'm coming with you," she says, promptly.

"You think a prisoner decides where she goes and where she stays?" I say. "Was that the case when I was in DesMax and you were the one on the other side of the table?"

Clare frowns. "It's not my fault you were in prison," she says. "And anyway, don't you want my help?" She falters. "I thought that's why you were keeping me with you…"

I see the fear in her eyes. The realization that I could have many reasons for keeping her, most of them unpleasant.

"No one is going to hurt you," I tell her, gruffly.

"No one but you," she says, the marks of my belt still visible on her ass and thighs.

"Do as I say and there will be no more occasion for punishment," I growl.

"I will," Clare says, her spirit rising again, "but I want to come with you."

"Why?"

"I want to know the truth," she says, staunchly. "If my father really is the sort of person to put an innocent man in prison... then I want to know."

"Well," I say. "Innocent is a stretch."

"Innocent of this particular crime," Clare says, a ghost of a smile on her lips.

"You think you want to know, Clare... but the truth can be painful. It can be destructive. It doesn't just kill the future...it decimates even the pleasant memories in your mind, changing the color of everything that came before."

Clare considers this, her face tense and somber.

"I understand," she says. "I still want to know."

"You can come with me," I agree. "But no interference this time."

After a moment's hesitation, she nods.

Our suite is stocked with toiletries and fresh clothes—this time, clothing actually purchased for Clare, not borrowed from Yury's sister.

I turn the water on in the shower, all five faucets. The glass box fills with steam, water raining down from overhead and thundering out from two sides.

I had intended to let Clare shower first, but as soon as I see her naked body, slippery with soap, I join her.

She's marked all over, not just on her ass. I was not gentle with her last night.

Perhaps remembering this, she soaps the washcloth and begins to wash my body, gently and carefully, like a servant. Hoping to please me.

Her delicate touch, combined with the hot water, is phenomenally relaxing. I lean against the cool glass, letting her soap my chest, my abdomen, and even my cock. It swells as she washes my balls, hanging heavy over the back of her hand.

Clare kneels down in the shower to wash my legs and even the tops of my feet.

There's something impossibly erotic in her bowed head, her slim shoulders, her attentive touch. She bites the edge of her lip. I'm certain if I were to touch her pussy lips, I would find them wet with much more than shower water. She enjoys this as much as I do. It makes her heart race, kneeling before me.

Now my cock juts straight out, stiff enough to split the skin.

Clare looks up at me, waiting for the order to put it in her mouth.

Instead, I say, "Go sit on that bench."

Confused, Clare rises and takes a new position on the shower's bench seat.

Now it's me who kneels before her, something new to my experience.

Clare has been such a good girl, she deserves a reward.

And I want something too—the taste of that sweet pussy in my mouth.

I push her knees apart, exposing her cunt.

I use my fingers to part her lips, examining her most private and intimate parts.

Clare blushes, raising her hand like she wants to push me away, but she knows better than to try to stop me.

With her pussy lips parted, I can see the smooth little nub of her clit, tiny and exquisitely sensitive. I rub the ball of my thumb across it. Her knees try to clamp together but they're spread by the width of my shoulders. Her thighs quiver, and she leans her head back against the shower wall, panting softly.

Her nipples stand out stiff on her chest.

I lean forward, pressing my mouth against her cunt. I inhale her scent, barely discernible through the soapy steam, but present nonetheless—a sweet, rich musk, finer than any perfume.

I run my tongue up her slit, dancing the tip across her exposed clit.

Now she can't help herself; she plunges her hand into my hair and moans helplessly, pressing my face against her pussy.

I lick her clit with long, flat strokes, reaching up with my hand to caress her soapy breasts. I was rough with her nipples last night, nibbling and pulling on them until she cried out over and over again.

Today I massage her breasts gently, running my palms over her nipples, making her moan deeply and helplessly, like she'll do anything as long as I keep going.

I put her thighs over my shoulders, my hands under her ass, and in one motion I stand up, lifting her in the air.

Now she's completely helpless, trapped on my shoulders, her hands gripping my hair. I plunge my tongue deep inside of her, her clit grinding against my face.

Her gasps are giddy and terrified. I'm sure she's lightheaded from the heat of the shower, the water pounding directly down on her head, the steam filling her lungs.

Still, she rolls her hips against my face, my fingers sinking into the soft flesh of her buttocks as I fuck her with my tongue.

She starts to come. I can taste the rush of pheromones, the delicious chemical alchemy of her climax. I lap against her clit, drinking every drop of her sweetness, eating her alive.

As the first wave passes, I grab her waist and slide her down my body, lowering her down on my raging cock. She gasps as I penetrate her swollen, sensitive pussy, her thighs wrapped around my waist, her arms around my neck.

We're fucking face to face now, something I do almost as rarely as eating pussy. I kiss her, letting her taste her own sweetness lingering in my mouth. Her lips are soft and swollen, her tongue warmer than I've felt it before.

She starts to come all over again, with almost no break in between, and I find myself coming too, without warning, without control.

Usually I have to work to come, I have to fuck hard and aggressive. This climax takes hold of me without my consent. I'm exploding inside of her before I know what's happening. The force of it is so powerful that my legs go weak; I can hardly hold us both up.

I pump and pump into her, still kissing her, still looking into those big, dark eyes.

A familiar feeling rushes through me, like when I visit the ocean or achieve an impossible goal. A sense of grandiosity and rightness that I've never experienced during sex.

It almost frightens me.

I put her down, breaking away, my whole body still shaking.

"What is it?" Clare says. "What's wrong?"

"Nothing," I say, roughly.

I can't look at her face, flushed with heat and pleasure. She's glowing like a goddess. I can't look at her.

"Get dressed," I order. "It's time to go."

CLARE IS quiet on the drive to the winery.

I know she's troubled by my abrupt switch in mood. And possibly by the sex as well. Did she feel it, too? That moment when I looked in her eyes and it felt like my chest would split open if I didn't look away?

The winery is in the posh part of Desolation, an area I really shouldn't go to under the circumstances. I should send Yury or Emmanuel to handle this errand, but I don't want to do that—I'm beginning to feel a strange sense of paranoia tightening around me concerning the circle of people I can trust.

I feel distinctly out of place parking in front of the forest-green awning with its ornate script reading *Baldacci's Fine Wine and Florals*.

The delivery truck is likewise parked out front—the same dark green van that Yury says was spotted stopping outside my house the day Roxy died.

I push my way through the front door, silvery bells jingling overhead, alerting the shop owner who bustles out of the back, wearing a crisp white apron, his dark hair neatly combed and a pair of spectacles perched on his nose. The scent of fresh flowers mingles with the richer smells of red wine and chocolates.

"Welcome!" he says. "What can I do for you?"

His eyes trace over the ink on my exposed skin. I wonder if he knows I'm Bratva.

"You can tell me who sent a bottle of Chateau Margaux to my house on March 5th."

The shop owner frowns, his thick black brows drawing together in one solid line over his beaky nose.

"I'm afraid that's quite impossible, sir—"

In one motion I seize him by the throat, slamming him against the nearest wine rack. Several bottles plummet from their berths, shattering on the tile floor, sending a flood of acrid wine across our shoes.

I can feel Clare tensing up behind me, but this time she doesn't try to intervene.

"You're going to tell me exactly what I want to know, or I'm going to smash every fucking bottle in this shop over your head, and set the whole place on fire," I snarl.

"But we—we—we don't sell Chateau Margaux!" he sputters, his face rapidly turning blue.

"Constantine," Clare murmurs, tugging at my arm.

I wheel around, just in time to see a skinny kid in a matching white apron slipping out a side door.

I drop the shop owner and bolt after the kid. He's trying to insert his key in the door of the delivery van, but when he sees me barreling after him at top speed, he drops the keys in the gutter and sprints off down the sidewalk instead. I race after him, my boots pounding the pavement, running with the speed and force of a linebacker.

I catch the kid four blocks away, plowing into him and taking him down hard.

He's already begging and pleading before he hits the concrete, his hands held up in surrender.

Unfortunately, this isn't the Warren where nobody would dare intervene in a physical confrontation like this—his shouts draw shoppers out of neighboring stores. I can see several people frantically punching three digits which are certainly 9-1-1 on their cell phones.

At that moment, the dark green van screeches up to the curb, Clare leaning out the driver's side window to shout, "Get in!"

I pick the kid up by his shirt and chuck him in the back of the van, amidst a half-dozen undelivered bouquets and several crates of wine.

"Drive!" I call to Clare.

"Where?"

"Anywhere!"

I turn to the kid.

"You have one fucking chance, exactly one, to tell me who hired you to deliver a bottle of Chateau Margaux to my house."

The kid is shaking so hard his teeth are chattering together, a long scrape down the side of his face where it met the cement at the culmination of my tackle.

"I don't know his name, I swear, he brought the wine, he paid me two hundred bucks to drop it off, I'm so fucking sorry man, I had no idea it was poisoned or whatever the fuck, I saw the news later about the girl, she was really nice when I dropped it off, she even tipped me, I never would have done it if I knew, I'm so fucking sorry!"

I stare at this kid in utter disbelief, realizing that he must have watched as I was convicted for what he believed was the murder he unwittingly committed.

I'd like to wring his scrawny neck.

But he got his facts wrong—the wine was drugged, not poisoned. I passed out on the floor. And Roxy died in a much more horrible way than from a bottle of tainted wine.

"Who paid you," I growl. "Tell me everything you know."

"He had dark hair, uh, maybe like thirty years old, wearing like a coat, a normal kind of black coat…"

"A *normal coat?*" I hiss.

I really, really want to murder this kid. That is the most useless description I've ever heard.

Instead, I yank my phone out of my pocket and pull up Roxy's Instagram.

I loathe social media, and never allowed Roxy to post a single picture of me or our house.

But if you go back far enough, there's plenty of pictures of Evan Porter.

"Is this him?" I demand, shoving the phone in the kid's face.

He examines Roxy's ex-boyfriend, squinting as if trying to be absolutely certain.

"No…" he admits, in a tortured tone. "That's not him."

I can tell he considered lying just to make me go away but was too scared to do it.

I want to fling my own phone against the floor of the van. How the *fuck* am I supposed to find some dude with dark hair and a normal fucking coat?

"Did you see his car?" I demand. "Anything else about him?"

"No," the kid moans. "Nothing."

Clare has been driving us through the pastoral upper-class neighborhoods of Desolation, carefully observing the speed limit to avoid drawing attention while I conduct my interrogation in the back.

"Pull over," I tell her.

She pulls to the curb.

I open the back door.

"Get the fuck out," I tell the kid. "And here—" I shove a plain white card with Yury's number on it into his hand. "If you think of anything useful, you call this number. You don't talk to anyone but me, you understand?"

The kid nods fervently.

"If I find out you're lying to me, I'll find you and kill you," I promise him.

As I shove him out and slam the door in his face, I can hear him calling, "Wait, how am I gonna deliver those flow—" before Clare speeds away.

I climb up to the front, dropping down heavily into the passenger seat.

"I'm sorry," Clare says, sympathetically.

"Well, it was good you spotted that kid. We know more than we did before."

"I suppose," she says, unconvinced. "What's next?"

"Now we talk to the Irish."

Clare sighs. "Because that went so well last time."

CHAPTER 14

CLARE

He's exhausted. I can see it in his features, written on his face like a road map.

We ditched the van and found our way to another hotel. He called his brothers, a sort of clean-up crew, I guess. They cleaned the van, wiped it of prints, ditched it. Got us a ride to another swanky hotel.

"Why couldn't we go back to the hotel we stayed in last night?" I ask, as he shuts and bolts the door of yet one more room reached from yet one more privacy entrance.

"It's harder to hit a moving target, *ptitsa*."

"Ah. Of course." My cheeks flush a little, but I turn away from him so he doesn't see me. I should've known that.

Still, always on the move like this, always on the run. I can't help but wonder if it takes its toll.

I have so many questions. He's been forthright with me, and I'd expect he'd continue to be, but we're both so weary after everything we've done.

When the door is sufficiently locked to his satisfaction, his guards discreetly stationed outside our door and our windows, as well as at the entrance and exit to every parking lot, he turns to me.

Even exhausted and weary, he stands tall. Powerful. I could put a sword in his hand and position him in the front line of battle, and he would strike with the power of an executioner. But there's no need for that. Not now.

He leans against the door and beckons to me with one of his thick, inked fingers.

"Come here, Clare."

I shiver at the low command in his voice. Even in the short time we've been together, my body's beginning to become conditioned to him. He punished me when I disobeyed him. Made me climax when he was done, rewarding me with the best, most teeth-clenching, most powerful orgasms of my life. So when he calls to me, desire threads through me like an electric current. Pulsing. Heated. Thrilling.

I walk to him across the thick, padded carpet, and when I reach him, he rests his hands on my hips. He gives me the trace of a smile, and my heart flutters. "Good girl. Daddy likes that."

So wicked. So wrong. And yet liquid heat pools between my legs at the taboo words.

I lick my lips and do what every girl wants to do when she sees a man as strong and mighty as Constantine. I rest my head on his chest.

His arms tighten around me, fully embracing every inch of me. I'm completely engulfed, and I love it. I draw in a deep breath and release it. I inhale his scent. If the scent of an alpha male could be bottled, it would smell like this—vigorous and indomitable, clean and woodsy.

"You comfort me, Clare."

His words surprise me. He's holding me as if I'm precious to him, and *I'm* the one who comforts *him*?

"Oh?"

Sometimes saying very little is the best approach. I don't want to push him away. I want to know why.

His shoulders shake with a chuckle. "Oh."

I smile against his chest. He runs his fingers through my hair, gently.

"I've never held a woman before."

Startled at this, I pull away from him and give him what must be a perplexed look, because he bends and kisses my forehead. "Don't look so surprised."

"I am. You're no virgin. You were engaged to be married. You've never held a woman?"

My heart sinks when he shakes his head. "Never."

"You've never... cuddled?"

He snorts. "I wouldn't even know how."

How could someone so strong and intelligent be so ignorant of one of the most basic human interactions? His must've been a miserable childhood, not that mine was much better. My heart aches.

"I could show you how."

My heart does a little somersault when he smiles at me. "I'm counting on it. For now, let's order dinner. I have calls to make."

We're going to see the Irish, that I know, but leaving unprepared would be like signing our death warrants.

Taking me by the hand, he leads me to a large, gleaming glass table in the corner of the room. He pulls out a chair. "Sit."

I obey without thinking.

When I was in grad school, we studied human behavior and conditioning, and I know exactly what he's doing to me. I don't even know if he does it all consciously or by instinct, but I'm as malleable to him as warmed taffy. He could twist and pull me into any shape.

I don't know if I like that.

"Do you expect blind obedience?" I hear the edge in my tone and feel it in my chest, a slight prickling of skin and nerves.

There's a warning edge to his tone when he replies, his accent thicker. "You feel the sting of my lash and yet you still question me, little bird?"

I swallow hard.

Why did that turn me on? Gah!

"I just mean, all the time, from all people. I know there are… times… when you've expected it from me."

I watch as he tugs a chair out across from me and folds his heavy frame into it, before he reaches for a folded menu labeled *Room Service* in large gold letters.

"Are you hungry?"

My stomach growls in response, earning another smile from him. God, I love it when he smiles.

"I'll take that as a yes."

"Yes. Starving. And you didn't answer my question."

"I was thinking how to formulate my answer."

Ah. So it's one of those questions, then, that deserves a calculated response? Interesting.

"From my men, I expect nothing short of blind obedience."

"Do you punish them if they disobey you, too, then?"

"Of course, but in a much different way than I would you."

I swallow hard, trying to focus on the menu. The words swim in front of me.

It's hard not to be attracted to him. He's absolutely nothing like any man I've ever dated, but that's exactly why I can't stop thinking about him. Every man I've ever dated fell short of what I wanted. What I needed. But Constantine…

Am I crazy that I'm even going there mentally?

"Baked stuffed haddock with a side of wild rice and side salad, please. Flourless chocolate cake for dessert." I fold the menu with a flourish, satisfied.

He nods, picks up the phone, and places the order. He tacks on a steak, an appetizer tray of antipasto, a bottle of wine, and sparkling water.

"So it makes sense that you expect your men to obey you."

He nods. "It's the way of the Bratva. We function within a solid hierarchy. There are men at the top and men who strive to be, as well as those who serve us and those who are paid by us."

I'm afraid to ask, but I need to know. "And what about your women?"

A shadow crosses his features. "What about them?"

"Do you all… expect obedience, too?"

A muscle ticks in his jaw. "That depends on the man."

Interesting.

"I see."

He leans across the table, his large, bulky frame pressed against his forearms as he folds his fingers together. "Do you, Clare? Do you see?"

No. Not at all.

I don't reply.

"I demand obedience from those under my care," he says in a gentler tone than I expect. "From my men and those beneath me. And since you are in my care, that would be from you as well. I cannot protect anyone who undermines me or seeks to take away my ability to do so in any way."

To him, the concept is clear as day. I nod.

"If I am willing to lay down my life to protect the life of another, it's only natural they grant me the gift of obedience to my command. Understood?"

Wait… what? Lay down his life?

Uncomfortable with the direction of the conversation, I mutter under my breath, "Well that got real intense real quick."

I jump at the sound of his loud bark of laughter. I blink. I've never heard him laugh before, and the sound does strange, wonderful things to my body. I squeeze my legs as heat pulses through my center.

I push myself to my feet. I don't have any plans or course of action in mind. I just stand. When I stand, he's so big that even sitting he's only a few inches shorter than I am.

I walk to him and slide myself onto his lap.

"Clare," he murmurs, his voice thick with arousal. I straddle him, my legs on either side of his large, solid ones, and face him. I cup his face in my hands, the feel of stubble prickling my palms. Without a word, I lean in and brush my lips against his.

The sound he makes is unadulterated passion and raw male wrapped together, and I swallow it whole. He tightens his grip on my waist, slamming me against him, and when I'm flush against his body, he stabs his fingers through my hair and yanks me closer.

I lick his tongue, and he groans. He releases his hand on my waist only to run one thumb along my breast. My nipples pebble, and I release a moan he quickly absorbs.

A sharp knock sounds at the door. We pull away with a shared groan.

"If that isn't our fucking food, I'll kill them." Something tells me he isn't joking.

I sigh, push myself off his lap, and stomp across the room to answer the door.

"No." I freeze at the authoritative sound of his voice. I look over my shoulder. "Stand behind me. You do not answer that door."

A sharp stab of fear grips my heart. There are long moments when I forget who I'm with, what the stakes are, and what could happen next. I watch as he glides a gun out of a holster like it's the most natural thing in the world to do. My pulse quickens.

A knock sounds again, louder. "Room service."

I sigh. Thank God. I'm so hungry my stomach rolls.

Constantine shakes his head, frowning, and pulls out his phone. He taps it, then mutters a few words in thick, rapid Russian. I watch as his eyes darken. He slides a knife out of his boot and hands it to me.

"Go to the bathroom," he says in a low voice. "Lock the door. Wait for me there. If anyone tries to hurt you, stab them. And if that doesn't work, you kick their balls as hard as you can."

What?

He growls at me. *"Now."*

I run to obey. My hands trembling, I shut and lock the door and hold the knife in front of me. I listen as if my life depends on it.

Maybe it does.

But there's no sound. No... nothing. The knife slips in my hand against my sweaty palm, and my pulse races. How long do I wait? I know by now that going against him would be a terrible mistake. Not only would it bring about his wrath, but he knows more about this world than I do by a long shot. I don't know what to expect or how to act, or who could be at the door. He's the one experienced in this.

It strikes me then that my years of studying, the number of my degrees, all the zeroes in my bank account and my place in society... mean absolutely nothing at a moment like this. My entire life my family's told me how important it was to build myself up, to secure my status in life. How crucial it was to be wealthy and elite. But it all means nothing in the face of danger, and less than nothing in the face of death.

And this is Constantine's everyday life.

This is the life he embraces.

The only one he knows.

I nearly sob with relief when I hear a soft knock on the door. "Open."

Constantine.

My hand trembles on the door handle as I gently unfasten the lock. He slides in quietly, a difficult feat for a man his size. He holds a finger to his lips and gives me a nod. His eyes go to the window behind me, then quickly back to me. I look at the window. It's large and airy with a generous tiled windowsill, framed by a gauzy white curtain, with a latch to the right to open it. Behind the window's the top edge of the rail of a balcony.

But wait. We didn't have a balcony.

My heart drops to the floor when I realize the balcony's *a floor below us.*

Oh, no. *No no no no no.* He wants me to *go out the window?*

I look back to him, panic-stricken, and shake my head wildly from side to side. There is *no way* I'm climbing out this window.

He leans in and brings his mouth to my ear. "My men at the gate saw four armored cars enter. The police have found us. We need to escape, and this is the only way out. My men have secured a car for me below this balcony, and we must go."

I shake my head. "I can't," I whisper.

His eyes narrow dangerously. "You must."

"I can't."

He shakes with fury as his fingers grip the back of my neck. "We're out of time. This discussion is over. You will, or I'll knock you out, carry you, and when you wake give you the punishment of your life, do you understand me?"

I'm shaking so badly my teeth rattle. He draws me to his chest and gives me a quick embrace so hard I can't breathe.

"You won't fall, Clare. I'll protect you."

I believe him. I have to.

I nod, shaking, as I walk to the little table below the window. I climb gingerly on top of it, and it wobbles beneath me. There's no way it will hold even half of his girth. "How are you—"

Wordlessly, he stands on the side of the tub, anchors his palms on the tiled ledge below the window, and vaults himself up. I stare, but not for long, because as soon as he's up there, he opens the window and steps right out. Leaning back in, half in, half out, he reaches his arms out to me, and before I can even think twice, he hauls me straight up and out onto the ledge with him.

Oh God. *Oh God.* Stars twinkle in the deep blue of the night sky. It's beautiful and glorious and so open and *free* out here, but we're *not near the ground.* I whimper and turn away from the yawning pavement that seems miles below us.

"Get on my back," he barks out. He falls to one knee and bends, giving me the breadth of his back. Wordlessly, I climb on, wrap my arms around his neck, and drape my body over his. I'm sniffling, tears wetting my cheeks from fear, but I blink them impatiently away as he crouches like a spring and *launches us.*

A scream wrenches from my lungs before I can stop myself, the need for quiet forgotten, but the night air and wind quickly swallow up the sound. We land with a heavy *thud*, he slings me down, then drags me to a spindly fire escape off the balcony.

I've barely recovered from the shock and fright of our crazy trek when I hear the sound of gunshots.

Instead of bolting, Constantine stares toward the source of that sound, squinting as if recognizing someone.

"Quickly, Clare. They've seen us."

The fire escape groans with our weight, swaying from side to side. Bright lights flood the night sky, illuminating the fire escape and blinding me.

"Freeze! Police! Freeze or we shoot."

"Keep moving," he growls. "They're too far to stop us."

A running car waits below us. "Jump! I'll catch you."

I freeze. We're two stories above the ground. He wants me to *jump*?

What?

With surprising grace, he swings himself off the balcony and lands on the ground like a panther. "Jump!"

He holds his arms out to me. *Oh my God.*

A shot rings out and pings the fire escape right above my head. With a terrified scream, I jump. I think I close my eyes. I know I don't look where I'm going, but in a split second I fall into his arms. He doesn't even lose his footing.

The car door opens, we jump in, and the car takes off.

CHAPTER 15

CONSTANTINE

I bundle Clare into the back of Yury's car. He hits the gas before the back door closes behind us. Several bullets pellet the side panel, loud as fireworks inside a tin can.

"Aghh!" Clare shrieks, probably never having been shot at before.

"Don't worry," Yury says, kindly. "I added after-market modifications —it's mostly bullet-resistant now."

"*Mostly* bullet-*resistant?*" Clare squeaks, not comforted in the slightest.

"Sure," Yury says. "Gives you better odds they don't hit you."

"How much better?"

"Mm…fifty-fifty."

"*Fifty-fifty!*"

Another spray of bullets attacks the rear of the car like angry hornets. Yury swerves around a tight corner, narrowly missing the side-view mirrors of several cars parked along the street.

The cop cars screech after us, sirens eerily silent. Both are stealth cars, black on black, their decals invisible at night.

"You see that?" I mutter to Yury.

"Yeah," he says. "And they aren't so careful where they shoot."

"What do you mean?" Clare demands, wide-eyed.

"It means trouble in paradise," I tell her. "I'm sure your father told Chief Parsons to be careful of his baby girl, but he isn't being very fucking careful. Valencia and Parsons may have been hand in glove while they were collaborating to chuck me in jail. Now—not so much."

The rear windshield shatters. Clare ducks down, chunks of glass scattered across her hair like diamonds. I brush the glass away, not caring if it cuts my fingers.

"You're saying Parsons doesn't mind if I get shot?" she says.

I can see the shock on her face.

She knows the chief of police personally. He attended her birthday party. He probably joked and laughed with her. Might even have called her one of those stupid nicknames the hoity-toity love so much.

A week later, he doesn't give a fuck if his off-the-books officers gun her down along with me and Yury.

He won't lose a moment's sleep as long as the evidence for this whole debacle dies along with us.

"It's never pleasant to learn who your real friends are," I tell her.

It's happened to me too many times to count.

On the other hand, I know who I can trust with my life. It's a short list, but immensely valuable to me. Yury, for instance. Like I told

Clare, I would put my literal lungs in his hands for safekeeping and never worry a moment.

Unconsciously, Clare's small hand steals into mine.

She wants to feel protected, while the man hired by the city to preserve the life of its citizens tries to shoot her fucking head off her shoulders.

I squeeze her hand tight, silently letting her know that I'll never let that happen.

"We switch cars up here," Yury grunts, wrenching the wheel to the right, taking us down a side alley.

My *bratoks* Czar and Remo are already waiting. As soon as our car passes, they shove a dumpster out into the alley, wedging the rusted metal bin in place. The cop cars brake hard, their doors flying open. Another volley of bullets hits the dumpster, but it doesn't matter— the bin is wedged into the alleyway like a cork in a bottle. The cops can't pass, they'll have to drive around. I hear them cursing, climbing back inside their vehicles, hastily reversing.

I'm already pulling Clare onto the back of Czar's sport bike.

"Wait, wait, wait!" Clare cries, eyeing the Kawasaki like it's a bucking bronco. "I've never been on a motorcycle before."

"You'll be fine," I say, shortly. "I'm the one driving. Just put your arms around my waist, hold on tight, and lean with me into the turns."

I seize her around the waist, lifting her up and physically setting her down on the seat like an argumentative toddler. Then I take the one and only helmet and shove it down on her head, silencing any further protests.

I take my position in front of her. Her arms wrap around my waist, her head turning so she can press her whole body against my back, clinging on tight.

Good. With that terrified grip, there's no way she'll fall off.

"I'll draw them off, boss," Yury assures me, staying behind the wheel of the Benz.

"Be careful," I tell him. "Parsons isn't fucking around."

"I noticed that," Yury grins.

"Should we follow you, boss?" Czar says. He's climbing onto the back of Remo's bike now that I've commandeered his ride.

"No," I say, surprising him. "Meet me at the next safe house in an hour."

Clare and I drive out the end of the alley first, taking a hard right. Yury heads off the opposite direction, where the cops will be speeding around the corner any second, trying to catch up after their unexpected detour.

I can feel Clare's fingertips digging into the hard muscles of my abdomen as she clutches me with every dip and sway of the bike.

We're roaring down the dark city streets, the streetlights blurring together into a steady stream of color.

With each corner I take, Clare fights me a little less, learning to lean along with the bike, so that she and I and the raging machine all move as one together.

I'm impressed by how quickly she picks it up. Clare may be sheltered and easily startled, but she has this grit down deep inside of her. When I scratch her deep enough, the steel glints through.

Slowly, her death grip relaxes, and she sits up a little taller, looking around as we speed through the city.

Eventually, she holds on with only one hand, flipping up her visor so she can call out to me, "Why didn't you bring your men?"

"Because they won't like where we're going," I grunt.

"Why do I get the feeling I'm not going to like it either?" Clare says.

She's right about that.

I pull the bike up in front of Maguire's pub, right in the heart of Little Dublin.

Maguire's is no dingy corner bar. It's a three-story, freshly painted, gleaming establishment, all rich dark wood, tightly stretched striped awnings, and photographs of famous Irishmen on every wall.

Usually it's packed with people, but the windows are dark an hour after closing. The gold gilt lettering across the glass reads, *Desolation's Original Local, Est. 1829.*

The Maguires have indeed been running this place for almost two centuries. You might be forgiven for thinking that old Cian Maguire, Roxy's great-grandfather, has been occupying his customary window booth for that entire duration—he looks more ancient and well-rooted than the oak bar itself, which he brags was taken from the hull of the ship that brought the first Maguires into New York's harbor.

There will be no boasting and no storytelling today. As soon as I step foot through the doors of the pub, Clare at my side, Cian gives a sharp whistle and four angry Irishmen come pouring out of the stock room. Niall Maguire is in the lead, his mouth still bruised from our last encounter. He looks as haughty and furious as a bantam rooster. Right next to him is Chopper, Roxy's pit bull, who can't seem to decide whether to snarl along with everyone else or dash over and lick my face. Connor Maguire brings up the rear, shirtsleeves rolled up to the elbow and his face almost as red as his thinning hair.

"You've got the fuckin' nerve, don't ya, boyo," he snarls as soon as he sees me.

"That's right," I growl right back at him. "And I'm gonna keep coming around until you dig the wax out of your ears and fucking listen to me."

"Oh, I'll listen to every word you say," Connor sneers. "When you're tied to a chair being beaten with a fuckin' pipe like you did to my boy. Then we'll have plenty of conversation."

Two of his goons step forward, moving to flank me, hands reaching for their guns.

I shove Clare behind me, roughly and unceremoniously, touching my own Glock, easily accessible in the double holsters inside my jacket. I'm waiting to see if they draw, or if they intend to take me down by hand.

"Your boy got home just fine," I say to Connor, keeping my eyes on his men. "I sent him back to you with barely a mark, even after he took a chunk out of my arm."

I turn my forearm into my body, showing Connor the ugly gash down the side of my bicep.

"You think I'd come in here if I killed Roxy? Do you?"

Doubt flares in Connor's eyes.

The man on the left—a tall, gangly ogre type with a blocky head and overlong sideburns—lunges for me. I shove his arms aside with a stiff-arm to the elbow joint, holding myself back from cracking him across the jaw for good measure.

"Easy!" I bark, and then to Connor, "I've got a recording for you. If you want to find out who's responsible for her death, you'll work with me."

Connor considers, making a hissing sound through the gap in his front teeth to tell his men to back off just a moment.

Niall hasn't made the same mistake of rushing me again. He's watching this whole exchange silently, hand resting lightly on Chopper's head, his expression dark and resentful.

I pull my phone out of my pocket, playing the recording I made of my interview with the florist's delivery boy.

His frantic sputtering and begging, while chaotic on the tape, has the ring of authenticity as he admits to the bribe and the delivery of the wine.

"So what?" Connor spits, unconvinced. "That could be anyone."

"I was there!" Clare cries. "The kid was terrified. He was telling the truth."

Connor turns to face her, his blue eyes so faded that they look like nothing more than black pin-prick pupils in a sea of grayish white.

"Don't think I don't know exactly who you are, little missy," he says, in his bitter-soft lilt. "Valencia's little bitch that nobody is supposed to know is stolen, but everybody fuckin' knows. What kind of favor do you think your father would owe me if I dropped you off on his doorstep, handcuffed to the body of your kidnapper? What a gift that would be."

"Constantine didn't kidnap me," Clare lies with an ease that startles me. "I'm with him willingly—because I believe him. He didn't kill Roxy. All he's done since breaking out of DesMax is try to find out who did."

She blushes slightly on this last sentence, as if recalling that we have taken a few breaks for other activities…

Connor Maguire narrows his eyes, considering her closely.

"And how does any of this concern *you*," he says, his lilt all the way down to a hiss now.

"Not everybody in Desolation is rotted black inside," I tell Connor, cutting across whatever Clare would have replied. "She's a good girl. She wants justice."

I can't have Connor suspecting Valencia in this—not yet, not with Clare right beside me. If Valencia was involved in Roxy's death, the surest way for Connor to get revenge for his daughter would be to kill *Valencia's* daughter right here and now. Something I cannot allow.

Catching the hint, Clare closes her mouth, carefully concealing the trembling of her hands by tucking them into her pockets. She's developing a better poker face, my little bird. She doesn't wear her emotions so much on her face, having learned better in the short time I've known her.

I can still read her thoughts, though, clear as a thirty-point newsprint headline.

She's terrified. She thinks this gamble isn't worth it, marching right into Maguire's pub. Trying to prove our innocence by exposing our throats to their knives.

"Kill them both," old Cian Maguire croaks, over by the window. "Make this whole problem disappear once and for all."

One of the Irish goons speaks up, breaking the brittle silence. I recognize him from Yama—he's still got a bruise in the shape of my fist down the right side of his face. "He might be telling the truth. He barely tried to defend himself at Petrov's."

Connor snorts like this means nothing, but I can tell from his frown that it bothers him—he's noted my behavior every step of the way. He knows I never used lethal force against his men, even when they were trying to kill me. He knows I interrogated his son with only a fraction of the cruelty I'd usually employ.

"The alliance could still be salvaged," I say, quietly.

"Not a chance!" Connor howls. "Not after what happened to Roxy! *You didn't protect her!*"

And now, for the first time, I see the truth; Maguire knows I didn't kill his daughter.

He's angry anyway. Because she died right next to me, a foot from my face, while I failed to stop it.

"You're right," I say, quietly. "And for that I'm deeply, deeply sorry."

Connor hears my sincerity. He looks at me, frowning slightly.

I never loved Roxy. Still, the greatest shame of my life is that I agreed to watch over her, and I failed to do it.

I woke to her wide-open eyes staring back at me, horrified, reproachful, drained of life. Begging me to help her, while gone to a place where no help is possible.

I will *never* let that happen again.

Especially not to Clare.

"Help me find who did this," I say to Maguire. "Work with me, not against me. We can both have our revenge."

"What about her?" Connor asks, nodding his head toward Clare without looking at her. "Your priorities are divided, Constantine."

"No, they aren't," I say, flatly. "I have one purpose only: to kill every last person who had a hand in this conspiracy."

In my peripheral vision, I see Clare flinch.

She knows I believe that includes her father.

"What do you want from us?" Niall demands.

He's quick on the uptake—much like his father.

"I want you to get the police file on the case," I say. "The full fucking file, not the bullshit Valencia brought to trial. I know you can get it—half the cops on the force are Irish. And I want access to your security footage before and after her death, particularly involving any possible intrusion on your property."

"The police may be Irish but they're not Maguires," Connor says, folding his beefy red forearms across his chest.

"They're still fuckin' Irish. You can get it," I say, forcefully.

Connor doesn't agree, but he doesn't argue, either.

"I'll be in touch," I say, taking Clare's arm and backing toward the door once more.

None of the Irish move, watching us leave with their pale, distrustful gazes fixed on our faces. Only Chopper bids me farewell with a soft whine.

As soon as we're outside, Clare wheels on me.

"You used me!" she cries.

"Quiet," I say, dragging her back toward the bike. "They'll hear you."

"I don't care if they do!" she shouts, sorely tempting me to clamp a hand over her mouth. Or maybe turn her over my knee again.

"You're gonna fucking care," I snarl. "Don't make the mistake of thinking they're on your side."

"Oh, I understand exactly what happened," Clare hisses at me. "You were gambling on the fact that they wouldn't want to kill you in front of me—that's why you brought me along. While knowing damn well they'd be happy to shoot me too, if they shared your opinion about my father."

"Well they don't just yet," I snarl back at her, "and I'd like to keep it that way, so keep your fucking voice down."

"I'm not going to stand by and watch you murder him," Clare says. "He's still my father, no matter what he's done."

"Oh yeah?" I sneer. "And what do you think should happen? You want me to turn the evidence over to the police? They're in on it, remember? Even if there was such a thing as justice, and they threw him in DesMax, he wouldn't last a fucking week. The outcome is the same either way."

Clare stares at me, really thinking this through for the first time.

She said she wanted the truth—but she doesn't want what follows.

She doesn't want the consequences.

CHAPTER 16

CLARE

I should've known better than to trust him. I should've known that he'd use me, that there was a reason that he broke me out of that prison.

I know he's capable of unspeakable violence. I've seen it with my own eyes. I know he's planning even more. And yet...

When he looks at me that way... with that glint in his eyes that tells me I'm special, I started to believe that it was true.

When he holds me that way... with that fierce possessiveness that only he has ever shown around me, I started to believe he meant it.

He makes me feel things I've never felt, makes me hope and dream and long for so much more. And I did what I *never* do. I let my logical brain be silenced by what my heart wants.

I didn't become who I was by allowing emotions to rule me, and I'm not going to start now.

"Get on the bike," he growls, in a voice still tainted by anger. I slam the helmet on my head.

"Fine," I snap. I'm just on the verge of snapping at him to take me home where I can nurse my wounds, until I remember that *we're not on a date.*

His eyes narrow on me as he holds the bike steady for me then jerks his chin at the bike to tell me to get on. I swing my leg over the side of the bike and cross my arms on my chest. It sways a little, but he quickly rights it. I relax when he bears the weight.

"Are you getting on *or what?*" My voice trembles with anger. He gives me what I might call a warning look, something that tells me not to push him too hard. I'd be smart to let things sizzle out right about now, to do what we refer to in academia as *de-escalating.*

I can still see it in my textbook.

De-escalation: the act of reducing or diminishing the intensity of a conflict or potentially violent situation.

I can still see the images of policemen, first responders, and medical personnel de-escalating a situation. I can still hear my professor reminding us how integral it is when dealing with those with mental illnesses or who are distraught to remain cool, calm, and collected, so we don't throw fuel onto the fire, so to speak.

But all my training, my experience, and my education mean nothing right now, and I can't seem to get a grip on my anger.

The air crackles between us, potent with electric sparks.

"Are you going to just stand there and glower at me? Last I checked, I don't know how to drive this thing, and I highly doubt it's one of those self-driving pieces of machinery."

Self-driving pieces of machinery? God, what am I even thinking?

His back goes rigid, and at first, he doesn't respond. Just when I've had it with him giving me the silent treatment or whatever the hell he's doing, and I open my mouth, he opens his and starts to talk.

"It is not. And yes, I am."

"Then why the hesitation?" I snap, my blood boiling.

A muscle jerks in his jaw. My heart thumps involuntarily. "I'm trying to decide if I need to put you over my knee right here, right now, or wait until we get to the safe house."

My jaw drops open and I stare, wide-eyed. I want to protest, but I don't know what to say or how to respond. He says it so... matter-of-factly. Like lighting my ass on fire is just something that has to happen, the only question is where and when.

"Excuse me?" I finally sputter, before I frantically look around to see if anyone overheard us. "I don't recall agreeing to—"

"And that gives me my answer." Holding the bike steady, he's careful to swing his leg over and take his place in front of me. When he starts the engine, it revs beneath me. I squeeze my legs together to stop the flare of erotic need, but it's hopeless.

Motorcycles turn me on.

Constantine turns me on.

Getting threatened with a spanking turns me on.

Fuck my life.

"What answer?" I ask, but as soon as I ask, the wind swallows my words and whips my hair around.

Against my better judgment, I wrap my arms around his waist, lock myself into place, and he takes off.

The engine purrs like a stallion. Between the humming between my legs, his sturdy, muscled back against my chest, and the fear of whatever will happen when this ride is over, I'm a damn mess when he turns into the driveway of a house that looks somehow vaguely familiar to me.

He pulls to a stop and cuts the engine. Silence echoes around us.

I look around us, trying to put some context to our location, but it's too dark here for me to really know where we are.

"Where are we?"

He grunts in response, as if expecting me to just accept that.

No explanation. No reasoning.

All of this—the way he comports himself, the way he talks, the way he makes decisions without a second thought—reminds me of who he is: a man who's used to leadership and knows no other way. A man who's used to responsibility. A man accustomed to being in charge. It's who he is, down to his very toes.

I cannot protect anyone who undermines me.

And for some reason, that knowledge, that actual understanding of who he is and what he does, diffuses *me* a little.

"Stay there, *ptitsa*. It's important to dismount carefully so you don't get hurt." One minute, he's spitting out orders that are hard to swallow and I wonder who he is and... moreover, who *I am to him.* The next, he's being gentle and careful with me. Protective.

I watch him put the bike in neutral and hold it steady so I can get off. I hold his shoulders to steady myself before I swing my leg over the side.

Even now, he doesn't want me to fall or injure myself. Even now, he's looking out for me. And for some reason, that makes me feel a little sad inside.

I don't know what's going to happen to Constantine. I don't know where we go from here. I do know the thought of him being caught and dragged back to DesMax, that hopeless, dismal place, makes a knot form in the pit of my stomach. I also know that being caught and brought back to prison might be a happy ending compared to the other outcomes he might face.

It isn't until we're halfway up the stairs to the house that I realize where we are — on a street I used to frequent with my parents when I was younger, a place of summer vacation homes and a boardwalk, a good distance away from the prison, but close enough to my childhood home that we could get there in a heartbeat. My father liked to vacation locally in case he needed to return quickly, and my mother was terrified of long flights, so it was an easy decision for them.

I almost tell him that I'm familiar with this street. I'm not sure we stayed in this exact home, but I've been in the close vicinity. Then it dawns on me, he knows where we are. He chose this place on purpose. Though he might not know that I vacationed here as a child, he's well aware of how close we are to my childhood home.

And right then, with the doubts of everything before us, the sadness of who he is and what he bears weighing heavily on me... I want to go home. I want my own bed again. I want to go back to who I was before all of this: a strong, independent woman, who knew what she wanted and where she was going in life.

I know I can't have that. I can't go there. I know now that who I was will never be the same.

And at this point? I'm not sure I even want to go back to the way things were.

It's my life's work to help others learn how to manage mental illnesses, to learn how to handle trauma, but right now, I'm not even sure how to begin.

Our heads bent, we walk quickly to the front door. He swipes at a number pad on the door, and the lock clicks open with a quiet snick. The muscles in his arms bunch and bulge as he pushes it open and gestures for me to go inside.

It's a modern, luxurious place, immaculately clean with comfortable-looking furniture, specifically geared for comfort and relaxation. I gasp when I look out the window at the night sky, the stars twinkling like diamonds in the valley below.

I open my mouth to speak to him when he barks out an order. "Strip."

I freeze and don't respond right away.

"You have thirty seconds, Clare, before I start counting."

"Counting... what?" I ask on a whisper, simultaneously turned on and terrified.

"How many more strikes you've earned with your disobedience."

Did I imagine it, or do his eyes look heated just now?

Do mine?

"Fifteen seconds."

It isn't enough time to think or plan. My eyes on his, I begin to strip.

As soon as the fabric of my clothes pools around my feet, I see I'm affecting him and realize... I can gain back control. Perhaps I never gave it up to begin with.

I could've demanded he take me home. I could've maybe even escaped. I didn't have to do what he told me. I didn't need to let him make me come.

I didn't have to enjoy it.

When I stand before him in nothing but a bra and panties, I know I've affected him. His Adam's apple bobs up and down, and his erection shows clean through the tightness of his pants. When I hold his gaze, his pupils dilate.

"So beautiful," he murmurs, before he speaks in ragged Russian.

"What was that?" I ask, my own voice thick with arousal.

A wicked glint lights his eyes. "I said *Yebat' yego konem*. Literally translated it means 'let the horse fuck it'."

"What?"

"In English you might say *goddamn*."

My heart thumps. "Oh. Well that's better than... horses... fucking." I flush.

"You're a treasure, Clare."

"Oh?" I ask in a teasing lilt. "Then why must you punish me?"

In one step, he's crossed to me. His fingers tangle in my hair. I gasp when he yanks it, my mouth dropping open when pain spikes down my scalp and tingles across my spine. Before I've recovered, he palms my ass and yanks me against him. I whimper just before he takes my mouth, lips pressed to mine with branding intensity.

I touch my tongue to his, relishing the low, sexy sound of his growl. My breasts feel heavy and full. His hand on my ass tightens painfully, and yet somehow, I crave more.

"Why do I punish you?" he grates against my ear. "Because you fucking love it."

"I don't," I lie, shaking my head, but I can't help the slow smile that spreads across my lips. "No one likes to be punished."

It's a dance we do, but in the end, we know where we'll end up.

"You lie, sweet girl," he drawls, his accent thickening. "Spread your legs and show Daddy how wet you are."

I obey so quickly he chuckles, the deep, dark sound melting straight between my thighs. He reaches his fingers past the waistband of my panties and teases me. I gasp, my legs wobbling when he fingers my slick, swollen folds. "*Khristos.* So fucking wet. So ready. I should punish you further for lying."

"And if I say no?" I can't help but tease.

"I wouldn't test me right now," he says in a warning tone that only makes me tremble harder. "Go. Finish stripping. When I come in, I expect your legs spread for me, you bent over the side of the tub. Stroke yourself while you wait for me, but you are not allowed to come."

Over... the side... of the bathtub?

Stroke yourself.

And then he's gone. His heat, his glorious fingers, and that sexy as fuck tone of voice in my ear. The smell of him and feel of him and the way he makes me wet with a mere look. I watch him lift a small remote and hit a button. The sound of water jets filling a tub echo behind me. I watch him stalk out of the room and give myself ten seconds of being dazed before I start to move.

Strip. Well, that part's pretty easy. Seconds later, I'm in the bathroom, staring at the tub. This is no mere tub. It's *enormous,* big enough for both of us to damn near swim laps. Nestled in a tiled corner of the room, it's backlit with a light blue glow, and blue and white lights twinkle like sparkling gems. The jets propel water into the tub, and steam rises. It's lower in the front, elegantly curved to allow one to lean back and bask in the warmth, with a higher back next to a small set of steps.

The cool tub presses against my belly, my ass on full display. Gingerly, I part myself and slide my fingers where his were. Mine are too small, too timid. I want his stronger, larger fingers inside me so badly I could cry.

I remember the way he pulled me over his knee, remember the way his belt landed on my ass. I remember the way he made me come. I imagine his tongue between my legs, bringing me to climax against his mouth, and I feel myself getting closer and closer to release, when I hear him enter.

"*Stop.*" My fingers freeze, dying to finish what I started, but I want him more.

Unprepared, I gasp when his palm slaps against my ass. I brace myself on the edge of the tub with my free hand, just before another smack follows the first. Heat flares across my skin, and my clit throbs. Oh, God, what he does to me when he punishes me…

I whimper and squirm when he fingers my folds, spreading my slick arousal along my seam then my ass. I couldn't have imagined anyone doing anything like this to me before, but right now, I can't imagine him stopping. I want all of it, and I want it fucking *now*.

"Touch yourself," he growls. My fingers move faster and faster. I feel myself on the edge. If he told me to stop right now, I'm not sure I could.

"You like to push, don't you, Clare?" he asks before he lands another hard, searing slap where my ass meets my thigh. "You like to see what Daddy will do, don't you?"

Oh, *God*, my clit throbs beneath my fingers as I work myself harder, faster, in rhythmic circles. I whimper when the pain of his palm melts to heat again.

I feel his thick, hot cock at my entrance, gliding between my folds, and brace myself hard. I need him in me so badly I'm trembling, grateful for the contrast of the cool, sturdy porcelain beneath my hand. Something warm and liquidy slides between my cheeks. Lubricant? I tremble when the head of his cock parts me.

Is he... *no*.

His huge body traps me beneath him, his sturdy legs on either side of me and his massive chest pressed to my back. He's fully clothed and I'm stark naked, the contrast somehow making me even hotter.

"I own you, woman," he growls in my ear. "I own that mouth, I own that hot, pretty pink cunt, and now I'll own this ass. No matter what happens, I want you to feel me. To remember. To know you're branded by me because you're mine." His cock teases my asshole and I tense, but he reaches one hand to cup my breast, and my whole body relaxes.

"Relax, little bird. Trust me. Trust me, Clare, and let your body take over." I close my eyes and do what he says. The fear seeps out of my body like rising smoke, as gone as quickly as it came, as he slowly, perfectly, enters me and fills me to completion. He stills, holding me against him, before he slowly builds a rhythm that makes me whimper with need and want.

Fuck yes. I've never had sex like this before. I'll never be the same again.

Constantine has ruined me for other men. For any other kind of sex.

For everything.

"Oh, God, oh *God*," I whisper at the same time he curses.

"*Khristos,* Clare. You're so fucking perfect. Jesus, woman." He mutters in Russian, and I don't know if he's cursing or praying, but it doesn't matter, his deep voice and the roughness of his words are pushing me straight over the edge of bliss.

I'm so full, so goddamn *full* I'm going to die, but I'll die a happy woman. I can't hold myself back as his flanks slam against my ass, all pain fading to perfect ecstasy. My clit throbs and my thighs clench. His fingers wrap around my throat as we near release.

"Come, little bird," he whispers against the shell of my ear. His hand flexes like a collar, reminding me of the power he wields and how I'm his, and at the feel of his fingertips against my skin, I shatter.

Ecstasy blinds me. I forget how to breathe. I whimper and writhe. Spasms ricochet through me. He comes with a roar that echoes around me, his seed lashing into me with hot insistence. I don't recognize my own voice when I scream his name.

I'm hoarse when I come back to earth. I'm panting, slumped over the side of the tub. He bends and kisses my shoulder and mutters something once more in Russian.

I imagine he says *I love you.*

CHAPTER 17

CONSTANTINE

I carry Clare to the large king-sized bed in the master suite.

This house is one of many properties held in common by the Bratva, sometimes used as a safe house, sometimes for fucking mistresses, sometimes simply for a break.

Even gangsters grow tired from time to time.

Even gangsters want to relax.

It's no coincidence that we're only a short distance from Clare's family home. I brought her into the heart of my world—sex clubs, gang territory, and underground fighting rings.

Now I want to stand in her world.

I want to show her that I can inhabit a palace of gleaming marble and polished wood. I could wear a suit, if I wanted to, and ride in the back of a limousine. I could drape diamonds around her neck and dance with her.

Or at least, I want to believe I could.

I want to believe that Clare and I are not so different.

I've stolen a princess, and now I want to keep her. But what kind of life could I possibly offer?

Clare is deeply asleep, curled up against my chest. She's exhausted from all this running and hiding, all this searching and fighting. She's not used to this desperate existence.

As exhausted as I am, I can't fall asleep alongside her. My mind is racing, trying to find some solution that could solve all our problems. That could make the impossible possible.

No matter which way I turn, one glaring issue remains.

I have to kill Valencia.

I know he's at the heart of this. He orchestrated it all. He killed Roxy and framed me for it. He intends to conquer the Bratva and the Irish, to bring the criminals of this city under his heel.

His actions require retribution; the Irish will expect it, and my own raging fury demands it.

He must be punished, tortured, obliterated.

How the fuck can I do that, while preserving any kind of relationship with Clare?

She's followed me every step of the way. I kidnapped her, broke out of prison, dragged her along on this mad dash. We've been threatened, shot at, almost killed.

But there has to be a line at which I'll lose her.

Valencia is her father. If I cut his throat in front of her, she'll never forgive me.

It will devastate her.

I know Clare well enough by now that I can perfectly picture the horror in those beautiful dark eyes, the guilt and misery it would cause her.

I don't want to hurt Clare. I can't stand the thought of it. I may have taken my belt to her ass, but punishment is not injury.

Clare is a good person, truly good. She came to that prison to try to help the worst kind of men—men like me. She saw me not as a monster in a cell, but as a human being with strength and intelligence, with the ability to change and grow.

I have never seen myself as someone who could change.

I believed that I was born a wolf, I would live a wolf and die a wolf. Subject to the laws of predators, not of philosophers.

Now my own vision of myself is cracking to the core, and I wonder what I could be with a woman like her by my side. What we could accomplish together.

Can mercy and power co-exist? Can love and domination?

Clare is naked in the bed, her soft, sensual body pressed up against mine. Her legs are wrapped around one of my trunk-like thighs, her bare pussy slotted against my skin.

While she dreams, she moans softly, her hips rocking ever so gently, her pussy grinding on my thigh.

I feel her nipples stiffening against my ribs.

This naughty little vixen... she's never satisfied. No matter how roughly I treat her, how deeply I fuck her, she still craves more.

When I pull my thigh away from her sweet little cunt, she lets out a pitiful sigh, her dark lashes fluttering against her cheek, her fingertips reaching for me.

I push her onto her back.

Her knees fall open, her pussy opening like a flower to me.

I stroke my fingertips across the exposed nub of her clit, swollen and warm from pressing against me.

She groans, her legs trembling at my touch.

I've never felt such velvet softness. I've never met a woman so responsive. I dip one finger inside her, feeling her clench around it, watching her rock her hips again, begging for me to penetrate her deeper, to rub her harder.

I could spend hours touching her like this.

This pussy is uncharted land, my fingertips Magellan. I want to explore every last bit of her. I slide my fingers up and down her folds, cup her pussy in my palm, and then I use her wetness to touch her ass again, so tightly puckered that I can't believe I fit my whole cock in there only an hour before.

My cock throbs at the memory.

There is no act more dominating than anal sex. It requires total submission from the woman. She has to be in a state of complete acceptance where her entire body relaxes, where she becomes soft and supple like warm taffy. What at first seems impossible and even painful turns into a deep and desperate pleasure so intense that by the end Clare begged me to take her harder, to explode inside her ass.

Clare is whimpering now, her legs spreading wider, her pussy aching to be filled.

Instead, I slide beneath the sheets, inhaling the warm, sweet scent of her skin all the way down to the delicate curve of her navel, over the ridge of her hip, down to my favorite place.

I push my tongue inside her.

Clare gasps, pressing her clit against my upper lip.

I fuck her with my tongue, rubbing the ball of my thumb over her clit.

Half asleep and half awake, she reaches down to run her fingers through my hair, scratching my scalp with her nails. Each point of friction sends delicious sparks of pleasure down my spine. Her scent fills my nose and mouth, rich and intoxicating. Her pussy is catnip and I'm fucking high.

She rolls her hips against me, my entire face wet and slippery. I want more, more, more.

I fuck her with two fingers, lapping my tongue against her clit. It's never been so swollen. I suck it gently, fluttering with the flat of my tongue.

Clare begins to come, still without entirely waking. Her moans are deep and guttural, drunk with slumber.

She comes against my tongue, her thighs clenching my ears.

Before the last shocks have run through her, I mount her and plunge my cock inside that achingly sensitive cunt.

Now her eyes flutter open, and she gazes up at me as if I've entered her dream, instead of the other way around.

"Tell me I belong to you," she moans.

"You're mine," I growl. "I'll never let you go."

"Tell me I'm your good girl…"

"You're my princess, my queen. I'll slaughter anyone who lays a finger on you. Only I touch you. Only I look at you. You're mine and mine alone."

She pulls me down on top of her, digging her nails into my back, holding me tight against her.

She's already coming again, her pussy spasming around my cock.

As she does, she sighs in my ear, "Oh... Constantine..."

The sound of my name on her tongue makes me erupt inside her. The orgasm is so powerful, so all-encompassing, the dark room becomes a sea of blackness around me, and all consciousness fades away.

“•

WHEN I WAKE, Clare has left the bed.

This is the only time in my life that a woman has woken before me. Usually the slightest sound, the slightest movement will jerk me awake.

I slept too deeply.

My whole body feels heavy and warm, still drugged with pleasure.

Clare is sitting in the window seat, gazing out, dressed in my discarded shirt. It hangs down almost to her knees like a dress, her bare legs tucked beneath her. Her hair is tousled, her face adorably puffy with sleep.

She hasn't noticed that I'm awake—I'm capturing a look at her when she believes she's unobserved.

I see her sadness.

She rose restless, unhappy. Maybe she doesn't even remember last night.

As I sit up, she startles and turns toward me.

"Good morning," she says.

The formality of the greeting is a far cry from what she moaned in my ear as she came all over my cock.

Already I feel my face stiffening, the shutters inside me slamming shut. I've never been vulnerable to hurt before—everything within me revolts against it.

"I can almost see my parents' house from this window."

"I know."

My voice comes out colder than I intended.

"I wondered…" she hesitates.

I already know what she's about to say, but I remain silent, playing out the rope. Something perverse inside of me wants to watch her hang herself.

"You want evidence on your case," Clare says. Her voice is soft but direct, her eyes fixed on my face. "I know my father's password to the computer in his office. I could look through his files. Then we'd both learn the truth."

"You want to go home," I say, flatly.

Clare flinches.

"I don't want—it's not like that. It's just… I have to know, Constantine. I have to know for certain."

"I've told you for certain."

"That's not the same!" Her cheeks are turning pink, her eyes glinting. Still, she's fighting for control, fighting to be understood.

I cannot understand her. Because I can't accept this.

"What about last night?" I bark. "When you belonged to me."

I twist the words in the ugliest way. Clare's chest rises and falls rapidly beneath my shirt. I know I'm upsetting her, but I can't seem to stop.

"Constantine... I... I care about you, about what happens to you—"

"Of course you do," I sneer. "You're a crusader. You wanted to save me from the moment we met. Before we even met. Me and every other lost soul."

"No! That's not what I—"

"I don't need your fucking pity," I snarl. "I don't need you at all. I can find the evidence with or without your help."

"But I want to—"

"I don't give a fuck what you want."

Clare recoils like I slapped her.

I would never slap her face.

But I would do this... I would push her away. Roughly and painfully.

Because Clare is bound to betray me. The moment she's back inside that house, safe with her parents, ensconced in her life of privilege and security, this thing between us will evaporate like dew on hot pavement.

I sucked her into this insane affair. This was never what she wanted for herself—a criminal. A killer.

She lost her mind for a moment and clung to me in the madness.

But she doesn't love me, how could she?

She wants to go home. Her old life calls to her.

Perhaps mine does, too.

It was much less complicated when I only had to worry about myself. When I could slash and beat and burn anyone in my path without a shred of remorse.

"You're right, Clare," I say, rising from the bed, naked and cold as solid stone. "It's time for you to go home."

CHAPTER 18

CLARE

I stare out the window of the bedroom and force myself to push past the sick, twisted feeling of nausea in my belly. The cool prickling sensation down the back of my neck that tells me something's terribly wrong.

I don't like the cold look in Constantine's eyes when they meet mine. Telling me to go home feels like the coldest of rejections. Like bone revealed with the deepest cut of a blade, it feels as if painful truth is revealed; we come from two different worlds and could never be together.

I reject this truth, though. I reject it with everything in me because I know it isn't true. I've seen the look in his eyes when he isn't guarded. I fit with Constantine like I was carved into him, and our being together completes the both of us. His brutal, fiery passion fuels me, and my steadiness calms his fire.

I know this. I'm not sure he does. I can't think of that now, though. If I do, the pressing weight of our future together might splinter me. The thought of never being with him again might shatter me.

So I hold it together.

I let his eyes shutter to black.

I bear the pain of the coldness in his gaze.

And I make a vow to myself. I will vindicate Constantine Rogov. Because he deserves the truth. And I love him.

So I go along with the ruse. I allow him to push me away from him. I have to… for now. Until I shed light on the truth, that needs to happen.

I gather up the few belongings I have while he talks on the phone in Russian, no doubt orchestrating the plans that will set me free, and for the hundredth time, I wish I spoke his native tongue. I can tell by the clenching of his fist and the tight, heated tone of his voice that he's angry.

When he disconnects the call, he whips the phone against the bed pillows so hard it flips into the air and lands unscathed a few feet away, at the foot of the bed. He sits on the edge of the bed and sighs, unable to mask the resignation in his features. Looking up at me, he crooks a finger.

"Come here, Clare."

My feet move of their own accord, as if my body knows the truth instinctively.

I belong to him.

I am his, and he is mine.

A part of me wants to stop a few feet away, to stay apart from him because if I draw too near, I know he'll touch me. I have to stay strong. I need to be sure that I don't waffle in the face of what I must do next. Because if he touches me…

I stand a few feet away from him, but it isn't good enough.

"No, little bird," he says, and for one minute, I think perhaps I'd imagined the cold rejection in his voice when he told me to go home. "Come closer."

I deliberate back and forth between obeying him and not, unsure of the right thing to do, when he leans forward and reaches for my hand. I'm standing closer than I thought, for in the next moment, he tugs me onto his lap. My pulse spikes when he anchors me to him with an arm around my lower back, my jaw trapped when his free hand grips me.

"No matter what," he says, his accent thick. "No matter what happens, you will always be mine."

I open my mouth to speak, and he takes it as an invitation to kiss me. My head tips back, his mouth on mine, hot and insistent. I moan, and he swallows every sound I make. His grip moves from my jaw to my throat, a gentle flex to remind me of his power, but I trust this man. He won't hurt me. His tongue licks mine, and the last of my resistance ebbs out of me. I'm putty in his hands.

A flare of pain bites my neck. I'm too stunned to react, still caught in the web of arousal and need. My eyes close, our lips unlock, and I slump against him. The world fades to darkness.

THE TWITTERING OF BIRDS. Car tires zooming. A slow trickle of rain hitting the roof. I try to open my eyes, but the lids are too heavy.

Where am I?

The smells are familiar... the slightest hint of vanilla and lavender, just like my —

202

I push my eyelids open with enormous effort and blink in the darkness of my bedroom. I look around me, disoriented and uneasy, but don't even have the strength to push myself to sitting. Am I alone?

My phone sits beside me, plugged into the charging base. My shoes are neatly lined up by my door. The blinds are half-open, revealing a blue tint of either dusk or dawn.

It's like I never left.

I'm in my bedroom, as if everything that happened was only a dream.

I try to sit up again. I need to see what day it is, what time it is. I need to prove to myself that it all happened. I close my eyes and assess my situation.

There are no other sounds in my apartment.

I remember… sitting on Constantine's lap. He was kissing me, then there was pain in my neck, and I—he drugged me.

He drugged me to take me home? Why would he do a thing like that?

Was he afraid I'd fight him? Run on my own?

Does he need to make it look legit, and drugging me and plunking me down in my own bed makes it look that way?

Or was he afraid I wouldn't go?

Is he watching me now?

My fingers feel like plump sausages, my joints creaky and swollen as well. I have no idea how long I've been under and no recollection as to how I got here.

I have to get to my father.

I reach for my phone, my fingers clumsy, and quickly swipe it on. I type in Constantine's name.

Convicted murderer takes DA's daughter.

The article is two days old—though still two days *after* I was kidnapped from the prison. Constantine was right—my parents tried to hush it all up, until they couldn't anymore.

My mother gave a statement:

PRAGMATIC AND STRAIGHTFORWARD, *Maria Valencia speaks plainly about the hunt for Clare Valencia.*

"I want my daughter back. We will use every resource available to us to ensure our daughter's returned home safe and sound, and the criminal responsible for her abduction is punished to the full extent of the law."

I FEEL as if I'm going to be sick, and I'm not sure if it's the effects of the sedatives or not.

No mention of her concern for me, nothing but a dedication to justice and enforcement of the law. In other words, typical.

My brain feels thick, even my thoughts slurred.

I sit up, rub a hand across my brow and, with effort, push myself out of bed. I look around my apartment. Everything appears untouched. My shoes neatly arranged in the closet, my clothes arranged by color and season. My laptop lays untouched on my desk, not a paperclip or speck of dust astray.

Did he bring me here himself? Did he carry me? Did he look around my private home?

Was it hard for him to leave me?

It's clean and organized, the way I left it. The mantle above my fireplace bare but for a few small, hand-carved ornaments I collected when my family vacationed on Martha's Vineyard.

Wait.

My gaze swivels back to the mantle again. I ignore the spasm of pain from the sudden movement.

There were six ornaments when I left. Now, there are five. Through the cloud of brain fog, I piece together what was there before I left and try to recall what's missing, when it dawns on me with vivid clarity. *A bird.* A little glass nightingale. It's gone.

Did he take it?

I close my eyes against the rush of emotion that floods me. Constantine was here, I know he was, right here in my apartment. He took the little bird as a memento.

I have to vindicate him.

I have to know if my father did what Constantine said he did.

My mouth feels as if it's stuffed with cotton. I stumble toward the kitchen to grab a bottle of water out of the fridge. I lean against the counter for support, but I'm too weak to even take the top off. Cursing under my breath, hating how weak and helpless I am, I focus. Take in a deep breath. Twist the cap off and guzzle half a bottle.

I slump against the counter, trying to piece together the next step.

I have to get to my parents' house. That might be the easiest step of all.

Holding the bottle of water as if it's my lifeline, I clumsily walk back to bed. Collapsing, I fall and let my weighted limbs sink into the mattress.

Okay, alright.

First step, call them.

Get back to Mom and Dad's house.

Evade police.

Feign confusion.

Sneak onto Dad's laptop.

Scour it.

I take another sip of water and clumsily spill it all over myself. I wipe it off my cheeks, surprised to find them wetter than I expected. Am I crying? I'm crying. No bother, it'll only add to my pleas for help when I call.

I tap the phone. "Dial Mom."

The phone rings. My mother answers on the second ring. "Clare?"

"It's me," I say, my voice rusty and ragged.

Her tone is sharp. "Where are you?"

"Home."

"You're here?"

Don't be so stupid, I want to tell her.

"My apartment."

"Are you alone?"

"Yes."

"Someone will be over to get you immediately." A pause. "Are you hurt?" She says it like it's an afterthought, and that stings.

I remember how Constantine held me. It would have been the first question he would have asked me.

I can't think like this.

I push my hand palm-down on my belly and ignore the aching in my heart.

"No," I lie.

She doesn't care if I'm hurt. Maybe she'd even prefer it if I didn't come back so she has an endless array of attention, a tragedy to wear like a cloak. A lump forms in my throat, and I swallow hard.

I have to stay focused.

Even if I never see him again.

Even if everything I felt was nothing but a sham.

Even if everything I hoped for was only in my mind.

He didn't kill Roxy, and I know that now.

I'll help him find who did.

The time passes slowly as I stumble around my apartment trying to right myself. No time for a shower, so I run my fingers through my hair and can almost hear him. *You look beautiful, just like that.*

A man like him doesn't lie. He may be a criminal, and he may have done terrible things, but lying to me was never one of them, unless —no, I won't think of that now. He never made a promise to me, and I can't question any of that now.

I splash water on my face and brush my teeth. I imagined it would feel nice to be home again in my own private sanctuary. I've worked for years to ensure my home was a place of comfort and luxury, a place to unwind and relax. But it doesn't feel like that now. Now, I feel alone and isolated. My skin crawls with the need to leave, and I vaguely wonder if it's the effects of the medication he gave me.

My heart says it's something else.

I laugh mirthlessly to myself when I remember my mother's words. *Someone will be over to get you.*

If Constantine had been afraid for my safety and then I called him, he wouldn't *send someone.* He'd come himself. Though I wonder if he'd ever let me out of his sight to begin with. Here I am now.

Is he watching me?

I look around my apartment, wondering if he's trained a camera on me.

He told me to go.

I close my eyes, willing myself to focus on what needs to happen next. I can't let my heart and brain war with one another and make me lose my focus. *I can't.*

I swallow down a few more gulps of water, stand straight, and pull my shoulders back.

I don't look the same. I look... older. More careworn. Almost haunted.

A knock sounds at the door. For one wild, crazy minute, I imagine it's Constantine.

"Hello?"

"I'm here to bring you to your father's house, Miss Valencia."

I sigh. Someone who works for my parents, then. Gingerly, I push myself away from the vanity and head to the door. I check through the peephole and see a uniformed driver waiting for me. With another forced sigh, I open the door.

He smiles at me, then gives me a curt nod. "Nice to see you're safe, ma'am. Your parents have given me instructions to bring you home."

"This is my home," I say, but I'm talking to his back, and my protests likely don't mean much to him anyway. My parents' house is not my home. I've worked too hard and too long to have the home that I've made for myself. I'm not sure why now, of all times, it's an important distinction for me to make.

I sit in the back of the car, buckle myself in, and close my eyes. I'm still woozy, almost like I've got a hangover. I hold my head as we drive over the streets that will bring me back to my father's house.

I wish Constantine was with me. I've never been afraid of my parents before. I'm not sure why I am now. Perhaps I'm afraid they'll see the truth without me saying a word. That they'll know I fucked Constantine. That he touched me. That he made me come, over, and over, and over again. That I screamed his name. Flailed over his knee while he whipped me then brought me to climax.

I've never been more alive than I was in the short time I spent with him, and everything else now seems so dull and muted I want to cry.

When I was with Constantine, I finally, for once in my life, felt I belonged somewhere.

"The press has been alerted, Miss," the driver says with pride. "I suspect we'll have some reporters back at the house ready for your statement. So good to have you home, Miss Valencia."

I don't even remember his name.

"Thank you." I look out the window, as the cars and streets whip by like we're on a carousel. "How's my father?"

"He's been distraught over your abduction, Miss, but otherwise in good health. Your mother's the same."

I didn't ask about my mother.

The drive is short, and we arrive at my parents' house just after dark. I feel disheveled and confused, my brain as jumbled as scrambled eggs. I swallow the remainder of the water in the bottle I brought with me, swishing it around to let it moisten my lips and mouth. My stomach drops when we pull up to the entrance to my parents' estate.

Red and blue flashing lights illuminate the night sky.

I stifle a groan.

This is going to be a very, very long night.

CHAPTER 19

CONSTANTINE

I left Clare sound asleep in her bed.

When she wakes in her own home, surrounded by all the things she knows and loves, our interlude together may feel like nothing more than a bad dream.

Walking through her apartment was far more painful than I anticipated. It was like stepping inside her skin. The scent of her perfume enveloped me the moment I walked through the door, Clare cradled in my arms. Everything inside—from the carpet to the throw pillows —was soft and gently textured, in shades of cream, pale blue, and dove gray.

I pulled back the coverlet and set Clare down on her bed, tucking her in like a child. She had been warm and sleep-heavy in my arms, her cheek nestled against my chest.

I intended to leave immediately, but I lingered in her living room, examining the neat rows of books on her shelves, and the carefully tended potted plants all along the windowsill.

The apartment was tidy and well organized, simple and comfortable. Welcoming and unfussy, like Clare herself.

Other than a few watercolors and an oil seascape, the only ornaments were the delicate glass figurines set on the fireplace mantle. Sitting at the very edge, as if it were about to take flight, perched a nightingale.

I picked it up, the fine glass resting weightless on my palm. If I closed my fingers around it, I could crush it to powder.

Instead, I slipped it carefully into my pocket.

I find myself touching it now, taking a strange comfort from the cool glass, like a talisman.

Other than that, I feel like shit.

I didn't expect to miss Clare this much. We've only been apart half a day and I already feel... empty.

This is how it has to be. We can't be together, so it's better that we part ways sooner than later.

And yet... for the first time in my life I wish I were someone else. Someone without a prison record, and a long history of bloodshed, and a future bound to be even more violent.

Clare is a good woman. A man like me doesn't deserve a good woman.

Just look at me now. I'm about to do something that would make Clare extremely upset. It might even make her despise me. If she were here, she'd certainly try to stop me—which is why she's not here.

I'm standing in the old slaughterhouse on Division Street, the tools of my trade laid out in front of me on a black silk cloth.

I've always been skilled at getting what I want out of people. I used these same techniques on Clare, though much more gently. I touched and teased her body, caressed and manipulated her. Made her feel exactly what I wanted her to feel. Convinced her to do things she never imagined she'd agree to, let alone enjoy…

Torture is the same.

It's bringing a man to the brink, over and over again, until his mind begins to fracture. Until he forgets everything he believed about himself. Until his will bends to mine, and he tells me everything I want to know.

I went easy on Niall Maguire, because I still hoped to salvage the agreement between his family and mine.

I'll offer no such leniency to my subject today.

Officer Wicker sits on the folding chair in front of me, his hands tied behind his back, a hood over his head.

I recognized him that night outside my uncle's hotel when six officers tried to turn Clare and me into bullet soufflé. Out of all the dirty vice cops, he's one of the filthiest. Whether Chief Parsons has confided in him or not, he's a sneaky motherfucker with his ear to the ground, and he'll know something.

I found him down under the overpass, getting a blow job from a teenaged prostitute. The cops take their cut from the girls, just like the pimps do.

Wicker was in an unmarked car, and the girl was young enough that she didn't know that Crown Vics are always cop cars, whether they've got lights on top or not. I assume Wicker rolled up, let the girl make her pitch, then grabbed her, cuffed her, and tossed her in the back. He took her beneath the underpass instead of to the station so she could "work off her infraction" without getting booked.

All of that was fairly routine. But Wicker is a sadistic motherfucker. He roughed the girl up even though she was cooperating, keeping her hands cuffed behind her back while he made her blow him. She was sobbing and snuffling, blood dripping down from her nose.

I smashed the driver's side window with a golf club, dragging Wicker out by the collar before he could grab his gun from the holster down around his knees. I flung him down on the cement, kicking him in the face for good measure.

The girl was screaming.

I said, "Shut the fuck up before you call all his buddies over here."

The girl shut her mouth fast. She had big blue eyes, unwashed hair, and a smattering of freckles. I could tell she was wondering whether she'd just fallen out of the frying pan into the fire.

Yury found the keys to the cuffs and unlocked her.

"Search the car," I told Emmanuel.

He found a kilo of snow in the trunk, as well as an envelope full of cash.

"Bribe?" Yury said, rifling through the bills curiously.

"That's a hefty fucking bribe," I said, counting ten thousand dollars at a glance.

I took the money from Yury, the thick envelope almost disappearing in my hand. I shoved it at the girl.

"Take it," I barked when she hesitated. "Get out of Desolation. Go to school. Don't let me see you down here again."

The girl clutched the envelope, staring back and forth between us like she didn't believe it. Then, with one last venomous glare at

Wicker groaning on the ground, she turned tail and sprinted away as fast as her stilettos and skin-tight skirt would allow.

"Starting a scholarship for hookers?" Emmanuel laughed, one eyebrow raised in disbelief.

Truthfully, the girl's freckles reminded me of Clare, though the rest of her bore no resemblance. It's why I kicked Wicker harder than was strictly necessary. But I wasn't about to tell Emmanuel that, or Yury either.

Yury might have guessed anyway. He was avoiding meeting my eye as he hauled Wicker up and chucked him in the back of Emmanuel's Escalade.

"Off we go," Emmanuel said, cheerfully.

"Just a second," I said, walking back around to the trunk of the Crown Vic. Emmanuel had left the brick of cocaine laying where he found it, under the spare tire.

"What do you want that for?" Emmanuel asked. "He probably just swiped it out of the evidence locker."

I picked up the brick, hefting it in my hands. It was densely packed, professionally wrapped and vacuum-sealed, with a black wax seal over the seam.

"You ever seen one like this?" I said to Yury.

He shook his head slowly.

"What about it?" Emmanuel said, edgy and glancing in the direction of the remaining sex workers hawking their wares along Joy Street.

The brick looked professional on a level I had never seen before in Desolation. This was no Ziplock baggie full of blow cut with baby powder.

"Take it with us," I said, tossing it to Yury.

Once we were back at the slaughterhouse, I told Yury to have the cocaine tested.

"We can test it ourselves," Emmanuel said, giving the brick a hungry look.

"Don't be a fucking fool," I told him. "You're gonna put something up your nose when you have no idea what's in it? If that's one hundred percent pure you might as well fire a .45 up there while you're at it."

Emmanuel turned away to hide his irritation, but I saw it anyway.

"Get the cop ready," I ordered.

Before Yury could leave, I grabbed his arm.

"Check on Clare," I said.

"I have been."

"Keep doing it. I want her watched at all times."

"Czar is outside her parents' house right now. She's safe," Yury promised.

I nodded, trying to ignore the tightness in my chest.

Now I'm standing in front of Wicker, waiting for him to adjust to the dim light of the slaughterhouse after I ripped the hood off his head.

He looks up at me, snarling like a junkyard dog. He's got a big, beefy face, one of those stupid too-short cop haircuts, and piggy little eyes that were already bloodshot before I ever touched him.

"You're in big fucking trouble," he hisses. "Parsons will have your head for this."

"Well, that's the problem with handing someone a life sentence, isn't it?" I say, calmly, picking up a cleaver and running a whetstone lightly down the edge of the blade. It makes a high, silvery sound, like a skate gliding over ice. Wicker's eyes are drawn to it involuntarily, his upper lip twitching. "Makes death seem appealing by contrast."

I set the cleaver down and pick up an ice pick instead, rotating the handle slowly between my thumb and index finger, so the point sparkles in the light of the overhead bulb.

Wicker stares at the cruel tip, mesmerized.

They always start out defiant, blustering.

And then they all break.

I've never had a man last longer than an hour.

"In fact," I say, softly, "when your buddies fired at me outside the hotel, they were shooting to kill. So I'm guessing Parsons is already hunting for my head."

Wicker's jaw tightens. We both know I'm right.

"Well, I don't know what you think I'm gonna tell you," he sneers. "I'm just a dumb grunt."

"Oh, I think you're going to tell me everything you know," I say. "Useful, not useful. Your darkest secrets and the shit you write on Facebook. What your mother said to you when you were four, and even what your wife likes in the bedroom... Once I go to work on you, I might as well be rifling through your brain. You'll keep nothing back from me, until there's nothing left. Because unlike you, I'm very good at what I do."

Wicker swallows, his throat jerking, eyes beginning to panic.

I trail my fingertips down the line of tools, watching to see which one elicits the strongest response.

Wicker is frozen in place, trying not to make a sound.

Until my index finger grazes the dental drill.

Then I hear the tiny, convulsive choking sound he tries to conceal.

I pick up the drill, switching it on to ensure it's fully charged. The high, whining sound pierces our ears, setting my own teeth on edge.

The effect on Wicker is instantaneous.

He begins to stutter.

"There's no—you don't have to—don't you fuckin'—"

"Hold his head," I say to Emmanuel.

Emmanuel grabs Wicker from behind, pinching off his nose and mouth, depriving him of air so that when Emmanuel lets go, he takes a great, gasping breath.

I shove the spreader in his mouth and crank it open.

The metal prongs hold his mouth wide open, no matter how he tries to thrash his head to loose it from Emmanuel's grip.

I set the drill down momentarily, though I leave it running so the high, insistent whine continues to burrow into Wicker's brain, maddening him like a bull that can't get away from a buzzing fly.

Instead I seize a pair of pliers and in one swift motion, close them around Wicker's right lower molar.

"Who killed Roxy?" I say.

Wicker lets out a gurgling scream, thrashing as best he can, which is barely at all within the tight bonds.

"*I duh nuhhhhhh!*" he howls.

"Wrong answer," I say, wrenching the tooth from its socket with one vicious flex of my arm.

"*Arghhhhhhhh!*" Wicker screams.

I hold the tooth up to the light so he can see it, ivory colored with long, bloodied roots.

"Now," I say quietly. "I know you think that hurt. But let me assure you, the pain you just felt is nothing compared to the agony you'll experience as I take this drill and apply it to your raw, open nerve. Men have killed themselves over a toothache, do you know that? They've blown their brains out when there was no dentist to give them relief. I'm no dentist... but I know exactly where to put this..."

I pick up the dentist's drill, revving it like a car engine.

Wicker screeches. He's gone past denial, past bargaining, all the way to pure desperation.

"Who killed Roxy?" I say, once more.

"*I don't know!*" he screams, his words mushy since his lips can't meet. "But *wait wait wait*! I did hear something."

"What?" I say, impatiently.

"It wasn't a cop—it was a lawyer. A senior prosecutor."

"What?" I say, even less patient this time.

"I heard him say something about an alliance. With the Russians and the Irish. How it couldn't go down... they couldn't let it go down."

I frown. "When was this?"

"I don't remember exactly—November! I know it was November," he adds, hastily, as my fingers clench around the drill.

I exchange glances with Emmanuel, who looks stunned and tense.

No one should have known about the alliance all the way back in November. Definitely nobody in the DA's office. My engagement to Roxy hadn't even been formalized yet.

I glare at Wicker, brandishing the drill.

"That doesn't make sense. How did they know?"

"I really don't fucking know," Wicker gurgles, blood dribbling down from his jaw. "He said there was a source. But I swear to God he didn't say who."

"What about the blow?" I say, swiftly switching tactics. "Where'd you get that?"

Wicker shifts in the chair, not wanting to answer. A flick of the drill toward his cranked-open mouth gets him talking real quick.

After several repetitions caused by the difficulty of speaking around the spreader, I gather that Wicker found out the higher-ups were stashing something juicy in the police vault. He broke in with a stolen key, hoping to liberate some of the booty for himself. He was surprised to find sixty keys of coke, an unusually large volume even in Desolation. He was only able to smuggle out a single brick, and when he went back for another, the rest had vanished. Nothing was ever written down in the evidence log.

I've never seen that black seal before, and I would have heard if there was a player that big in town—especially if they lost such a massive shipment to the cops.

"You have no idea where it came from?" I ask.

Wicker shakes his head, making spit and blood fly from his mouth.

"I believe you," I say, quietly. "But there's only one way to be sure."

With that, I shove the drill in his socket and bear down hard.

The screams shake the slaughterhouse to its foundations.

AN HOUR LATER, I'm washing my hands at the sink.

Emmanuel watches me, pale and slightly shaken.

"Been a while since I watched you work," he says.

I dry my hands on a fluffy white towel.

"Thought I lost my touch?" I ask.

Emmanuel shudders. "Obviously not."

Yury cracks open the back door, stepping through with the brick tucked under his arm.

"Tested it. Purest product I've ever encountered," he says.

"How can that be?" I frown. "How can there be a new supplier in Desolation with sixty keys of premium-grade snow seized by the cops, and we don't hear a peep about it?"

Yury shakes his head, equally mystified.

I don't understand what the fuck is going on.

But there's no way in hell this is all a coincidence.

CHAPTER 20

CLARE

I hate it here. How this was ever a place I called home seems impossible now.

A perfectly manicured front lawn landscaped to within an inch of its life welcomes me. A large, nearly ostentatious wreath adorns the front door, a pathetic attempt at making the sterile home inviting. A curtain flicks, telling me my mother's resumed her typical peeping view of the front lawn and neighborhood.

And of course, the camera crews are already here, too.

When I was younger and attended private school, I'd occasionally have friends over. When I was much younger, anyway. "Oh, I wish I lived here," they would say, eying the glimmering pool out by the deck and the lounge chairs, my massive room decorated in pinks and purples, the heart-shaped vanity I'd sit in front of. But appearances can be deceiving, and they didn't know how miserable it actually was.

My childhood was stifling, and my friends who envied the patio and deck didn't know what it was like living here. How my mother would scold and nag me if a single thing was out of place, a single smudge on a glass or crumb on the floor. Her endless cleaning frenzies *before* the cleaners came, and the way she and my father would fight about the money she spent on the upkeep of the house. To my mother, appearances are everything.

As a child, I found that stifling. When I became an adult, it made me physically nauseous. And now? I want to slap her.

I'm actually relieved when she comes out to the front stoop and shoos the camera crews away, though. "You aren't supposed to be here for another hour. We won't answer any questions until then."

Some camp out and others leave, but enough stay that when I exit the vehicle, lights flash all around me.

"Go!" my mother screeches. It sounds like nails on a chalkboard to me. She eyes me coming up the walkway with a scowl, then forces her lips upward. "Hello, Clare." When I draw nearer, her voice drops to a whisper. "Get in the house quickly so we can clean you up before the camera crews come back."

"Oh, yes, of course," I say in a voice dripping with sarcasm. "So glad I'm alive, too. Makes perfect sense your first priority is how I appear on the big screen."

She opens her mouth to protest, but I brush past her. I never talked back to her before, never really stood up to her. My silent victory came when I found my own personal place and success in this world, when I didn't bow to her whims or cater to her requests.

Things are different now… since Constantine. I don't have any patience for her bullshit. I feel a corner of my lips quirk up when I wonder if Constantine would feel the same way, before the realization that I won't ever see him again dawns.

There's a gnawing feeling in the pit of my stomach, a yearning I can't quite identify. It takes me a minute to really understand, to fully grasp that the one person I want right now, the one person I *need* right now… can't be here. It feels like mourning.

Constantine doesn't put up with anyone's crap, and he wouldn't do it now.

He'd be proud of me for standing up to my mother and her bullying ways. But something tells me if he was with me, she wouldn't even try.

It's a moot point, though. It doesn't matter.

I'm here for a reason, even if he never knows what happens next. Even if I never see him again. I swallow the stab of pain that threatens to choke me.

I enter the double doors to the entryway and hear my father's voice in the distance. In my mind's eye, this would have gone so differently. I imagined coming back here and that they'd be glad to see me. Relieved of the fears they had around my abduction and safety. Instead, my mother wants to make sure I brush my hair, and my father's on the phone, likely for yet another press conference, his absolute fave.

Even the housekeeper stays away from me, likely warned by my mother to leave me be. We wouldn't want any of *them* on an interview, now, would we?

After my mother's assured herself that no one's absconded with her daughter or taken any pictures, she hurries in the house and slams the door.

"Oh, Clare," she says in a pitying voice. "You do look a sight."

"Do I? Can't imagine why." The dry sarcasm seems lost on my mother as she frowns, mulling over the stray lock of my hair she twists in her fingers.

"What can we do in such a short time," she mutters to herself. "The hair is hopeless, but we can at least tuck it up and apply some decent makeup."

I ignore the tingling in my nose and burning in my belly. Her rejection burns, but I've been here before. I've been rejected by someone who actually loved me.

I will survive again.

There are so few things in my control right now, it's maddening, but I do have a few.

Top of the list, I need to see what the hell my father had to do with setting up Constantine, if anything. I wish my gut still said he was innocent, but for some reason, being back here, back in my childhood home, is making my doubts evaporate. I hate that.

Heavy footsteps sound behind me, and I turn just in time to see my father, his arms extended toward me.

"Clare! You made it home safely," he says, tucking me against his chest. "My God, you gave us a scare." I close my eyes, and for one brief moment, let myself feel his embrace. Smell the scent I'm so familiar with I could pick it out in a line up, bourbon and cigar smoke and a hint of cologne. I cling to an innocence I have to give up.

If he did what Constantine said he did …

I draw in a breath and release it slowly. Remind myself of my purpose.

I'm here for a reason. Whether I ever see Constantine again doesn't matter, not now. What matters is that I find out the truth.

About who killed Roxy.

About who framed Constantine.

And why.

"She needs to freshen up," my mother sniffs. "Let her go. Clare, dear, go wash your hands and face and brush your hair." Like I'm five.

I step away from my father and turn to my mother. "I'm fine, Mother. Thanks for asking. No, I don't believe I need to see a doctor. It was *indeed* a traumatic situation, but imagine, I actually survived it. All on my own. Now if you'll excuse me, I'm in need of some food and water."

Before she can reply, I head to the kitchen. I hear her talking to my father in a hushed tone. "Just give her time," he says, but I feel both of them watching me like I'm a bomb about to go off... and maybe I am.

I miss Constantine.

I miss everything about him—his ferociousness and fearlessness. His fierce dedication to those in his inner circle—his brotherhood, his family... and, at times... me.

I *will* vindicate him.

As I make my way to the kitchen, it amuses me to imagine their reaction if I stepped into this room holding Constantine's arm. His large, imposing frame would barely fit through that doorway. My mother has "opinions" about men with tattoos, and my father, of course, would not get past the fact that he's a criminal.

Constantine and I live in two different worlds. Two such very, very different worlds.

That doesn't mean we don't belong together. Sometimes, when two forces of nature collide… they make something new.

Something beautiful.

I decide right then and there. I will fight for him. I will fight for *us*.

Certain my parents haven't followed me, I grab a sandwich and bottle of water from the kitchen. Thankfully, it's the kitchen staff's day off, so I can wander around without repercussion—no fearful gazes or prying questions. I need answers, and I need to find a way to my dad's laptop.

My parents are having a heated discussion in the living room when I return. My father stands, his face flushed.

"Were you or were you not taken by that man in prison, Clare?" he asks, his eyes bulging dangerously with the look he gets that I know all too well, the warning sign that he's going to explode.

"Of course I was. You saw the news." I look away, not wanting to talk to him. Not wanting to even look at him. I hate referring to the only man I've ever cared about as "that man."

After a beat, I force myself to look back because I have questions that he can answer, but before I do, I feign that I'm weaker than I appear. I place my hand on my forehead and sigh. "I have a headache. Why are you questioning me?"

"*I'm* not the one who questioned it," he says with an angry glare at my mother.

My mother leaps to her feat, flushing red. "I never said she lied!"

"You wondered why she was there to begin with. You implied it was her own damn fault."

She doesn't deny this. A sick, twisted feeling takes root in the pit of my stomach. I shouldn't be surprised. Such behavior is terribly consistent for my mother. But what if I *had* been abused and hurt? Would I have to defend my choices even then?

My mother turns to me. "Why were you there?"

"At the prison?" I ask, pulse racing. I don't want to answer her questions. I don't want her to see through anything.

She rolls her eyes. "Of *course* the prison. Where else?"

I decide she doesn't deserve my answer. I'm a full-grown woman who's been independent of her parents for years. They aren't owed the full reasoning.

"You know, I don't believe I owe you an explanation. I was taken by a convict. I was used as a means to an end. For all you know I've been violated."

I can still feel his hands on my hips. His mouth on mine. Still feel his powerful fingers digging into my thighs, anchoring him in place before he—

"Clare," my mother says with a gasp, her eyes widening at the very thought of her precious daughter being violated by a *prisoner.*

"Mother," I say in the same offended whisper. "You didn't even ask me if I was hurt. You don't even care." I don't have to work very hard at infusing pain into my tone before I leave. I don't have to work very hard to make tears come to my eyes, nor to swipe them away angrily as I start toward the guest room.

"Clare, you get back here."

I ignore her. This is part of my plan. Let them think I'm injured, delicate, and they'll give me wide berth. Be difficult, and they won't want to put a spotlight on me.

My mind reels, trying to grasp the most effective way to get to my father's computer. To find out what I need. To vindicate Constantine.

I'll have to get to my father's office.

"Oh, don't worry. I'll make sure I'm here when the reporters are ready for me."

I stomp up the stairs, feeling not a little like the petulant teen raised under this roof. I can imagine the look on Constantine's face at my behavior, his arms crossed over his chest. That implacable look he gives when he goes all alpha caveman on me.

I miss it.

I have to stop thinking about him.

I walk into the guest room and shut the door hard. I listen. No footsteps.

Good. I'm alone for now. The guest room's adjacent to a shared bathroom with a second guest room my father's used as his office for years. My mother never comes to this floor, and I'll have at least a few minutes of quiet while the two of them argue.

I turn on a bedside alarm clock to a low-key jazz station someone traumatized might listen to, then roll my eyes at my intentional dramatics. I step into the bathroom and turn the shower on. The steaming hot water hits the wall and sides of the tub, billows of steam clouding my vision. I close my eyes when I'm assaulted with another memory of Constantine's large body dwarfing mine while I'm bent over the tub...

Stay. Focused.

My hand shakes on the knob of the door to my father's office. I take a deep breath, and open it.

The shades are drawn, casting the room in total darkness. I blink, trying to adjust my eyes to the dim lighting and quickly put the flashlight on my phone to bright. I swing the light around the room until I see it—his desk, cluttered and messy, the one "fuck you" to my mother's compulsive dedication to neatness, the one space she doesn't touch.

Crumpled papers and notebooks lie on the desk. But there's no laptop in sight.

"Shit," I mutter to myself, scanning everything and anything I can to find what I need. The shower runs in the background, and the music plays on.

He only takes his laptop out of the office when he's in court. He's home now, so it's here somewhere. I race to the desk and try the drawers. They're all open except for the bottom one, strangely locked with a padlock. I don't remember him ever having a locked drawer before. Odd.

The laptop's nowhere to be found.

I push myself to my feet, partly to get a better look around the office, partly because my nerves are on fire. Every second that ticks by feels loaded, weighted, as if they have a greater significance somehow. I need to find answers, and I need to find them now.

I glance at the locked drawer and wonder… is that where it is? Where's the key?

When I was little, my parents had a secret stash of cookies and chocolate. My mother didn't like me having sugar and would restrict junk food, but I found their stash, "hidden" in plain sight—right in my dad's office closet.

In other words, my father isn't terribly clever or conniving. I lift the padlock, frowning, and spin the dial to my dad's birthday.

Nothing.

I try my parents' anniversary. Again, nothing.

On a whim, I spin the dial to my own birthday. When the lock opens with a soft *click,* a lump knots my throat. With trembling hands, I open the drawer, knowing what I'll find inside.

I expect the laptop. Slim, silver, it sits atop a small stack of papers with little else. Quaking, I remove it, open it, and quickly fire it up.

The laptop password is also my birthday, not surprisingly. The screen comes to life, and I quickly scroll.

His history's filled with nothing but news articles, including a few recent searches involving Constantine. A cold trickle of fear and apprehension trace down my back when I narrow the search to dates and find Constantine's name listed long before he was ever imprisoned.

Bratva heir

I close my eyes against the heady rush of emotion at seeing those words. It doesn't take much to imagine Constantine sitting on a throne.

I haven't really processed what any of that means yet. I swallow, hands trembling as a few more search histories come up that give me pause.

Alliance with Irish and Bratva.

Illicit drugs.

Nothing too incriminating for a DA, I tell myself. Until I come to his email.

The standard folders are filled with so much minutia, I don't see it at first, but when I do, reality dawns on me so hard I can't breathe. There's an encrypted folder on his desktop with a little lock beside it.

For anyone else, that wouldn't seem out of the ordinary. For my father who considers his birthday a secure password and still carries a flip phone... it's a red flag.

I click the file. *Encrypted* flashes in yellow. I've been here before, though. I know how to do this. Quickly, I right-click the file and bring up the menu selection until I see "properties." I navigate to "advanced," then scroll again until the details pop up. Shaking, I remove the encryption. I breathe heavily when the file pops open.

Every email in here is from the chief of police.

I scroll through, reading as rapidly as I can while copying the file to a flash drive, when voices sound in the hallway outside. I look around me, panic-stricken, as the voices come nearer. I read through what I can as quickly as possible, shaking like a paper in the wind as the flash drive finishes copying, when I hear someone at the door.

I bite my lip, my whole body shaking now as I yank the flash drive out, drop the laptop like it's made of fire, shut the drawer, snap the lock back on and jumble the numbers. I sprint to the shared bathroom just as the handle of the office door turns.

I'm in the shower, fully clothed, when I hear him enter his office. Thankfully, he's on the phone and doesn't seem to suspect a thing. The shower washes away my tears.

Constantine was right.

My father was involved.

My father was behind everything.

CHAPTER 21

CONSTANTINE

I've been hunting all across the city. Nobody knows of a new supplier bringing in high-quality product. Yet, somehow, the streets are flush with drugs.

I shake down the dealers, demanding to know where they're getting their product. Slowly but surely, Yury, Emmanuel, and I trace the source back to a warehouse in the old textile district.

The warehouse is in a pocket of Desolation cut off from the rest of the city by the new freeway route. These eight blocks are like a branch lopped off a tree, left to rot. Most of the businesses have boarded up their windows, and a few have burned to the studs, either from vandals or desperate owners hoping to collect insurance money.

Still, I notice brand new security cameras mounted on the corners of the warehouse, a sure sign that somebody thinks the contents are worth protecting.

Yury parks a street over. We approach from the back of the building, breaking in through the loading bay doors.

Stacks of plastic-wrapped pallet boxes fill the dark, cavernous space inside.

Yury moves to cut one open, but I hold up a hand to stop him.

"Don't you want to see what's in them?" he murmurs.

"That's not the real product," I tell him. "Look…"

I draw my finger across the top of the closest pallet, leaving a trail through the thick dust. Nobody has moved these pallets in months.

Emmanuel peers around through the gloom, edgy and keyed up.

"Maybe it was a bullshit tip," he says.

"No," I shake my head. "This is the place."

I can feel it, a silent, thrumming energy that tells me the warehouse is not as deserted as it's supposed to look. People have been coming through here, recently.

In fact, I can see footprints in the dust on the floor. Following the tracks further into the warehouse, we come to several crates that look much fresher than the others.

The lids have already been pried up, nails scattered around and a crowbar resting next to the crates.

I lift the lid, peering down onto dozens of neatly wrapped packages of pure Colombian cocaine. They're all vacuum packed and sealed with the same black wax stamps.

"Guess we found the missing stash from the police locker," Yury grins.

"What are we gonna do with it?" Emmanuel says, gazing down at all that beautiful white powder like we just opened a vein of pure gold in the heart of a mountain.

Before I can reply, a rough voice barks, "Don't fucking move."

When someone tells you not to move, the worst thing you can do is stay still. You turn around with your hands up, and you might as well kneel down and shoot yourself in the back of the head, saving them the trouble.

Yury and Emmanuel know this too, so at the same instant, all three of us dart apart, diving down behind the crates.

Bullets fly all around us, ripping chunks of wood out of the crates, sending splinters flying through the air.

I'm already pulling out my own Glock to return fire.

"Fuck," Yury hisses, "It's the cops."

Sure enough, when I poke my head around the nearest crate, I see two uniformed officers hunkered down, firing at us.

Three more run down the cramped aisles, trying to surround us.

I shoot the closest one, hitting him above the knee. His leg crumples beneath him and he tumbles over. Emmanuel fires and misses. Yury hits a cop in the shoulder, but he's wearing full Kevlar and it barely slows him down.

Bullets sink into the crates inches from my face as the cops fire recklessly and relentlessly, driving us back the way we came. I can still see Yury on my left, but I've lost sight of Emmanuel.

Gunfire echoes through the warehouse, the already dusty air filling with smoke. The smoke darkens and I hear a crackling sound. Rushing heat hits the side of my face.

"Fire!" someone shouts.

The warehouse is a tinderbox, the old crates dryer than dust and the air full of tiny flammable particles. The fire spreads rapidly, the air so thick and black that coughing overwhelms the sound of firing guns.

Yury and I are falling back toward the exit, but I still don't see Emmanuel. I can't call out to him, for obvious reasons.

I also can't leave without him. Yury and I pause by the loading bay doors, peering through the gloom.

I see a glint of metal and Yury shouts, *"Boss!"* The gun fires louder than a cannon as Yury dives at me, knocking me sideways. The bullet hits him instead, right below the ribs. We both tumble over, Yury falling heavily over my legs. I jump to my feet, hauling him up as well, slinging his arm over my shoulder. Yury clutches his side, blood seeping through his fingers.

"Fuck, I always forget how much this hurts," he groans.

I'm still searching for Emmanuel, cursing under my breath. I hear the shouts of cops searching through the pallets for us. Yury is reeling, his face pale and smoke streaked.

Finally Emmanuel darts out from the furthest aisle, his boots pounding on the dusty cement, firing back over his shoulder at the two cops hot on his heels. I provide cover fire, driving them back while Emmanuel grabs Yury's other arm. We duck out of the warehouse, sprinting back to the car with Yury limp and reeling between us.

Emmanuel drives this time, while I pull my shirt over my head and press it hard against Yury's side.

"How'd the cops get there the exact same time as us?" Yury groans.

"They didn't," I say, shaking my head grimly.

Emmanuel glances back over his shoulder, eyebrow raised in confusion.

"That's their fucking stash," I say. "It wasn't stolen out of the police locker. They moved it."

Yury's mouth makes a comical "o" of surprise as comprehension sweeps over his face.

I say it out loud anyway, just so we're all on the same page.

"We couldn't find the new supplier, because there isn't one. The cops *are* the supplier."

I TAKE Yury to my father's house so his private physician can dig the bullet out of his side.

"You again," Dr. Bancroft says, gruffly. "What is this, the fourth time?"

"Only the third," Yury groans, sighing gratefully as Dr. Bancroft shoots a hefty load of Demerol into his arm. "Second time doesn't count though—that was only an ex-girlfriend."

"That's the bullet that almost killed you," I remind him.

"Yeah, well," Yury shrugs. "She was pretty pissed."

My phone vibrates in my pocket.

When I see the name on the screen, my heart jolts like it just got hit with a defibrillator. It's Clare.

The message is short and to the point.

YOU WERE RIGHT. *I'm sorry.*

. . .

I TYPE BACK, still so excited at the sight of her name that my hands are shaking slightly.

WHAT DID YOU FIND?

I WAIT, my mouth too dry to swallow the lump in my throat.

I can see the three little dots that mean she's composing her response. At last I read:

EMAILS. Lots of them.

HOLY FUCKING SHIT. Clare found the evidence that could exonerate me. The problem is, I'm not just looking to clear my name. I'm looking to clear the slate—by wiping out her father and everyone else who conspired against me.

She's still typing. In a moment, another message pops up:

I HAVE them saved on a flash drive. I'll give them to you—but you have to promise you won't kill him.

I CONSIDER.

I don't want to hurt Clare. But Valencia stole six months of my life. He orchestrated Roxy's death, or at least collaborated in it. The

Maguires won't be satisfied with anything less than his head on a platter.

And most of all, he killed my son. That can never be forgotten or forgiven. Not even for Clare.

I type back:

I can't promise that.

A moment later:

Then you don't get the emails.

I want to strangle her, yet I can't help smiling. My little bird has grown quite the spine in the time I've known her. Unconsciously, my hand steals into my pocket to feel the cool glass of the nightingale.

I type:

Where are you? I want to talk in person.

She replies:

Do I have to be kidnapped or drugged to meet with you?

. . .

OH, she's definitely in a feisty mood.

I'M SORRY. That was for your own protection.

THAT'S the closest I've ever come to lying to Clare. The truth is that I couldn't bear to say goodbye to her. I didn't want her to see my face as I left her on that bed in the apartment that smelled like my favorite thing in the world.

Maybe Clare knows that because she doesn't press on that particular point.

Instead, after a longer pause, she responds:

I CAN'T TONIGHT. My father's parading me around at some stupid gala.

I CAN ALMOST HEAR the irritation in her voice, and I can perfectly picture the adorable scowl that creases her face when she's annoyed.

I've watched the media circus since Clare returned home. Her parents have been giving carefully curated sound bites about "the lack of proper security in the prison system," the "need for privatization," and "the deep roots of organized crime that the district attorney will rip out of this city." I've heard them say everything except how happy they are to have their daughter back.

They don't appreciate Clare. They don't deserve her.

She's talking about the Policemen's Gala, I assume. It's an annual event—a chance for the cops to spend their remaining budget on shrimp skewers and champagne so they can toast themselves all night long.

"Who are you texting?" Emmanuel demands.

Instead of answering, I say, "Do you have a tux?"

"Yeah," he says. "Why?"

"Because we're crashing a party tonight."

"What party?" he frowns, already suspicious.

"The Policemen's Gala."

Emmanuel shakes his head at me, shocked beyond words.

"Have you lost your mind? Every cop in the city is looking for you."

"I know. It's not gonna be a problem."

"How do you figure that?"

I grin. "It's a masquerade ball."

THE GALA IS NOT JUST for cops—all the wealthiest and most influential citizens of Desolation are here, the women dressed in gowns as fanciful and frilled as pastel wedding cakes, the men in dark dinner jackets. Every face is masked, and every person who passes through the doors bears a heavy gilt invitation.

I secured the invitations for Emmanuel and me at great cost and no small inconvenience.

The price is well worth it when we pass inside with a respectful, "Enjoy your evening, gentlemen," from the guards at the door.

Emmanuel is wearing a pale white mask with a devilish grin that covers his whole face. Mine is black and covers only the upper half, leaving my mouth bare.

It won't matter—everyone is already well on their way to drunk, and far more interested in schmoozing than trying to guess the identity of two more dark-suited men in a crowd of two hundred.

I, on the other hand, am searching carefully for the one person I want to see.

Masked or not, I know I'll recognize Clare.

Sure enough, it only takes me a minute to pick out her unmistakable figure gliding across the dance floor.

She's dressed in a silvery gown, lighter than a cloud, that seems to float around her, glittering gently under the dozens of chandeliers lining the hall. Her hair is pulled up in an elegant updo, the dark waves held in place with two jeweled combs. Her silver mask looks like the open wings of a swan.

She's never looked more stunning.

Just the sight of her would fill me with pure, bright happiness all over again.

Except that she's dancing in the arms of another man.

Instead of joy, I'm filled with hot, boiling jealousy. All in an instant, I forget why I'm here. I forget that this room is filled with a hundred cops. I forget that I'm already a wanted man.

All I see is that suicidal motherfucker with his hands around Clare's waist. He's touching her, holding her, looking into her eyes. I decide right then that I'm going to break every finger that touched her, and then I'm gonna snap his neck for good measure.

I'm already storming across the dance floor, shouldering aside anyone who stands in my way.

I grab him by the shoulder, wrenching them apart, saying, "Excuse me," in the tone of voice that really means, "Fuck off right now if you know what's good for you."

"Hey!" the guy says, indignantly.

"Don't say another word if you want to keep that tongue attached to your head," I snarl.

The guy gives me one shocked stare through his knocked-askew mask, then he sees the crazed look in my eyes and he hustles off toward the open bar instead.

"Smart decision," I grunt, already sweeping Clare into my arms where she belongs.

Her outraged sputtering turns to stunned silence as soon as she recognizes me. Now her hand is shaking inside of mine as she looks up at me, squeaking, "Are you out of your mind?".

"I told you I wanted to see you."

"And I told you that it would have to wait until tomorrow! *Every cop here is looking for you!*"

"I don't want to wait."

Her eyes are darting around wildly from behind the mask as she notes how close we're standing to the mayor and the chief of police.

"This is insane!" she hisses. "You can't be here!"

I shrug. "Obviously I can."

"They're going to catch you!"

"They definitely will if you keep dancing like a hostage instead of my date."

I twirl her around, expertly taking her through the steps of the waltz played by an eight-piece orchestra.

"I can't believe you!" Clare murmurs, still flushing red under her mask. "And how do you know how to dance?"

"I know how to do a lot of things."

After a moment, Clare says quietly, "I suppose your mother taught you."

I nod, pleased that she guessed.

"She would have liked you," I say.

"Really?" Clare says. Then, laughing softly, "My mom's not going to like you at all, but if she did, then *I* probably wouldn't."

I snort. "You planning to introduce me to her?"

"No," Clare says, not smiling anymore. "But only because I'd never inflict my parents on you."

Yet another cement barricade against the possibility of us ever being together.

I don't give a fuck. I want Clare. In fact, I need her.

"Who was that guy?" I growl.

"We went to school together. And he's gay, so there was no need to threaten to rip out his tongue. He's not interested in me."

"I really don't give a shit," I tell her. "The only hands that touch this waist are mine."

"Are you serious?" Clare scoffs. "You drugged me and dumped me off at my house! We're not exactly exclusive."

My hands tighten around her, reminding her of my strength. Reminding her to yield to me.

"You're mine, little bird. Don't make me take this belt off and remind you of that fact."

"Unbelievable!" Clare cries.

She's seriously annoyed with me. I don't care—being this close to her again, holding her in my arms, seeing the fire in those brilliant dark eyes, smelling the warm, sweet scent of her perfume... it's an irresistible combination.

I want to kidnap her all over again. I want to throw her over my shoulder and carry her out of this place, right under the noses of Valencia and Parsons and every other person who knows her.

I came here to get the flash drive from Clare, but now that I see her in the flesh, I can't bring myself to give a shit about the evidence. I want her a thousand times more than I want those emails.

"Come on," I growl, seizing her by the arm and pulling her off the dance floor.

"Where are we going?" she hisses.

I'm pulling her out the side doors of the ballroom, into the botanical gardens adjacent to the hotel.

The gardens are enclosed inside a vast glass greenhouse, the air humid and redolent with chlorophyll and freesia blossoms. Fairy lights sparkle in the greenery, illuminating the leaf-choked paths through the trees.

"Constantine, I'm not going to—" Clare begins.

I silence her with my mouth on hers, kissing her wildly like I haven't seen her in years instead of a matter of days. I press her up against the trunk of an ornamental cherry, the drooping branches shielding us from view. Groping her body through the diaphanous dress, I feel her warm, firm flesh. I bite the side of her neck so I can taste the light salt of her skin.

She only resists for a moment before sinking against me helplessly, letting out a moan as I run my tongue along her jaw, before plunging it into her mouth.

I'm addicted to this woman.

I went into withdrawal without her.

I'm beginning to realize that nothing matters to me next to Clare—not my business, not the Maguires, not even clearing my name. I want her more than any other goal. Any achievement seems pointless without her.

"I'm taking you," I tell her, "and this time I'm not giving you back."

She pulls back, looking up into my eyes.

"What about what I want?" she says.

I seize her by the throat. Lifting the skirt of her dress, I shove my hand underneath, feeling her velvet soft pussy lips, warm and wet and ready for me.

"I already know what you want," I say, thrusting two fingers inside her. "You want this."

Clare moans, head tilted back, throat exposed.

I suck on the side of her throat while I fuck her with my fingers, feeling her warm, soft grip, feeling her clench and squeeze with every thrust.

"Oh my God. Oh my God…" she pants.

"Tell me you're mine," I growl.

"I'm yours…"

"Tell me you're coming with me, wherever I go…"

Her eyes lock with mine.

"I will," she says. "Anywhere."

I kiss her again, unzipping the trousers of my black tux. Then I take my fingers out of her and shove my cock in instead. I fuck her up against the tree, cherry blossoms raining down around us with every thrust. The air is sweet with the scent of crushed petals. Clare's mouth is even sweeter as I kiss her again and again and again.

The party continues behind us, all my enemies assembled in one place.

I'm not thinking about any of them.

All I care about in this moment is the perfect fit of Clare's pussy clenching around my cock, the feel of her tight waist gripped between my hands, and her tongue lapping against my lips.

This is what falling in love feels like.

It's delirium.

Stripping your cares away from everything that mattered to you before and wrapping them around one person instead.

Nothing has ever felt as good as my cock sliding in and out of her. I'm high on her taste and smell, my head floating, my body soaked in bliss.

She's mine, and no one is going to take her away from me.

With that thought, I explode inside of her.

Clare is coming too, crying out so loud that I have to smother her mouth under my hand.

Even while I'm coming, I keep fucking her, because I never want to stop.

CHAPTER 22

CLARE

I know it isn't safe here, not with every Desolation officer only paces away. Not with my *father* nearby. But I still can't help but take a minute to rest my head against Constantine.

I'm filled by him. Branded by him. I didn't know how badly I needed his hard, firm body against me, his raw and honest passion, him *inside* me until we were together again. It should come as no surprise to me that he couldn't stand to see another guy's hands on me. Furthermore, it should come as no surprise that he had to make it super abundantly clear to anyone and everyone that I belonged to him. He's left me panting and branded, sated and... alive. So goddamn *alive*.

Too soon, I pull away.

"My hair must be a wreck," I say in a whisper. The upturned corner of his mouth makes me smile. "Oh, you're *proud* of yourself, aren't you?"

"Proud?" he says in that thick accent of his that makes my heart unfurl. "The only one I'm proud of is you." He draws me to his chest in a fierce embrace and plants a heated kiss on my forehead. "You found what we needed. You waded into a den of vipers and came out unscathed." His voice cracks on the last word, and he kisses me again. "Tell me everything."

So I do. My back to the others, in a rapid whisper I tell him about the emails, the correspondence with the police. I tell him about the locked drawer, the encrypted files, the evidence I found poorly hidden on my father's laptop.

"An alliance between my family and the Irish would've been an unbreakable fortress," Constantine says, almost sadly, as if he still mourns the loss of what should have been. "Your father knew that. He couldn't have been successful with his plans if he'd had to defeat the power of two families joined together."

Constantine explains what he found in the warehouse—the pallets of cocaine smuggled in by the cops, now being distributed all across Desolation.

"Your father gets to look like a hero, taking down the Bratva, and Parsons gets to put the Irish out of business by becoming the fucking drug kingpin himself," he scoffs.

I nod. He's right. I know this now. I easily fill in the blanks.

"The easiest way for him to break that alliance was to paint you as Roxy's murderer. He knew if he could get the Irish to believe that story, and get you in jail…"

Constantine nods. "He could do what he needed to. The only question is…" Constantine's voice tapers off, as if he's thinking over a conundrum.

"What?" I whisper. My heart slams in my chest. The only question is… how to deal with my father? How to bring the truth to light?

Or how to end my father's life.

Constantine gives a hard shake of his head. "Clare, I don't want you to get hurt. What happens next will not be easy. It will be bloody, and violent."

I lift my chest and square my shoulders. "I know."

I can't see his full face because of the half-mask he wears over his nose and eyes, but I can see the battle that rages in his eyes. "I want to protect you from this," he says in a fierce whisper. "You weren't supposed to know any of this."

I shake my head. "And I wasn't supposed to fall in love."

My heart staggers in my chest. I'm a bundle of nerves after my declaration, more than I was even when I was looking through my father's laptop.

I've just confessed my love to the most dangerous person I know.

I don't quite know how to feel about that.

I open my mouth to speak, but I don't know what to say. He needs to respond.

Doesn't he?

I hear voices over my shoulder and realize with a sudden stab of fear that it's my father, with none other than the chief of police himself.

"You must go," Constantine whispers in my ear. Exactly what every girl wants to hear when she's just declared her love to a man.

I nod, my throat tight and my nose tingling.

"Let me eavesdrop," I whisper. "If I'm caught, the consequences for me are far less dangerous."

"No," he hisses in a vehement whisper. "You've done enough. This is my battle now, Clare." He pulls me to him, his mouth to my ear. "And before you get another thought in your head, know this. I love you, too. You are my light, shining like a beacon. You led me out of darkness." His arms around me tighten like a belt pulled taut while I try to compose myself. "Now go, little bird. *Fly.*"

I won't. I *won't.*

I shake my head vehemently from side to side.

"Clare," he says warningly. I know that look in his eyes all too well, but I stand my ground.

"No," I repeat. "It's inevitable. I'm as much a part of all of this as you are, now."

His jaw tightens, as his eyes watch my father and the chief share a drink.

Behind my father, I see a uniformed waiter with sandy blond hair pass between the gardens and the back access to the kitchens.

"Constantine," I gasp. "It's Niall Maguire…"

"I know," he murmurs back. "I brought the Irish. Now go Clare, do not force my hand. I need you safe."

"I will stay safe," I say, as I pull my hand away and glance back at him over my shoulder. "Watch me. I'm counting on you to keep me safe."

He reaches for me, but I've already stepped into the limelight. I hear him curse, then see him pull out a cell phone in my peripheral vision as I turn away. My mother sees me a few paces off and waves to me. I'm glad I have the mask on to hide the tears in my eyes, the panic that sweeps over me like a waterfall.

It felt a lot safer by his side. So much safer.

His scent still clings to me, the press of his fingers still lingering on my sides, and I bear the marks of his perfectly savage brand of love-making on my body.

I make sure to wave to my father as I watch Constantine—the mysterious cloaked stranger, only one of many at the masquerade ball—fall into the shadows to my right. A few of the masked men standing against the wall casually follow. *His* men, or maybe more Irish.

"Clare, I'd like to introduce you to a few of my friends," my mother says. Her friends, as tacky as she is, ask me questions about being taken by "that monster." They listen with wide eyes and open mouths before I even speak.

"It was terrible," I tell them. "He was so strong and fierce, I saw him rip the door off a car without breaking a sweat." I'm having fun with this. I can almost imagine Constantine shaking his head, that smirk on his face before he smacks my ass for being so cheeky.

"Were you scared?"

"Terrified," I say in a breathy whisper. I shiver when the dark-cloaked men pass by, masked and incognito. "But he never hurt me," I lie. I'll never forget that whipping while splayed over his lap in the car and wish I could understand why my body heats at the memory. "He only used me to get out of jail. That's how I escaped so easily." My voice sounds a little hollow when I finish my story. "I was never part of his plan."

He just told me he loved me.

I have to stay strong.

When I see my father and Parsons going to a more private location, I pretend I'm choked up, and it isn't very hard to do. "Now, if you'll excuse me, I'm going to get a little bite to eat."

The food's right out in the open courtyard where my father's headed.

Dread gathers in my chest; the pounding of my heart wants to come next. This is where the proverbial shit hits the fan. I need to hear what these two will say to each other, when they think they're safe behind their masks and with their crowds of people nearby. I need to record this for evidence and find out if there's anybody else implicated in any of this. I look wildly around me for one quick second to try to catch Constantine's eye, but he's nowhere to be found.

A rowdy group of younger people, around college-aged, steps in front of me. I let them go so they camouflage me. Thankfully the color of their dresses and gowns and masks is similar to my own. I head straight into the crowd, allowing their boisterous enthusiasm to buoy me along until I see them—my father and his friend, out by the bar, each with a drink in hand.

Even a day ago, I'd have wanted to cry thinking about my dad embroiled in any of this.

But I saw the inside of that prison.

I know my father's not innocent.

But Constantine is.

I slip casually to the side, just as one of Constantine's men brushes by me. I look at him in surprise, but he's already gone.

To the left, there are none of the twinkling fairy lights lighting up the garden, just a couple talking quietly to each other but no one else.

My phone buzzes.

I look at the screen and see a text from Constantine.

CONSTANTINE: *You're a stubborn brat.*

Me: And you love that about me.

Constantine: You tell a girl you love her ONE TIME…

I TUCK my head and stifle a smile.

CONSTANTINE. We'll talk about your willfulness later, alone.

Me: And naked?

Constantine: Absolutely.

NOW THAT WE'RE back together, I feel as if my world is brighter again, more vivid. I feel like I can smile. I feel like everything will be okay, even if we still have to walk across hot coals to get there.

CONSTANTINE: Clare, you'll find a small recording device in your pocket. It's designed to look like a rock. Open it and click it on. Gently roll it beneath your father's chair, then walk away. We'll take it from there.

Me: Got it.

AH. So that's what his friend was doing.

With shaking hands, I reach into the gauzy pocket of my costume. Huh. I didn't even know it had a pocket, but Constantine was one step ahead of me.

I turn so my back's to everyone and look at it. It's obviously something high tech and beyond my capabilities, similar to a surveillance camera tucked into a boulder. When I hold it in the palm of my hand, it just looks like any old rock, but when I tip it upside down, I can see little filigree wiring and a tiny microphone.

Alrighty then.

I draw in a deep breath. I walk over to the garden where a variety of rocks lay, and wonder how I'll get this over to them without anyone noticing.

I have to do this.

It feels almost surreal that after everything that's happened—the brutal death of Roxy, and Constantine's incarceration, nameless deaths and crimes committed—that the outing of the truth comes down to a fake rock being rolled under the seats of the guilty parties.

Thankfully, the rowdy crowd comes back my way just in time. I pretend to trip, fall to my knees, and roll the rock just as they walk by me. I hold my breath—I haven't even come up with a plan B— then release it with a silent thrill of victory. It's there.

It lands.

I turn, pretending I didn't just drop a bug that probably signed the death sentence for my own father.

I'm a different woman now, though. I've seen the rawest side of humanity and the evil people are capable of. I'm not as innocent as I once was. Now, I've chosen the side of the men who know the meaning of loyalty and honor.

When I reach the landing, I see Constantine's cousin Emmanuel standing beside me. I look at him in confusion. I didn't expect him to be the one Constantine sent to me.

"This way. Follow me." His hand on my elbow, he guides me none too gently to a hallway that leads to the exit. He quickens his step, and I look wildly about me for Constantine.

"Where's Constantine?"

"Waiting for us."

Something isn't right. Something's gone wrong, I know it.

"I don't believe you," I say. I pause at the door, shaking off his hand and refusing to go another step.

He turns to me, his eyes furious, and grabs for me, but I won't let him touch me. I dodge his arm, and by instinct, kick him straight between the legs, just as a hulking shadow rises behind Emmanuel.

"Of all the people to betray me," Constantine says in a furious whisper. Emmanuel's on the floor, cursing me out and grabbing his balls. I'm shaking with nerves and anger, but Constantine's ready to kill.

"You dare to touch my woman!"

"I didn't—didn't—touch her!" Emmanuel gasps.

"You tried to, and that's the same fucking thing," Constantine growls. He kicks Emmanuel in the belly, then drags him to his feet by his hair. "You will pay for that."

He shoves Emmanuel at two of his men behind him. "Bring him with us to listen to the recording. Leave his punishment for me."

Constantine turns to me. "Well done, little bird," he says in a voice affected by emotion. "Come with me, now. You deserve to hear the truth as much as any of us do."

Constantine leads me to a room with him, and he never takes his eyes off me, his hands on me at all times.

"I lost you once," he says in a heated whisper. "I don't want to ever lose you again."

Emmanuel is cursing behind us. Constantine turns to him and curses back in a heated whisper.

"Wish I knew Russian," I mutter.

Yury laughs beside me. "Those are not the words you'd want to hear. It would be hard to imagine your lover kissing you with a mouth like that."

Constantine's eyes twinkle.

I wonder at their lightheartedness. After everything Constantine's been through, how can he smile like this?

Maybe it's because for the first time in so long... he's on the cusp of being *free*. Free from the bonds that held him. Free from the accusations of the Irish.

I want this all over now. I want this all behind us.

It feels surreal to sit in what looks like a meeting room, Constantine beside me and his men all around us. Someone hits a speaker, and my father's voice comes loud and clear, along with that of the chief of police.

"WHAT HAPPENED AT THE WAREHOUSE?" my father demands.

"It was Rogov. It doesn't matter—we moved the product again."

"We should have just killed him," my father says, annoyed.

. . .

A CHILL GOES DOWN my spine. Even after all I've seen, I can't believe my father is discussing murder in the same tone of voice he employs when instructing our gardener.

Constantine's jaw is set. He runs his thumb along the top of my hand, thoughtfully.

"IT WAS you *who wanted the conviction," Parsons snarls back. "You had to have the whole media circus, as per fucking usual."*

"That 'circus' got me re-elected," my father says, coolly. "But he's outlived his usefulness. No more trials—tell your officers to execute on sight."

"I already have," Parsons says.

I FEEL as if I'm not in my body, like I'm suspended above the room watching and listening as someone else. It's all so surreal. I never could have imagined myself in this position a week ago. This man was at my birthday party! He brought me a card with purple sparkles all over the front. God, I was so naïve.

"WILL the Irish back down once we've gelded the Bratva?" my father asks.

"They want revenge. I don't think they believe it was Constantine anymore."

There's a pause as my father muses. Then he says, "Then we'll have to find a scapegoat."

"Another one, you mean," Parsons laughs.

"Who?"

It's Parson's turn to pause.

"The cousin," he says at last. "He's also outlived his usefulness."

. . .

I LOOK AT CONSTANTINE, but his eyes drill into Emmanuel's.

"You were the source," he says in a cold, ruthless voice that makes me shiver. "You told them about the alliance. And you ordered the wine."

Emmanuel hangs his head and doesn't speak.

To Yury, Constantine says, "Bring Parsons to me. I will deal with Emmanuel." He looks my way. "Out of respect for Clare, I'll leave Valencia's reckoning to the Irish."

Yury nods, shooting one last look at Emmanuel, torn between repulsion and sorrow.

"Take Clare to a safe house," Constantine says, standing. "I don't want her injured."

No. No!

"Constantine, I want to stay with you." I get to my feet. I won't leave him again.

He turns to me. "Do not defy me in front of my men, Clare."

There will be rules in this new world of mine, and if I stay I choose that life.

I put my hands on his shoulders.

"You want me in this world, Constantine?"

He nods. "You know there's nothing I want more."

"Then let me stay."

Slowly, he shakes his head and cups my jaw. He leans in closer so only I can hear him. "When I touch you, I don't want you to know

259

what my hands have done. I don't want what's between us tainted by my work and the life I live." He swallows hard. "I want our life together to be *all ours.*"

I nod, sudden emotion washing over me.

"I'll give you that," I whisper.

Constantine opens his mouth to say something else, but it's drowned out by an explosion that deafens us all.

CHAPTER 23

CONSTANTINE

An explosion rockets through the hotel, shaking the building.

Instinctively, I dive on top of Clare, knocking her to the ground, covering her with my body.

This moment of distraction is all Emmanuel needs to escape. He bolts in the direction of the kitchens, sprinting off like his life depends on it, which it absolutely fucking does.

The Irish have likewise vanished, with a coordination and speed that tells me they're not at all surprised at the sudden blast. In fact, I'd bet my pinky finger they're the ones who set it.

The Maguires have never been patient. Apparently, Connor has no intention of seeing Valencia behind bars before he exacts his revenge —he wants it here and now, tonight.

When it seems that no second explosion is imminent, I pick Clare up off the floor, smoothing her hair back out of her eyes, holding her face steady between my hands so I can look into her eyes and be sure she isn't injured. Her eyes are wide open and terrified, but the pupils are even, no sign of concussion, despite the force of the blast that slapped us like an invisible hand.

The air is full of smoke and screams.

Holding tight to her hand I murmur, "Follow me."

People are fleeing in all directions, chaotic and frenzied. A man slams into Clare, almost knocking her over. I seize him by his lapel and fling him away from her, snarling, "Don't fucking touch her!" I stiff-arm the next two people before they can bowl her over. My petite little bird would be trampled in minutes without me by her side. I tuck her under my arm, close against my side, as we shoulder our way through the crowd.

Gunfire breaks out in the garden where Clare and I were entangled such a short time ago. Pulling her over to the windows, I peer through. The Irish are shooting at Chief Parsons and several officers in formal clothes. They're trying to get to Valencia, but slippery eel that he is, he's crawling back through a tangled maze of rose bushes, his tuxedo torn by the thorns and his bow tie askew. Connor Maguire roars with rage, only to take a bullet to the shoulder a moment later, dropping him from view.

Valencia is fleeing in the same direction as Emmanuel. I'm torn between my desire to get Clare to safety and my need to wrap this up once and for all.

Clare looks up at me.

"I want to be with you," she says, quietly. "Wherever you're going. Whatever you're doing."

I hesitate only long enough to pull one of the Glocks from the holsters concealed beneath my jacket.

"Do you know how to shoot?" I ask her.

She nods, taking the gun in her small, slim hand. "My father showed me."

"You stay behind me, and if I tell you to hide, you hide."

She nods again.

With the second gun clasped tight in my own hand, I head toward the kitchens. Shouldering my way through the swinging double doors, I see a scene of total chaos: shattered dishes, water overflowing from the sink onto the floor, smoking frying pans left burning on the stove. The kitchen staff fled at the sound of the blast. But I have a feeling Clare and I are not actually alone in here.

A moment later, a bullet shatters the wine glasses directly behind my right ear.

"*Get down!*" I roar to Clare, following that advice myself as I dive behind a trolley laden with pastries. Two more bullets ricochet off the vent hood as Clare ducks inside a lower cabinet. I shove the trolly in front of her, covering her from view, while I run, crouched down, between the crowded service stations.

Valencia keeps shooting at me, exploding serving platters and a massive cruet of olive oil. The oil topples onto the floor, adding to the slippery morass already coating the tiles.

I return fire, forcing Valencia back toward the walk-in freezer. I'm a better shot than him—I could finish this right now. But I still don't know who actually killed Roxy. Valencia wouldn't have the balls to do it himself, or Parsons either. I need to know whose hands were wrapped around her neck. Who snuffed out her life, and the life of my son.

So instead of firing a bullet right between his eyes, I grab a heavy pewter dish and fling it at his head instead, striking him in the temple. He slips on the wet floor and stumbles, losing his grip on his gun. Roaring, I dive at him, seizing him around the waist and knocking him backward. I hit him in the face, one, twice, three times, until his nose is shattered, his mouth full of blood.

The smoking frying pans have finally set off the fire alarm, or perhaps it was the bomb itself. With a frantic hissing sound, the sprinklers activate. Water pours down from the ceiling. It drenches me in seconds, and Valencia too, blood running away from him in long, winding threads.

Seizing him by the throat, I snarl, "It's over! I have your drugs. I have your emails. I've got you on tape admitting everything. The only thing you have left is your life, and I will throttle it out of you unless you tell me right now who you hired to kill Roxy."

Valencia laughs, hair plastered to his head, his teeth a gory, broken mess.

"I didn't hire anyone," he chokes.

I resist the overwhelming urge to tear out his larynx with my bare hands.

"What the fuck does that mean?" I snarl.

"I didn't hire anyone. He volunteered."

"Who!?"

Valencia looks me right in the eyes.

"Her brother," he says. "Niall Maguire."

I stare at him, uncomprehending, unbelieving.

Then the last pieces fall into place, and I see it all clearly. Why the dog didn't bark. Why the doors weren't forced. Why Roxy failed to defend herself against the man she welcomed into our home as friend and family. Her own little brother.

"We weren't the only ones unhappy with your alliance," Valencia says, his voice strangled but surprisingly calm. "As soon as Connor Maguire knew about the pregnancy, he started planning for a new successor. Which of course displeased his son. Niall was only too happy to help us get rid of you all. No one wanted an heir."

"*I did,*" I say, furiously.

With that, I lift a massive copper platter over my head, planning to bring it smashing down on Valencia's skull.

"Constantine!" Clare cries, a high note of pleading in her voice.

I turn to look at her.

She doesn't ask me to stop.

She just stands there, water running down her face, those big dark eyes full of tears.

And in that moment, I realize that while I may have lost my son, Valencia has given me something else. Without meaning to, without wanting to, he gave me Clare. And I love her with an intensity that may, in time, eclipse even the deepest hurts.

Slowly, I set down the platter.

At that moment, the door to the walk-in freezer bursts open and Emmanuel comes barreling out. He's clutching a butcher knife, his face a mask of rage. He sprints at me, blade swinging down toward my face. All I can do is put up my forearm to block it.

But Emmanuel isn't aiming for me. He buries the knife hilt-deep in Valencia's chest. He stabs him over and over while Clare's scream pierces the air.

Then, sobbing, Emmanuel sits back on his heels saying, "*Izvini, kuzen!* I'm so sorry, cousin. They picked me up in a bar uptown. They beat me, tortured me. I was so blitzed, I didn't know what I was saying. I never meant to tell. I should have confessed in the beginning when the mistake was small, when you could have forgiven me. I had no idea what they had planned. I did order the wine, but I swear to God, I didn't know what it was for... I never thought they would dare..."

He kneels before me, head bowed.

"I accept any punishment," he says. "Even if I have to pay with my life."

This time, I comprehend in an instant.

Emmanuel did spill intel on the alliance, probably drunk and high, just like he said. Then Parsons and Valencia used that leverage to blackmail him. But he didn't kill Roxy. He didn't intentionally betray me.

Before I can open my mouth to speak, a shot rings out. Emmanuel's expression of contrition turns to one of mild surprise. He looks down at his chest where blood spreads across his white dress shirt in a dark flood.

I turn to the doorway. Chief Parsons stands between the open double doors, the barrel of his gun still gently smoking.

"You're welcome," he says to me.

Then he points the gun right at my face.

"Unfortunately, you won't have long to enjoy it."

His finger curls on the trigger.

I lift my chin, ready to meet the fate that lies at the end of the road for all men like me.

The second shot rings out, and strangely, it's Parsons who stumbles. He clutches his side, turning in shock and horror.

Clare shoots him twice more in the chest.

He tumbles to the ground, his gun skittering away across the tiles, disappearing under the stove on which the fires have finally been extinguished.

Clare is still holding the gun in both hands, her arms rigid, her teeth bared.

I have to pry the gun out of her hands and pull her against my chest before she can take a full breath, at which her teeth rattle together like castanets.

"Oh my God, oh my God!" she cries. "What did I do!"

"You saved my life," I say.

I can hear sirens approaching from all sides. I no longer hear the Irish shooting out in the garden. I don't know if they were all killed, if they fled, or if they're still hunting the grounds for Valencia.

At this moment, I really don't care. All that concerns me is getting Clare out of here.

Swiftly, I wipe the prints from her gun, and then, with a napkin wrapped around my own fingers, I press it into Emmanuel's limp hand and fire twice more. The sprinklers may wash away the gunshot residue, but I don't want to take any chances.

Then I seize Clare by the arm and we run.

EPILOGUE

CLARE

Time lessens pain, and my break with my past and all that transpired is no exception. With my father's death came my mother's unraveling. She played the part of the mourning victim for as long as she could muster, until she simply stopped.

I think the truth about my father's guilt and his lack of concern for anyone in his life except himself helped. With her cool dismissal of her past, and the way she almost painlessly took up the next stage of her life, I couldn't help but wonder if she knew what he was up to all along.

If only I'd been so wise.

"What are you thinking, *ptitsa?*"

I look out over the smoky mountain view outside our window, twiddling with the thick band on my finger. It was only a week ago we took our vows, a full year after the scandal that broke my family. I begged Constantine to take us to his native land to start a new life together, and he didn't have to be asked twice. I'm leaning against his thick, muscled body, comforted by the weight of his arm on me.

"I wonder how much my mother knew about my father's plans."

"I'd guess quite a bit, if you were to ask me." He doesn't change the subject or chide me for bringing this up for the umpteenth time. He allows me as much time to process and grieve as I need. Constantine understands the complexities of a painful past.

I roll over toward him, toward his bare chest, and smile.

"Thank you."

A corner of his lips quirks up, and he brushes the pad of his thumb over my cheek. "For what?"

"For letting me talk about this wherever and whenever I need to. For not telling me to let it go by now."

"I wouldn't," he says simply. "Your past is who you are, and I have no need to fear it."

His pragmatic view of life is one of the things I love best about him.

"I will," he says, with a teasing lilt of his voice, "suggest a form of distraction from time to time."

"Mhm," I say on a moan, as he pins me beneath his large, heavy frame and begins to kiss his way down the side of my jaw to my neck. "And I may—*ooh.*" I gasp. "Agree to that."

My eyes flutter closed when he clamps his mouth on one bare nipple and suckles. I bite my lip to keep from gasping as he cups my ass so hard it's painful. The sexy session over his knee the night before doesn't help. I'm still raw, still aching from him, even as I crave more.

He swallows my gasp with a kiss that makes me whimper, dragging his already-hard cock between my legs. My wrists are trapped between his fingers as he glides himself in me.

I moan, the feel of him in me so perfect. He stretches me and fills me, and my mind goes blank. All I want is to feel, to revel in my skin against his, and as he thrusts in and out, he pulls nearly fully out of me, only to splinter me with jolts of ecstasy when he slams back in.

He lets my wrists go, and I automatically throw my arms around his thick, muscled shoulders. When he thrusts and dips his head to mine, I kiss his shoulder. With a wicked grin he can't see, I sink my teeth into the muscle there, relishing the salty taste of him.

"*Khristos!*" he curses, stilling his thrusts. I whimper with the need for more. With surprising grace, he rolls over, taking me with him. When I'm well situated on his cock, he gives me one of his rare grins. "What a bad girl you are," he says, before he gives me a teasing swat. I bite my lip, and he lifts me by the hips, then slams me back down on his cock. "Just for that, you'll have to do the work."

I grin back at him, moving my body in perfect time with his. This angle gives me a perfect view of him, and I pause in our lovemaking just long enough to run my fingers through his dark hair. "I love you, Constantine."

His hands travel up my sides, then back down, as if he's assuring himself that he's really there. "And I love you, Clare." His voice drops to a growl. "Now fuck me, woman."

He rolls me onto my back again, impatient for me to ride him, pinning me beneath him and pounding into me until I think I'm going to shatter.

"Oh God," I moan. "Constantine, *fuck.*" My eyes close as my body shudders beneath his. With another hard thrust, he comes inside me. I take all of him as my body surrenders fully. Bliss floods me from head to toe, until his forehead drops to mine and we're panting together.

"There, now," he says with a teasing smile. "You were saying something?"

I mumble something incoherent and jumbled.

"What was that?" He's still grinning, only now his eyes are half-lidded. "You were saying?"

"Coffee. I want coffee."

He pulls out of me with a chuckle and heads to the bathroom to get a washcloth. "Stay there. I'll bring it to you."

I gaze out of the window at the mountains, the brilliant blue of the sky, and in the distance, the stately buildings that dot his native land in a breathtaking skyline of pale blues and pinks. I sigh. "I'm not going anywhere."

Constantine

I TAKE CLARE TO KARELIA, the place I used to come with my mother as a small boy. Here the trees reach prehistoric proportions, growing atop boulders larger than a house, while sparkling waterfalls crash down into bottomless pools. It's the loveliest part of Russia. After all the ugliness she endured in Desolation, I want to show Clare that the world is still beautiful and safe for her. As long as she's with me.

Every time I pull her close, I rest my hand possessively over hers, touching the gold band on her finger, the shackle that binds us together forever. This is the one imprisonment I never wish to escape. She is mine and I am hers until we are nothing but atoms... and perhaps even beyond that.

I am filled with a deep contentment that I never thought possible for me.

Clare brings me peace, every minute, every hour.

Her warm, sweet scent and her low, soft voice have become the bedrock of my life. The things I live for now.

I thought we would return to Desolation once the madness of the gala had subsided. I released the emails, the recordings, and all the evidence I had on Valencia and Parsons. My lawyer had my conviction overturned in absentia, and my father brokered a deal with the new chief of police which would have allowed the Bratva to operate quite comfortably as we always had.

Instead, I find myself on the first holiday of my life, touring Clare through Moscow, St. Petersburg, Sochi, and now Karelia. My business concerns seem distant and dreamy. Only Clare and the here and now interest me.

Niall Maguire fled to Dublin, and Connor Maguire allowed him to flee. I'm sure Connor's rage is all-consuming, and yet he couldn't bring himself to punish his son in the way he deserved.

I planned to hunt Niall down myself and kill him. Yet even for that, I find myself loathe to leave Clare. Even for a single day, even for a single hour.

I have not become a more merciful man, but perhaps I've become a more patient one.

Clare's light footsteps creep up behind me, across the ancient oriental rugs that carpet the dacha. She may be as quiet as ever, but she'll never be able to sneak up on me. I whirl around and seize her, swinging her through the air and kissing her hard.

"Careful!" she says, breathlessly.

I set her down, looking at her bright eyes and flushed cheeks.

"When did you ever tell me to be careful?" I demand. "Or to go lighter on you?"

Clare tries to hide her smile, but it's impossible.

"Some things change," she says.

"What things?"

"The number of people in our party, perhaps…" she says.

Now my heart is racing, and a rare emotion hits: I'm afraid. Afraid that I'm not understanding her correctly.

"Are you telling me what I think you're telling me?"

She nods, blushing prettily. "I think it happened a few weeks ago. In the back of that convertible…"

A shout of joy bursts out of me, startling us both. I want to sweep her up in my arms again, but instead I summon every ounce of self-control I possess to lay my hand gently on her belly instead.

"Do you feel it moving?" I ask.

"Not yet," she says. "It's too early. But I definitely feel… different."

We're both quiet for a moment, listening, as if we might hear the tiny heartbeat beneath my hand.

"I'm different, too," I tell her. "You've changed me. I never could have felt like this before."

"Like what?" Clare asks.

"Happy. I'm so, so happy."

WE HOPE YOU ENJOYED OUR CO-WRITE,
THANK YOU! 🤍
WE RECOMMEND THESE BOOKS NEXT →

KEENAN
DANGEROUS DOMS

USA TODAY BESTSELLING AUTHOR

JANE HENRY

KEENAN

I watch from where I sit on the craggy cliffs of Ballyhock to the waves crashing on the beach. Strong. Powerful. Deadly. A combination so familiar to me it brings me comfort. It's two hours before my alarm goes off, but when Seamus McCarthy calls a meeting, it doesn't matter where you are or what you're doing, the men of The Clan answer.

I suspect I know why he's calling a meeting today, but I also know my father well enough not to presume. One of our largest shipments of illegal arms will arrive in our secured port next week, and over the next month, we'll oversee distribution from the home that sits on the cliff behind me. Last week, we also sealed a multi-million-dollar deal that will put us in good stead until my father retires, when I assume the throne. But something isn't right with our upcoming transactions. Then again, when dealing with the illicit trade we orchestrate, it rarely is. As a high-ranking man of The Clan, I've learned to pivot and react. My instincts are primed.

The sun rises in early May at precisely 5:52 a.m., and it's rare I get to watch it. So this morning, in the small quiet interim before daybreak and our meeting, I came to the cliff's edge. I've traveled the world for my family's business, from the highest ranges of the Alps to the depths of the shores of the Dead Sea, the vast expanse of the Serengeti, and the top of the Eiffel Tower. But here, right here atop the cliffs of Ballyhock, paces from the door to my childhood home, overlooking the Irish Sea, is where I like to be. They say the souls of our ancestors pace these shores, and sometimes, early in the morning, I almost imagine I can see them, the beautiful, brutal Celts and Vikings, fearless and brave.

A brisk wind picks up, and I wrap my jacket closer to my body. I've put on my gym clothes to hit the workout room after our meeting if time permits. We'll see. My father may have other ideas.

I hear footsteps approach before I see the owner.

"What's the story, Keenan?"

Boner sits on the flat rock beside me, rests his arms on his bent knees, and takes a swig from a flask. Tall and lanky, his lean body never stills, even in sleep. Always tapping, rocking, moving from side to side, Boner has the energy of an eight-week-old golden retriever.

My younger cousin, we've known each other since birth, both raised in The Clan. He's like a brother to me.

"Eh, nothing," I tell him, waving off an offer from the flask. "You out of your mind? He'll knock you upside the head, and you know it."

If my father catches him drinking this early in the day, when he's got a full day of work ahead of him, heads will roll.

"Ah, that's right," he says, grinning at me and flashing perfect white teeth, his words exaggerated and barely intelligible. "You drink that energy shite before you go work on yer manly *physique*. And anyway, get off your high horse. Nolan's more banjaxed than I am."

I clench my jaw and grunt to myself. *Fuck*. Nolan, the youngest in The Clan and my baby brother, bewitched my mother with his blond hair and green eyes straight outta the womb. Shielded by my mother's protective arms, the boy's never felt my father's belt nor mine, and it shows. I regret not making him toe the line more when he was younger.

"Course he is," I mutter. "Both of you ought to know better."

"Ah, come off it, Keenan," Boner says good-naturedly. "You know better than I the Irish do best with a bit of drink no matter the time of day."

I can toss them back with the best of them, but there's a time and place to get plastered, and minutes before we find out the latest update of the status of our very livelihood, isn't it. I get to my feet, scowling. "Let's go."

Though he's my cousin, and I'm only a little older than I am, Boner nods and gets to his feet. As heir to the throne and Clan Captain, I'm above him in rank. He and the others defer to me.

He mutters something that sounds a lot like "needs to get laid" under his breath as we walk up the stone pathway to the house.

"What's that?" I ask.

"Eh, nothing," he says, grinning at me.

"Wasn't nothing."

"You heard me."

"Say it to my face, motherfucker," I suggest good-naturedly. He's a pain in the arse, but I love the son of a bitch.

"I *said*," he says loudly. "You need to get fuckin' *laid*. How long's it been since the bitch left you?"

I feel my eyes narrow as we continue to walk to the house. "Left *me*? You know's well as I do, I broke up with her." I won't even say her name. She's dead to me. I can abide many things, but lying and cheating are two things I won't.

"How long?" he presses.

It's been three months, two weeks, and five fucking days.

"Few months," I say.

He shakes his head. "Christ, Keenan," he mutters. "Come with me to the club tonight, and we'll get you right fixed."

I snort. "All set there."

I've no interest in visiting the seedy club Nolan and Boner frequent. I went once, and it was enough for me.

Boner shakes his head. "You've only been to the anteroom, Keenan," he says with a knowing waggle of his eyebrows. "You've never been *past* there. Not to where the *real* crowd gathers."

"All set," I repeat, though I don't admit my curiosity's piqued.

The rocky pathway leading to the family estate is paved with large, roughly hewn granite, the steep incline part of our design to keep our home and headquarters private. Thirty-five stones in the pathway, which I count every time I walk to the cliffs that overlook the bay, lead to a thick, wrought-iron gate, the entrance to our house. With twelve bedrooms, five reception rooms, one massive kitchen, a finished basement with our workout rooms, library, and private interrogation rooms, the estate my father inherited from his father is worth an estimated eleven million euros. The men in The Clan outside our family tree live within a mile of our estate, all property owned by the brotherhood, but my brothers and I reside here.

When I marry—a requirement before I assume the throne as Clan Chief—I'll inherit the entire third floor, and my mother and father will retire to the east wing, as my father's parents did before them.

When I marry. For fuck's *sake*. The requirement hangs over my head like the sharpened edge of an executioner's blade. No wedding, no rightful inheritance. And I can't even think of such a thing, not when my ex-girlfriend's betrayal's still fresh on my mind.

I wave my I.D. at the large, heavy black gate that borders our house, and with a click and whirr, the gates open. When my great grandfather bought this house, he kept the original Tuscan structure in place. The millionaire who had it built hailed from Tuscany, Italy, and to this day, the original Tuscan-inspired garden is kept in perfect shape. Lined with willow trees and bordered with well-trimmed hedges, benches and archways made from stone lend a majestic, age-old air. In May, the flowers are in full bloom, lilacs, irises, and the exotic violet hawthorn, the combined fragrances enchanting. The low murmur of the fountain my mother had built soothes me when I'm riled up or troubled. I've washed blood-soaked hands in that fountain, and I laid my head on the cold stones that surround it when Riley, my father's youngest brother and my favorite uncle, was buried.

We walk past the garden, and I listen to Boner yammer on about the club and the pretty little Welsh blonde he spanked, tied up, and banged last night, but when he reaches for his flask again, I yank it out of his hand and decidedly shove it in my pocket.

"Keenan, for fuck's—"

"You can have it after the meeting," I tell him. "No more fucking around, Boner. This is serious business, and you aren't going into this half-arsed, you hear?"

Though he clenches his jaw, he doesn't respond, and finally reluctantly nods. I'm saving him from punishment ordered by my father and saving myself from having to administer it. We trot up the large stairs to the front door, but before we can open it, the massive entryway door swings open, and Nolan stands in the doorway, grinning.

"Fancy meetin' you two here," he says in a high-pitched falsetto. "We won't be needin' any of yer wares today."

He pretends to shut the door, but I shove past him and enter the house. He says something under his breath to Boner, and I swear Boner says something about me getting laid again. For once in my life, I fucking hope my father assigns me to issue a beating after this meeting. I'm so wound up. I could use a good fucking fight.

"Keenan." I'm so in my head, I don't notice Father Finn standing in the darkened doorway to our meeting room. He's wearing his collar, and his black priest's clothes are neatly pressed, the overhead light gleaming on his shiny black shoes. Though he's dressed for the day, his eyes are tired. It seems Boner isn't the only one who's pulled an all-nighter.

"Father."

Though Father Finn's my father's younger brother, I've never called him uncle. My mother taught me at a young age that a man of the cloth, even kin, is to be addressed as Father. It doesn't surprise me to see him here. He's as much a part of the McCarthy family as my father is, and he's privy to much, though not all, of what we do. It troubles him, though, as he's never reconciled his loyalty to the church and to our family.

Shorter than I am, he's balding, with curls of gray at his temples and in his beard. The only resemblance between the two of us are the McCarthy family green eyes.

Vicar of Holy Family, the church that stands behind my family's estate, Father Finn's association with the McCarthy Clan is only referenced by the locals in hushed conversation. Officially, he's only my uncle. Privately, he's our most trusted advisor. If Father Finn's come to this meeting, he's got news for us.

He holds the door open to my father's office, and when I enter I see my father's already sitting at the table. He's only called the inner circle this morning, those related by blood: Nolan and Cormac, my brothers, Boner, Father Finn, and me. If necessary, we'll call the rest of The Clan to council after our first meeting.

"Boys," my father says, nodding to Nolan, Boner, and me in greeting.

My father sits at the head of the table, his back ramrod straight, the tips of his fingers pressed together as if in prayer. At sixty-three years old, he's only two years away from retirement as Chief, though he keeps himself in prime physical shape. With salt and pepper hair at his temples, he hasn't gone quite as gray as his younger brother. He jokes it's mam that keeps him young, and I think there's a note of truth in it. My mother is ten years his junior, and they've been wed since their arranged marriage thirty-three years ago. I was their first-born, Cormac the second, and Nolan the third, though my father's made mention of several girls born before me that never made it past infancy. My mother won't talk of them, though. I wonder if the little graves that lie in the graveyard at Holy Family are the reason for the lines around my mother's bright gray eyes. I may never know.

I take my seat beside my father, and pierce Nolan and Boner with stern looks. Boner's fucking right. Nolan's eyes are bloodshot and glassy, and I notice he wobbles a little when he sits at the table. Irishmen are no strangers to drink, and we're no exception, but I worry Nolan's gone to the extreme. I make a mental note to talk to him about this later. I won't tolerate him fucking up our jobs because he can't stay sober. I watch him slump to the table and clear my throat. His eyes come to mine. I shake my head and straighten my shoulders. Nodding, he sits up straighter.

Cormac, the middle brother, sits to my left and notices everything. Six foot five, he's the giant of our group, and, appropriately, our head bonebreaker. With a mop of curly, dark brown hair and a heavy beard, he looks older than his twenty-five years.

He nods to me and I to him. We'll talk about our concerns about Nolan later, not in the presence of our father. Or any of the others, really.

"Thank you for coming so early, boys," my father begins, scrubbing a hand across his forehead. I notice a tremor in his hand I've never noticed before and stifle a sigh. He's getting older.

"It came to my attention early this morning that Father Finn has something to relay to us of importance." He fixes Boner and Nolan with an unwavering look. "And since some of you haven't gone to bed yet, I figured we should strike while the iron's hot, so to speak."

I can't help but smirk when Nolan and Boner squirm. When Boner's father passed, one of the few gone rogue in our company, my father took Boner under his wing and treated him as one of his own. I love the motherfucker like a brother myself. Though he's got a touch of the class clown in him, he's as loyal as they come and as quick with a knife draw as any I've seen, his aim at the shooting range spot-on. He's an asset to The Clan in every way. When he's fucking sober, anyway.

Now, under both my gaze and my father's, he squirms a little. My father keeps tabs on everyone here, Boner no exception.

"I think it best I let the Father speak for himself, since he needs to leave early to celebrate mass." None of us so much as blink, the Father's duties as commonplace as a shopping list. We're used to the juxtaposition of his duties to God's people and to us. We have long since accepted it as a way of life. He has a certain code he doesn't break, though, and out of respect for him, we keep many of the inner workings of The Clan from him. We give generously to the church, and though God himself may not see our donations as any sort of indulgence, the people of Holy Family and Ballyhock certainly do.

Father Finn sits on my father's left, his heavy gray brows drawn together.

"Thank you, Seamus." He and my mother are the only ones who call my dad his Christian name. Finn speaks in a soft, gentle tone laced with steel: a man of God tied by blood to the Irish mob.

My father nods and sits back, his gaze fixed on his younger brother.

Father clears his throat. "I have news regarding the… arms deal you've been working on for some time."

My father doesn't blink, and I don't make eye contact with any of my brothers. We've never discussed our occupations with Father so out in the open like this, but like our father, he sees all. The church he oversees is sandwiched between our mansion that overlooks the bay to the east, and Ballyhock's armory to the west. Still, his blatant naming of our most lucrative endeavor is unprecedented.

Though we dabble in many things, we have two main sources of income in The McCarthy Clan: arms trafficking and loansharking. Though neither are legal, Father Finn's insisted we keep out of the heavier sources of income our rival clan, the Martins from the south, dabble in. They're known for extortion, heroin imports and far more contracted hits than we've ever done. Rivals since before my parents married, we've held truce ever since my father took the throne. Both his father and our rival's former chief were murdered by the American mafia; the dual murders formed a truce we've upheld since then.

"Go on," my father says.

Father Finn clears his throat a second time. "There's no need to pretend I don't know where you're planning to get your bread and butter," he says in his soft voice. "Especially since I've advised you from the beginning."

My father nods, and a muscle ticks in his jaw. His brother takes his time when relaying information, and my father's not a patient man. "Go on," my father repeats, his tone harder this time.

"The Martins are behind the theft of your most recent acquisitions," he says sadly, as he knows theft from The Clan is an act of war. "Their theft is only the beginning, however. It was a plot to undermine you. They fully plan on sub-contracting your arms trafficking by summer. They have a connection nearby that's given them inside information, and I know where that inside information came from."

Boner cracks his knuckles, ready to fight. Nolan's suddenly sober, and I can feel Cormac's large, muscled body tense beside me. My own stomach clenches in anticipation. They're preparing to throw the gauntlet, which would bring our decades-long truce to a decided and violent end.

"Where would that be?" I ask.

Finn clears his throat again. "I'm not at liberty to give you all the details I know," he begins.

Boner glares at him. "Why the fuck not? Are you fucking kidding me?"

The Father holds up a hand, begging patience.

"Enough, Boner," I order. There's an unwritten rule in my family that we don't press the Father for information he doesn't offer. I suspect he occasionally relays information granted him in the privacy of the confessional, something he'd consider gravely sinful. Father Finn is a complex man. We take the information he gives us and piece the rest together ourselves.

"I can give you some, however," the Father continues. "I believe you'll find what you need at the lighthouse."

I feel my own brows pull together in confusion.

"The lighthouse?" Nolan asks. "Home of the old mentaller who kicked it?"

"Jack Anderson," the Father says tightly.

The eccentric old man, the lighthouse keeper, took a heart attack last month, leaving Ballyhock without a keeper. Someone spotted his body on the front green of the lighthouse and went to investigate. He was already dead.

Since the lighthouses are now operated digitally, no longer in need of a keeper, the town hasn't hired a replacement. Most lighthouse keepers around these parts are kept on more for the sake of nostalgia than necessity.

The man we're talking of, who lived in the lighthouse to the north of our estate, *was* out of his mind. He would come into town only a few times a year to buy his stores, then live off the dry goods he kept at his place. He had no contact with the outside world except for this foray into town and the library, and when he came, he reminded one of a mad scientist. Hailing from America, he looked a bit like an older, heavier version of Einstein with his wild, unkempt white hair and tattered clothing. He muttered curse words under his breath, walked with a manky old walking stick, and little children would scatter away from him when he came near. He always carried a large bag over his shoulder, filled with books he'd replenish at the library.

Father Finn doesn't reply to Nolan at first, holding his gaze. "Aren't we all a little mental, then, Nolan?" he asks quietly. Nolan looks away uncomfortably.

"Suppose," he finally mutters.

The Father sighs. "That's all I can tell you, lads. It's enough to go on. If you're to secure your arms deals, and solidify the financial well-being of The Clan, and most importantly, keep the peace here in Ballyhock, then I advise you to go at once to the lighthouse." He gets to his feet, and my father shakes his hand. I get to my feet, too, but it isn't to shake his hand. I've got questions.

"Was the lighthouse keeper involved?" I ask. "Was he mates with our rivals? What can we possibly find at the lighthouse?"

Inside the lighthouse? I've never even thought of there being anything inside the small lighthouse. There had to be, though. The old man lived there for as long as I can remember. There's no house on property save a tiny shed that couldn't hold more than a hedge trimmer.

My father holds a hand up to me, and Cormac mutters beside me, "Easy, Keenan."

Father Finn's just dropped the biggest bomb he's given us yet, and they expect me just to sit and nod obediently?

"You know more, Father," I say to him. "So much more."

Father Finn won't meet my eyes, but as he goes to leave, he speaks over his shoulder. "Go to the lighthouse, Keenan. You'll find what you need there."

READ MORE

AIDA GALLO

Fireworks burst into bloom above the lake, hanging suspended in the clear night air, then drifting down in glittering clouds that settle on the water.

My father flinches at the first explosion. He doesn't like things that are loud or unexpected. Which is why I get on his nerves sometimes —I can be both of those things, even when I'm trying to behave myself.

I see his scowl illuminated by the blue and gold light. Yup, definitely the same expression he gets when he looks at me.

"Do you want to eat inside?" Dante asks him.

Because it's a warm night, we're all sitting out on the deck. Chicago is not like Sicily—you have to take the opportunity to eat outdoors whenever you can get it. Still, if it weren't for the sound of traffic below, you might think you were in an Italian vineyard. The table is set with the rustic stoneware brought from the old country three generations ago, and the pergola overhead is thickly blanketed by the fox grapes Papa planted for shade. You can't make wine out of fox grapes, but they're good for jam at least.

My father shakes his head. "It's fine here," he says shortly.

Dante grunts and goes back to shoveling chicken in his mouth. He's so big that his fork looks comically small in his hand. He always eats like he's starving, hunched over his plate.

Dante is the oldest, so he sits on my father's right-hand side. Nero's on the left, with Sebastian next to him. I'm at the foot of the table, where my mother would sit if she were still alive.

"What's the holiday?" Sebastian says as another round of fireworks rocket up into the sky.

"It's not a holiday. It's Nessa Griffin's birthday," I tell him.

The Griffins' palatial estate sits right on the edge of the lake, in the heart of the Gold Coast. They're setting off fireworks to make sure absolutely everybody in the city knows their little princess is having a party—as if it wasn't already promoted like the Olympics and the Oscars combined.

Sebastian doesn't know because he doesn't pay attention to anything that isn't basketball. He's the youngest of my brothers, and the tallest. He got a full ride at Chicago State, and he's good enough that when I go visit him on campus, girls stare and giggle everywhere he goes, and sometimes pluck up the courage to ask him to sign their t-shirts.

"How come we weren't invited?" Nero says sarcastically.

We weren't invited because we fucking hate the Griffins, and vice versa.

The guest list will be carefully curated, stuffed with socialites and politicians and anybody else chosen for their usefulness or their cache. I doubt Nessa will know any of them.

Not that I'm crying any tears for her. I heard her father hired Demi Lovato to perform. I mean, it ain't Halsey, but it's still pretty good.

"What's the update on the Oak Street Tower?" Papa says to Dante while slowly and meticulously cutting up his chicken parm.

He already knows damn well how the Oak Street Tower is doing, because he tracks absolutely everything done by Gallo Construction. He's just changing the subject because the thought of the Griffins sipping champagne and brokering deals with the haute monde of Chicago is irritating to him.

I don't give a shit what the Griffins are doing. Except that I don't like anybody having fun without me.

So, while my father and Dante are droning on about the tower, I mutter to Sebastian, "We should go over there."

"Where?" he says obliviously, gulping down a big glass of milk. The rest of us are drinking wine. Sebastian's trying to stay in tiptop shape for dribbling and sit-ups, or whatever the fuck his team of gangly ogres does for training.

"We should go to the party," I say, keeping my voice low.

Nero perks up at once. He's always interested in getting into trouble.

"When?" he says.

"Right after dinner."

"We're not on the list," Sebastian protests.

"Jesus." I roll my eyes. "Sometimes I wonder if you're even a Gallo. You scared of jaywalking too?"

My two oldest brothers are proper gangsters. They handle the messier parts of the family business. But Sebastian thinks he's going to the NBA. He's living in a whole other reality than the rest of us. Trying to be a good boy, a law-abiding citizen.

Still, he's the closest to me in age, and probably my best friend, though I love all my brothers. So, he just grins back at me and says, "I'm coming, aren't I?"

Dante shoots us a stern look. He's still talking to our father, but he knows we're plotting something.

Since we've all finished our chicken, Greta brings out the panna cotta. She's been our housekeeper for about a hundred years. She's my second-favorite person, after Sebastian. She's stout and pretty, with more gray in her hair than red.

She made my panna cotta without raspberries because she knows I don't like the seeds, and she doesn't mind if I'm a spoiled brat. I grab her head and give her a kiss on the cheek as she sets it down in front of me.

"You're going to make me drop my tray," she says, trying to shake me loose.

"You've never dropped a tray in your life," I tell her.

My father takes fucking forever to eat his dessert. He's sipping his wine and going on and on about the electrical workers' union. I swear Dante is drawing him out on purpose to infuriate the rest of us. When we have these formal sit-down dinners, Papa expects us all to stay till the bitter end. No phones allowed at the table either, which is basically torture because I can feel my cell buzzing again and again in my pocket, with messages from who knows who. Hopefully not Oliver.

I broke up with Oliver Castle three months ago, but he isn't taking the hint. He might need to take a mallet to the head instead if he doesn't stop annoying me.

Finally, Papa finishes eating, and we all gather up as many plates and dishes as we can carry to stack in the sink for Greta.

Then Papa goes into his office to have his second nightcap, while Sebastian, Nero, and I all sneak downstairs.

We're allowed to go out on a Saturday night. We're all adults, after all—just barely, in my case. Still, we don't want Papa to ask us *where* we're going.

We pile into Nero's car because it's a boss '57 Chevy Bel Air that will be the most fun to cruise around in with the top down.

Nero starts the ignition, and in the flare of the headlights, we see Dante's hulking silhouette, standing right in front of us, arms crossed, looking like Michael Meyers about to murder us.

Sebastian jumps and I let out a little shriek.

"You're blocking the car," Nero says drily.

"This is a bad idea," Dante says.

"Why?" Nero says innocently. "We're just going for a drive."

"Yeah?" Dante says, not moving. "Right down Lake Shore Drive."

Nero switches tactics.

"So what if we are?" he says. "It's just some Sweet Sixteen party."

"Nessa's nineteen," I correct him.

"Nineteen?" Nero shakes his head in disgust. "Why are they even— never mind. Probably some stupid Irish thing. Or just any excuse to show off."

"Can we get going?" Sebastian says. "I don't wanna be out too late."

"Get in or get out of the way," I say to Dante.

He stares at us a minute longer, then shrugs. "Fine," he says, "but I'm riding shotgun."

I climb over the seat without argument, letting Dante have the front. A small price to pay to get my big brother on team Party Crashers.

We cruise down LaSalle Drive, enjoying the warm early summer air streaming into the car. Nero has a black heart and a vicious temperament, but you'd never know it from the way he drives. In the car, he's as smooth as a baby's ass—calm and careful.

Maybe it's because he loves the Chevy and has put about a thousand hours of work into it. Or maybe driving is the only thing that relaxes him. Either way, I always like seeing him with his arm stretched out on the wheel, the wind blowing back his sleek dark hair, his eyes half-closed like a cat.

It's not far to the Gold Coast. Actually, we're practically neighbors— we live in Old Town, which is directly north. Still, the two neighborhoods aren't much alike. They're both fancy in their own ways—our house looks right over Lincoln Park, theirs fronts onto the lake. But Old Town is, well, just what the name implies—pretty fucking old. Our house was built in the Victorian era. Our street is quiet, full of massive old oak trees. We're close to St. Michael's Church, which my father genuinely believes was spared the Chicago Fire by a direct act of god.

The Gold Coast is the new hotness. It's all pish-posh shopping and dining and the mansions of the richest motherfuckers in Chicago. I feel like I sprang forward thirty years just driving over here.

Sebastian, Nero, and I thought we might sneak in around the back of the Griffin property—maybe steal some caterers' uniforms. Dante, of course, isn't participating in any of that nonsense. He just slips the security guard five Benjamins to "find" our name on the list, and the guy waves us on in.

I already know what the Griffins' house looks like even before I see it, because it was big news when they bought it a few years back. At the time, it was the most expensive piece of residential real estate in Chicago. Fifteen thousand square feet for a cool twenty-eight million dollars.

My father scoffed and said it was just like the Irish to flash their money.

"An Irishman will wear a twelve-hundred-dollar suit without the money in his pocket to buy a pint," he said.

True or not as a generality, the Griffins can buy plenty of pints if they want to. They've got money to burn, and they're literally burning it right now, in the form of their fireworks show still trying to put Disneyworld to shame.

I don't care about that, though—first thing I want is some of the expensive champagne being ferried around by the waiters, followed by whatever's been stacked into a tower on the buffet table. I'm gonna do my best to bankrupt those snooty fucks by eating my weight in crab legs and caviar before I leave this place.

The party is outdoors on the sprawling green lawn. It's the perfect night for it—more evidence of the luck of the Irish. Everybody's laughing and talking, stuffing their faces and even dancing a little, though there's no Demi Lovato performing yet, just a normal DJ.

I guess I probably should have changed my clothes. I don't see a single girl without a glittery party dress and heels. But that would have been annoying as hell on the soft grass, so I'm glad I'm just wearing sandals and shorts.

I do see Nessa Griffin, surrounded by people congratulating her on the monumental achievement of staying alive for nineteen years. She's wearing a pretty, cream-colored sundress—simple and bohemian. Her light-brown hair is loose around her shoulders, and she's got a bit of a tan and a few extra freckles across her nose, like she was out on the lake all morning. She's blushing from all the attention, and she looks sweet and happy.

Honestly, out of all the Griffins, Nessa's the best one. We went to the same high school. We weren't exactly friends, since she was a year behind me and a bit of a goody-two-shoes. But she seemed nice enough.

Her sister on the other hand . . .

I can see Riona right now, chewing out some waitress until the poor girl is in tears. Riona Griffin is wearing one of those stiff, fitted sheath dresses that looks like it belongs in a boardroom, not at an outdoor party. Her hair is pulled back even tighter than her dress. Never did anybody less suit flaming red hair—it's like genetics tried to make her fun, and Riona was like, *"I'm never having one goddamned moment of fun in my life, thank you very much."*

She's scanning the guests like she wants to bag and tag the important ones. I spin around to refill my plate before she catches sight of me.

My brothers already split off the moment we arrived. I can see Nero flirting with some pretty blonde over on the dance floor. Dante has made his way over to the bar, cause he's not gonna drink froofy champagne. Sebastian has disappeared entirely—not easy to do when you're 6'6. I'm guessing he saw some people he knows; everybody likes Sebastian, and he's got friends everywhere.

As for me, I've got to pee.

I can see the Griffins brought in some outdoor toilets, discretely set back on the far side of the property, screened by a gauzy canopy. But I'm not peeing in a porta potty, even if it's a fancy one. I'm gonna pee in a proper Griffin bathroom, right where they sit their lily-white bottoms down. Plus, it'll give me a chance to snoop around their house.

Now, this does take a little maneuvering. They've got a lot more security around the entrance to the house, and I'm skint of cash for bribes. But once I throw a cloth napkin over my shoulder and steal the tray abandoned by the sobbing waitress, all I have to do is load up with a few empty glasses and I sneak right into the service kitchen.

I drop the dishes off at the sink like a good little employee, then I duck into the house itself.

Jiminy Crickets, it's a nice fucking house. I mean, I know we're supposed to be mortal rivals and all, but I can appreciate a place decked out better than anything I've ever seen on *House Hunters*. *House Hunters International*, even.

It's simpler than I would have expected—all creamy, smooth walls and natural wood, low, modern furniture, and light fixtures that look like industrial art.

There's a lot of actual art around, too—paintings that look like blocks of color, and sculptures made of piles of shapes. I'm not a total philistine—I know that painting is either a Rothko or supposed to look like one. But I also know I couldn't make a house look this pretty if I had a hundred years and an unlimited budget to do it.

Now I'm definitely glad I snuck in here to pee.

I find the closest bathroom down the hall. Sure enough, it's a study in luxury—lovely lavender soap, soft, fluffy towels, water that comes out of the tap at the perfect temperature, not too cool and not too hot. Who knows—in a place this big, I might be the first person to even step foot in here. The Griffins probably each have their own private bathroom. In fact, they probably get tipsy and get lost in this labyrinth.

Once I finish up, I know I should head back outside. I had my little adventure, and there's no point pushing my luck.

Instead, I find myself sneaking up the wide, curved staircase to the upper level.

The main level was too formal and antiseptic, like a show home. I want to see where these people actually live.

To the left of the staircase, I find a bedroom that must belong to Nessa. It's soft and feminine, full of books and stuffed animals and art supplies. There's a ukulele on the nightstand, and several pairs of sneakers kicked hastily under the bed. The only things not clean and new are the ballet slippers slung over her doorknob by their ribbons. Those are beat to hell and back, with holes in the satin toes.

Across from Nessa's room is one that probably belongs to Riona. It's larger, and spotlessly tidy. I don't see any evidence of hobbies in here, just some beautiful Asian watercolors hanging on the walls. I'm disappointed that Riona hasn't kept shelves of old trophies and medals. She definitely seems the type.

Beyond the girls' rooms is the master suite. I won't be going in there. It seems wrong on a different level. There has to be some kind of line I won't cross when I'm sneaking around somebody's house.

So, I turn the opposite direction and find myself in a large library instead.

Now, this is the kind of mysterious shit I came here for.

What do the Griffins read? Is it all leather-bound classics, or are they secret Anne Rice fans? Only one way to find out . . .

Looks like they favor biographies, architectural tomes, and yes, all the classics. They've even got a section dedicated to the famous Irish authors of yesteryear like James Joyce, Jonathan Swift, Yeats, and George Bernard Shaw. No Anne Rice, but they've got Bram Stoker at least.

Oh look, they've even got a signed copy of *Dubliners*. I don't care what anybody says, no one understands that fucking book. The Irish are all in on it, pretending it's a masterwork of literature when I'm pretty sure it's pure gibberish.

Besides the floor-to-ceiling shelves of books, the library is full of overstuffed leather armchairs, three of which have been arranged around a large stone fireplace. Despite the warm weather, there's a fire going in the grate—just a small one. It's not a gas fire, there are actual birch logs burning, which smells nice. Above the fireplace hangs a painting of a pretty woman, with several objects arranged along the mantle underneath, including a carriage clock and an hour-glass. Between those, an old pocket watch.

I pick it up off the mantle. It's surprisingly heavy in my hand, the metal warm to the touch instead of cool. I can't tell if it's brass or gold. Part of the chain is still attached, though it looks like it broke off at about half its original length. The case is carved and inscribed, so worn that I can't tell what the image used to be. I don't know how to open it, either.

I'm fiddling with the mechanism when I hear a noise out in the hallway—a faint clinking sound. Quickly, I slip the watch into my pocket and dive down behind one of the armchairs, the one closest to the fire.

A man comes into the library. Tall, brown hair, about thirty years old. He's wearing a perfectly tailored suit, and he's extremely well-groomed. Handsome, but in a stark sort of way—like he'd push you off a lifeboat if there weren't enough seats. Or maybe even if you forgot to brush your teeth.

I haven't actually met this dude before, but I'm fairly certain it's Callum Griffin, the oldest of the Griffin siblings. Which means he's just about the worst person to catch me in the library.

Unfortunately, it seems like he plans to stick around a while. He sits down in an armchair almost directly across from me and starts reading emails on his phone. He's got a glass of whiskey in his hand, and he's sipping from it. That's the sound I heard—the ice cubes chinking together.

It's extremely cramped and uncomfortable behind the armchair. The rug over the hardwood floor is none too cushy and I have to hunch up in a ball so my head and feet don't poke out on either side. Plus, it's hot as balls this close to the fire.

How in the hell am I going to get out of here?

Callum is still sipping and reading. Sip. Read. Sip. Read. The only other sound is the popping of the birch logs.

How long is he going to sit here?

I can't stay forever. My brothers are going to start looking for me in a minute.

I don't like being stuck. I'm starting to sweat, from the heat and the stress.

The ice in Callum's glass sounds so cool and refreshing.

God, I want a drink and I want to leave.

How many fucking emails does he have?!

Flustered and annoyed, I hatch a plan. Possibly the stupidest plan I've ever concocted.

I reach behind me and grab the tassel hanging down from the curtains. It's a thick gold tassel, attached to green velvet curtains.

By pulling it out to its furthest length, I can just poke it in around the edge of the grate, directly into the embers.

My plan is to set it smoking, which will distract Callum, allowing me to sneak around the opposite side of the chair and out the door. That's the genius scheme.

But because this isn't a fucking Nancy Drew novel, this is what happens instead:

The flames rip up the cord like it was dipped in gasoline, singing my hand. I drop the cord, which swings back to the curtain. Then that curtain ignites like it's paper. Liquid fire roars up to the ceiling in an instant.

This actually does achieve its purpose of distracting Callum Griffin. He shouts and jumps to his feet, knocking over his chair. However, my distraction comes at the cost of all subtlety, because I also have to abandon my hiding spot and sprint out of the room. I don't know if Callum saw me or not, and I don't care.

I'm thinking I should look for a fire extinguisher or water or something. I'm also thinking I should get the fuck out of here immediately.

That's the idea that wins out—I go sprinting down the stairs at top speed.

At the bottom of the staircase, I plow into somebody else, almost knocking him over. It's Nero, with that pretty blonde right behind him. Her hair is all messed up and he's got lipstick on his neck.

"Jesus," I say. "Is that a new record?" I'm pretty sure he only met her about eight seconds ago.

Nero shrugs, a hint of a grin on his handsome face. "Probably," he says.

Smoke drifts down over the bannister. Callum Griffin is shouting up in the library. Nero gazes up the staircase, confused.

"What's going on—"

"Never mind," I say, seizing his arm. "We've gotta get out of here."

I start dragging him in the direction of the service kitchen, but I can't quite take my own advice. I cast one look back over my shoulder. And I see Callum Griffin standing at the head of the stairs, glaring after us with a murderous expression on his face.

We sprint through the kitchen, knocking over a tray of canapés, then we're out the door, back out on the lawn.

"You find Sebastian, I'll get Dante," Nero says. He abandons the blonde without a word, jogging off across the yard.

I run in the opposite direction, looking for the tall, lanky shape of my youngest brother.

Inside the mansion, a fire alarm starts to wail.

KEEP READING – FREE KINDLE UNLIMITED

USA Today bestselling author Jane Henry pens stern but loving alpha heroes, feisty heroines, and emotion-driven happily-ever-afters. She writes what she loves to read: kink with a tender touch. Jane is a hopeless romantic who lives on the East Coast with a houseful of children and her very own Prince Charming.

You can find Jane here:

Join My Newsletter

The Club (Jane Henry's fan page)

Website

BB bookbub.com/profile/jane-henry

facebook.com/janehenryromance

instagram.com/janehenryauthor

amazon.com/Jane-Henry/e/B01BYAQYYK

Amazon Bestselling Author

Sophie lives with her husband, two boys, and baby girl in the Rocky Mountain West. She writes intense, intelligent romance, with heroines who are strong and capable, and men who will do anything to capture their hearts.

She has a slight obsession with hiking, bodybuilding, and live comedy shows. Her perfect day would be taking the kids to Harry Potter World, going dancing with Mr. Lark, then relaxing with a good book and a monster bag of salt and vinegar chips.

The Love Lark Letter
CLICK HERE TO JOIN MY VIP NEWSLETTER

COME JOIN ALL THE FUN:

Made in the USA
Las Vegas, NV
04 August 2022

52647962R00174